WHERE WE HOLD EACH OTHER

WHERE WE HOLD EACH OTHER

A Novel

Alberta Lampkins

A.L. Savvy Publications

Published by A.L. Savvy Publications ISBN: 979-8-9925291-2-8 Printed in the United States of America

This is a work of fiction. While certain real locations and community settings are referenced, all characters and events are products of the author's imagination. Any resemblance to actual persons, living or dead, or to actual events is coincidental.

Cover art by an unknown Kenyan artist, source during travel. Cover design by Taherul.

DEDICATION

For my parents and my Aunt Alberta, the first hands that held me. For Buffalo, where I learned the meaning of community. For my husband, Al, whose devotion and service reflect the heart of this work. For my children and grandchildren, the future I rise toward. For my friends and family who have lifted me with love, and for my best friend, Lakesha, whose sisterhood shaped the way I understand loyalty, laughter, and being held across a lifetime. And for the sociological journey that taught me to see people fully, honor their stories, and believe in the quiet power of community care.

May we all rise in purpose and in community.

AUTHOR'S NOTE ON THE COVER ART

The painting on the cover of this novel was created by an unknown artist whose work I encountered in a small market in Kenya. Though I do not know their name, the piece carries a spirit of movement, community, and ancestral presence that echoes the heart of this story.

Its colors and rhythm reminded me that art — like care, like lineage — often comes to us without introduction, yet leaves a lasting imprint. I offer it here in gratitude, honoring the hands that shaped it and the stories it continues to hold.

A LETTER TO THE YOUTH

To every young person holding this book — this is for you. For the ones still figuring out who they are. For the ones carrying stories they've never spoken aloud. For the ones who feel too much, dream too big, or fear they're not enough. For the ones who rise anyway.

I wrote this story because I've met you — in classrooms, community centers, church basements, military towns, HBCU hallways, and quiet corners where you thought no one noticed. I've seen your brilliance long before you believed in it. I've watched you carry more than you should have had to, and still find ways to laugh, to lead, to love.

You are not invisible. You are not alone. You are not too late or too complicated to become who you were meant to be.

Inside these pages, you'll meet characters who stumble, fall, question themselves, and rise again — not because they are perfect, but because they are held. By mentors. By community. By each other. By the belief that becoming is not a straight line, but a journey shaped by every hand that reaches back to lift us.

If you take nothing else from this book, take this: Your story matters. Your voice matters. Your becoming matters.

You deserve spaces where you feel safe, seen, and supported. You deserve mentors who show up. You deserve communities that make room for your growth. You deserve to take up space without shrinking.

And when the world feels heavy, remember this: You don't have to carry it alone. Move boldly. Stand in your purpose. Trust your unfolding.

May this book remind you that you are held — by ancestors, by community, by the future you are already shaping with your courage.

Keep rising. Keep growing. Keep choosing yourself.

With deep belief in you,
Alberta Lampkins

DEAR READER

Thank you for opening *Where We Hold Each Other.* This story began in the quiet places — the in-between spaces where memory lingers, where mentorship takes root, where community becomes a kind of prayer. It was born from the moments when we learn, often gently and sometimes through ache, that we were never meant to carry life alone.

I wrote this novel for anyone who has ever been carried through by a guiding hand, lifted by a soft word, or reminded — in the smallest, most unexpected ways — that they are worthy of being held. It is a love letter to neighborhoods stitched together by resilience, to women whose laughter carries generations, and to the mentors who show up with open palms and open hearts.

Within these pages, you'll meet characters who are imperfect, tender, and brave. You'll walk with them through living rooms warmed by memory, church basements humming with hope, and bus stops where healing begins in whispers. You'll witness how choosing to hold space for one another — even when it's uncomfortable, even when it's hard — can transform a life.

Whether you're reading this with a book club, curled into your favorite chair, or offering it to someone who needs a reminder of their own strength, my hope is simple: that you feel seen, that you feel held, and that you feel the quiet power we carry when we choose each other.

With gratitude,
Alberta Lampkins

Chapter One

When the World Shifts Beneath You

The bus ride from Philadelphia to North Carolina blurred into gray highway and muted emotion. Tyashia stared through the rain-streaked window, her world reduced to the cheap plastic bag at her feet. It sagged with everything she had left — not much, yet somehow more than she could carry. Inside were the only things she cared about: a change of clothes, her headphones, and a pair of old-school white leather roller skates with cheerful blue-and-white pom-poms.

Roller skating had been her thing with Aunt Asiah. Asiah loved the rink — the rhythmic glide, the freedom, the music. Tyashia could still hear her aunt's laughter echoing over the speakers, warm and encouraging.

"In life, Tye," Asiah would say during a slow song, "you have to keep rolling even through the tough times. Don't stop moving forward, no matter how hard it gets."

But now the wheels felt stuck.

Asiah was gone — cancer had taken her in just two short months. Her mother had abandoned her years ago, leaving behind a dull ache Tyashia refused to acknowledge. And now she was being shipped off to live with Aunt Sylvia in Fayetteville, North Carolina — a place she only knew as "near a military base."

Military life. Great.

She shoved the skates deeper into the bag, rejecting the optimism Asiah had tried to leave her with. It was hard to "keep rolling" when your entire foundation had crumbled.

The bus shifted under her, and a sudden memory rose — sharp and uninvited.

For a split second, she felt the familiar sway of the SEPTA Regional Rail pulling out of 30th Street Station. She could almost hear the conductor's muffled announcement, the soft rumble of the tracks beneath her feet. She and Aunt Asiah used to take that exact route — SEPTA to Trenton, quick transfer, then the NJ Transit train thundering into New York Penn Station. Those trains had carried them straight into New York City, into dim theaters and off-Broadway stages where Asiah insisted Tyashia learn to dream bigger than their block.

Those trips weren't casual outings. They were hard-earned. They were stitched together from long days, low wages, and the determination of a Black woman who refused to let the world shrink her niece's imagination.

Asiah would pick up extra shifts at the department store on weekends when she wasn't teaching — stretching a teacher's salary the way so many Black women had to, making joy possible one overtime hour at a time. And after the diagnosis, those hours became a necessity; insurance covered some things, never enough, leaving her to shoulder the kind of burden people expected her to carry quietly. She never said it outright, but Tyashia knew: those shows were her aunt's way of giving her a world bigger than their block, bigger than the classroom, bigger than the life she feared Tyashia might settle for.

Those trips had been their ritual. Their escape. Their little pocket of joy.

She could still smell the popcorn in the Broadway lobby, see the tickets clutched in Asiah's hand, feel the excitement buzzing through her aunt's body as the curtain rose on *Sista's*. Asiah had loved that show — the music, the history, the sisterhood. They had even stayed afterward one night to meet the cast. Marlaina Powell had taken a picture with them both, but what Tyashia remembered most was the way Asiah smiled — like she had all the time in the world.

Those train rides had felt like movement, like love, like the world was stretching open just for them.

Another memory surfaced — quieter, but just as alive.

Harriett's Bookshop.

She and Asiah had gone once on a warm Saturday, walking down Girard Avenue with the sun bouncing off the rowhomes and the El rattling overhead. The street had that Philly mix — corner stores, murals, bikes weaving through traffic, somebody blasting Jill Scott from a cracked window. Asiah had squeezed her hand and said, "This is a place built for us, Tye. You'll feel it when we get inside."

And she had.

Harriett's was small but mighty, tucked between a café and a tattoo shop, its front window filled with books by women who looked like her aunt — bold, brilliant, unbothered. Inside, the air smelled like paper, sage, and possibility. The walls held the faces of women who had moved mountains. The owner, Miss Jeannine, had greeted them like she'd been expecting them all along.

Tyashia remembered how Asiah's whole spirit shifted in that space — shoulders dropping, breath deepening, like she'd stepped into a room that understood her without explanation. Asiah lived with the burden of being a Black woman educator in a world that underpaid her and over-relied on her, and Harriett's felt like a place that finally saw all of her.

They'd wandered the aisles slowly, reverently, touching the spines of books by Black women writers Asiah called "our ancestors in print."

Tyashia had stopped at a display of journals — bright covers, affirmations stamped in gold.

"Pick one," Asiah had said. "A place to put your truth."

She'd chosen a teal one with the words *Your story matters* on the front. She hadn't written in it yet. But she remembered how it felt to hold it — like holding a future she wasn't sure she deserved.

Outside, the street had been loud again — buses sighing, bikes zipping past, the El roaring overhead — but inside Harriett's, she had felt something she didn't have a name for then.

Presence. Power. A reminder that Black girls had stories worth holding, worth reading, worth fighting for.

Now, on this bus headed south, that memory pressed against her chest like a hand she wished she could hold.

The memory dissolved, leaving the ache sharper than before.

She put on her headphones, letting conscious rap — all truth, grit, and survival — drown out the world. She wouldn't cry. She wouldn't break. The bus rumbled on, carrying her farther from everything she knew and toward a future that didn't feel like hers.

Hours later, the bus hissed to a stop at the Fayetteville station. The air outside was thick with humidity and that familiar Carolina sharpness that clung to summer nights, even here in the middle of downtown. Sylvia was waiting at the curb — arms crossed, posture rigid, expression unreadable.

The drive wasn't long. Downtown Fayetteville unfolded around them almost immediately — brick sidewalks, small boutiques with bright window displays, the minor league baseball stadium rising clean and modern against the sky. A couple of soldiers crossed Hay Street, and a group of teenagers laughed loudly near a smoothie shop. Everything felt too open, too slow, too unfamiliar.

Sylvia pointed stiffly out the window, her voice trying for casual and landing somewhere closer to strained.

"They've really built this area up," she said. "People like to walk around down here."

Tyashia didn't respond. She just watched the storefronts blur past, each one reminding her she was far from Philly's noise, far from the life she knew.

Traffic slowed as they approached the Market House, its arches catching the late-afternoon light. The building rose in the center of the roundabout like something out of a history book — old, complicated, impossible to ignore.

"There," Sylvia said suddenly, gesturing past the Market House. "That's that rapper y'all like. He's from here."

Tyashia followed her gesture.

On the wall just beyond the roundabout, the mural spread wide — a young man in a hoodie, eyes soft but rooted, painted in colors that seemed to vibrate against the brick. The artist had captured something real, something real, something that felt like it belonged to the city and the city belonged to him.

Her breath caught — just a spark — before she forced her face back into its practiced blankness.

"Oh," she said, flat.

But her eyes lingered on the mural as they passed. Even in the shade, the paint held its presence, the expression familiar — like someone who knew what it meant to leave and return changed.

Sylvia kept talking, trying too hard. "He does a lot for the youth here. Quietly. Folks say he still comes back around."

Tyashia turned her gaze to the window, pretending she wasn't listening.

But inside, something shifted — a tiny spark she didn't have a name for yet. A reminder that someone who once felt out of place in this city had still found a way to rise from it.

Sylvia didn't notice. Leonard didn't notice.

But the mural stayed with her long after they turned off Hay Street and the downtown noise faded behind them.

The scent of eucalyptus and mint air freshener hit her like an insult the moment she stepped inside Sylvia's house. It clung to the walls of the big, quiet home — so different from the city grime and the warm, lived-in scent of Asiah's apartment, where shoes piled up on a mat by the door, replicas of paintings by Black artists lined the hallway, affirmations curled slightly at the edges on the kitchen walls, and a soft, overstuffed couch welcomed anyone who sat. The yellow old-school tea kettle always sat on the stove — Asiah refused microwaved tea, insisting on waiting for the whistle, insisting on making time instead of rushing through it.

Now she stood in the room that was supposed to be hers. Sterile. Perfect. Wrong.

Her grief clung to her like a fever: the dull headache, the vanished appetite, the sleepless nights. She'd kill for a real cheesesteak — the grease, the provolone, the foil. Instead, she was promised baked ziti.

She was forced to live with Sylvia, her husband Leonard, and their three kids. Sylvia was nothing like Asiah — feisty, superior, and proud of her GS status on Fort Bragg. Leonard, a retired First Sergeant turned ROTC instructor, followed her lead with quiet, practiced deference. Asiah's life had been shaped by soft things — books, students, roller rinks — but also by the hard truth of a teacher's paycheck. Sylvia's world ran on rank, routine, and the reliable promise of a GS salary. Two sisters shaped by the same city but different systems.

A cardboard box sat by the door, "TYASHIA" scrawled across it. It held the pieces of her life that hadn't been packed by strangers.

"They don't get it. Nobody gets it."

She kicked the box.

Stupid North Carolina. Stupid sunshine. Stupid new high school.

A memory flashed — not Broadway lights this time, but the small pool of the kitchen lamp during one of their "tea talks." Asiah in her pink rollers and light purple terry-cloth bathrobe, smooth brown skin carrying its own richness even under the dim bulb — not a faint brown, not dark brown, just a perfect shade of her own. Gentle eyes. Small frame. A presence that filled a room without ever raising her voice.

She was stirring honey into her mug, laughing so hard her tea splattered when Tyashia teased her about being that old lady at the roller rink.

"You're gonna be seventy-five still rolling to 'Roll, Bounce, Rock, Skate' like you're the queen of the rink," Tyashia had said.

"And I'm gonna look good doing it," Asiah shot back, hips rolling in a slow, exaggerated skate move that made them both fold over with laughter.

The memory of that night closed in on her, sharp enough to hurt.

Now it all felt impossibly far away.

A knock, then the door swung open. Sylvia stood there, arms crossed.

"Dinner's in an hour," she said. "Curfew is nine-thirty. Lights out at ten."

"Nine-thirty? I'm sixteen, not ten."

"You're sixteen and living under my roof," Sylvia snapped. "And in this house, we keep things orderly. Something your Aunt Asiah never quite mastered."

The jab landed like a slap.

"Aunt Asiah knew how to actually live," Tyashia shot back.

"You'll learn our ways. Mentor orientation is coming up, and you will attend. No arguments."

She left.

Tyashia's anger rose to shield her anxiety.

She pulled out her phone. A photo of her mother stared back — a stranger. A ghost.

"They left me. Both of them."

She tossed the phone aside and unpacked. Her hand froze on her favorite shirt: the one Aunt Asiah gave her, soft gray cotton, with white script reading *Faith over Fear.*

"What faith," she whispered.

She shoved the shirt to the bottom of the box.

Her fingers brushed something else — smooth, warm, familiar. A slim Be Rooted journal, the one Asiah had slipped into her bag during their last hospital visit. A gift from a woman who had spent her life giving more than her paycheck ever reflected.

Tyashia snapped it shut before the memory could rise.

She wasn't becoming anything. Not here. Not now.

She would not cry.

Somewhere in the house, Sylvia moved with the precision of someone who believed order could fix anything.

Chapter Two

What We Carry Before We Know We're Carrying It

The feel of polished wood beneath her fingertips was Sylvia's anchor — specifically the curio cabinet she and Leonard bought when he was active duty and they were stationed in Bamberg, Germany. She kept it immaculate, the Windex-cleaned glass shelves gleaming, each piece of Czech crystal arranged by height and purpose. That cabinet was proof of a life built through discipline, sacrifice, and order — the opposite of the cluttered, lived-in chaos of Asiah's Philadelphia apartment. Sylvia had spent her entire adulthood distancing herself from that kind of disorder. Stability was something she believed she had earned — a reward for choosing the right path, the disciplined path, the government-paycheck path. In her mind, order wasn't just preference; it was protection, a buffer between her and the kind of financial uncertainty she'd watched swallow people back home.

Even now, a single unlit candle from So Lit Candle Company — a veteran-owned brand she liked to mention but never actually burned — sat perfectly centered on her dresser, untouched. Order was something she curated. Chaos was something she refused.

She leaned against the doorframe of the guest room, watching Tyashia glare at the walls. The girl was a mirror image of her mother, Sarah — the same defiant eyes, the same inherent belief that rules didn't apply to her.

Sylvia had tried with her sisters, on her own terms. But Asiah had always acted like a martyr, pouring her childless yearning into every stray student and project, never accepting that Sylvia's structured life was a valid path. Sylvia had even returned those ridiculous gifts Asiah kept sending Tasha, Cassidy, and Simon; she didn't want Asiah's soft, undisciplined view of life influencing her perfectly managed children. To Sylvia, Asiah's life had always looked unstable — a teacher's salary stretched to its limits, side jobs, hand-me-down furniture, joy carved out of scarcity. Sylvia mistook that for chaos, never quite understanding that Asiah's world ran on community, not rank.

Sarah had run off with that man, Henry, then disappeared completely after the scandal broke. Sylvia, the practical one — the one who married a good, dependable soldier and built a stable life — was left to pick up the pieces.

She remembered the last time she'd tried to discuss boundaries with Asiah, when Asiah had scoffed at Sylvia's clean house and rigid rules.

"Lighten up, Syl," she'd said with that easy laugh that always annoyed Sylvia. "It's just a house, not the White House."

Sylvia believed in boundaries, discipline, and respect for authority. She wasn't just a GS employee; she was a Grade 12 — a position earned through hard work and dedication, a badge of honor her sisters had never understood or respected. The title held her in place. In a world where budgets shifted and commanders rotated and nothing on base stayed the same for long, her GS-12 felt immovable — a guarantee she clung to more tightly than she admitted. The idea that anything could threaten that stability never crossed her mind.

She saw her civilian government rank as a permanent position of authority that extended well beyond the base gates and, apparently, into family dynamics. Rank had shaped her entire adulthood — Leonard's stripes, her GS grade, the invisible ladders everyone on base climbed. It was the language she trusted, the structure she believed kept the world from slipping into the kind of unpredictability she'd grown up with.

Now this broken girl, full of Asiah's "keep rolling" nonsense, was her responsibility. Tyashia needed structure, not clichés. She needed a schedule, a curfew, and guidance from strong, local community members like Leha Harrington.

Mentoring. It's mandatory, Tyashia. Good for you.

Watching Tyashia stuff those ridiculous roller skates into a bag was a small victory. The girl needed to lose her romanticized Philadelphia memories and focus on her new reality. Fayetteville wasn't glamorous, but it ran on the constant heartbeat of federal paychecks — soldiers, civilians, contractors, retirees. People built whole lives around the promise that the government would always keep moving, always keep paying. Sylvia never questioned it. She couldn't imagine what would happen if that rhythm ever stopped.

She needs a solid foundation, Sylvia thought, her hands tightening on the polished wood of the doorframe. *And I'm the only one who can give it to her.*

She glanced toward the hallway where Leonard had just walked past, his posture straight, his expression careful. Their marriage ran on structure — on routines, on rules, on silence. Predictability was the glue that held her world together. As long as the routines stayed intact — Leonard's schedule, her work hours, the kids' activities — she could pretend the ground beneath them was solid.

Some things stayed unspoken in a marriage. Some things stayed unspoken in a family. Sylvia preferred it that way.

She packed her sister's death away — neat, contained, sealed. Just like she'd packed away everything from their childhood. The three of them had learned early how to survive without softness, how to keep secrets even from each other. They never talked about what happened back then. Never talked about why Sylvia really kept her distance. Some things were easier to bury under polish and order than to face in the light.

She was sympathetic to Tyashia's loss on a superficial level, but she didn't know how to help the girl through her pain — or perhaps didn't want to try — preferring a solution that fit into a structured checklist she could manage.

The problem with grief, Sylvia thought, was how messy it was, how it resisted organization. It scattered like leaves in a storm — impossible to sweep into neat piles, no matter how hard she tried. Messiness reminded her too much of the past — overdue bills, eviction notices slipped under the door, the kind of instability she'd sworn she'd never return to. Order had saved her once. She believed it would save her again.

Too bad, she decided, turning away from the guest room door. This house runs on order, not emotions.

She didn't know it yet, but the world she trusted — the one built on pay grades, protocols, and predictable checks — was more fragile than she allowed herself to believe.

But Sylvia wasn't the only sister shaped by fear. Years earlier, in a different city, another woman had made a choice that would change all their lives.

Chapter Three

Where Fear Learns to Speak

Philadelphia in the mid-to-late 2000s was a city of harsh contrasts: the rich aroma of street vendors selling cheesesteaks mixing with the choking smell of exhaust and urban decay. For Sarah, the air had taken on a sharp, metallic residue of fear that clung to the back of her throat. She worked for City Councilman Davis, a man whose charisma matched his political ambition. She had fallen for the illusion, the glamour — chasing the joy she couldn't find in her simple life, despite the enduring love of Henry, the real father of her child.

The political world had seemed so clean and powerful from the outside.

The news broke like glass: a front-page scandal in the local paper. The mainstream stations ran the story with their usual detached spectacle — grainy photos, dramatic music, newscasters speaking about her life like it was a plotline instead of a person.

But on Black radio and the independent news streams, the tone was different.

Roland Martin's voice cut through the noise one evening, not naming her but naming the pattern — how powerful men hid behind their wives' rage, how Black women became collateral damage in political storms they never asked to enter. Then he said something that made Sarah's blood run cold:

"Whenever the story is too neat, too convenient, too focused on a woman's alleged morality, you can bet there's a bigger machine behind it. Sex scandals are the oldest distraction in the political playbook. Follow the money, not the gossip."

Sarah stood frozen at the sink, dishwater cooling around her hands. He didn't know her name, but he knew her story. He knew there was more.

And there was.

It had started with a misfiled email — a late-night request from the councilman's wife asking her to "clean up the inbox." Sarah clicked too fast, opened a thread she shouldn't have, and froze. It wasn't gossip or flirtation. It was a chain of messages linking city contracts to shell nonprofits, federal grant money rerouted through organizations that didn't exist, signatures that looked copied and pasted. And the wife — not the councilman — was at the center of it all.

At first Sarah thought she misunderstood. But the deeper she looked, the more the pattern sharpened. The wife wasn't just angry. She was connected — to the mayor's office, to a congressional aide, to people whose names Sarah had only heard whispered on Black talk radio when hosts discussed "the quiet machinery of corruption."

The councilman had no idea. He was too busy chasing headlines and shaking hands. But his wife? She was the architect. And Sarah had stumbled into the blueprint.

When the scandal broke, the public latched onto the easiest story — the alleged affair, the supposed love child. A narrative designed to humiliate her, to distract from the truth. The wife weaponized the rumor with surgical precision. A sex scandal was digestible. Federal corruption was not.

The threats weren't about jealousy. They were about silence.

The councilman's wife, a woman known for her vicious temper and connections in high places, believed the baby was her husband's — or rather, she wanted the public to believe it. The threats started as whispers over the phone line, then escalated into outright calls filled with acid and venom.

"That little love child of yours won't see her next birthday," the voice hissed — a voice Sarah recognized from political dinners. The words were delivered with a calm malice that terrified her more than shouting ever could.

Fear had a way of threading itself through their family — quiet, inherited, almost invisible unless you knew where to look. Their father lived with it first. Each sister just learned her own way of outrunning it.

It lived in her gut, a cold knot of dread that never loosened. Every time little Tyashia laughed in the other room — a pure, innocent sound — Sarah flinched internally. Every time a car door slammed on the street, her heart hammered against her ribs like a drum solo of panic.

I have to protect her. I have to protect my little girl. I have to be her harbor, even if it breaks me.

She was sitting at her small kitchen table when she made the decision. The evening news blared in the background, a local anchor discussing the scandal with a dispassionate tone. Tyashia was in the other room, sleeping soundly in the small apartment they called home, the only brightness drifting in from the faint orange cast of the streetlights outside the window.

Sarah grabbed a pen and a pad of paper, her hands trembling so hard the words were barely legible. The cheap paper felt rough under her shaking fingers. She wrote a quick note to her sister, Asiah, who lived just a few blocks away in Philadelphia. Asiah was strong, dependable, deeply rooted in her community as a schoolteacher. She would love Tyashia with the kind of unwavering care Sarah feared she could no longer provide.

For a fleeting second, the thought of reaching out to their other sister, Sylvia, in North Carolina crossed her mind. Sylvia had stability and rules, but she quickly dismissed it. Sarah wanted Tyashia to be nurtured by Asiah, even if it meant remaining in

Philadelphia, still close to the danger. Sylvia's cold efficiency could never replace Asiah's heart.

Sarah had even named her daughter partly after her sister, a testament to the bond they shared. Asiah always said Tye was her namesake, her mini-me.

Sarah packed two small suitcases, her movements quick and frantic. The zipping sound seemed too loud in the quiet apartment. She stopped by the crib, pressing a kiss to Tyashia's forehead, the smell of baby lotion and sleep becoming a tenderness she knew would haunt her.

"I love you, baby," she whispered, tears streaming down her face. "Mommy has to go, but Aunt Asiah will take care of you."

Leaving Henry was a different kind of pain, a heartbreak born of necessity. He was a good man, dependable, but he couldn't fight City Hall and a vengeful wife armed with money, power, and federal connections. Sarah knew she had to disappear completely.

She walked out the door, into the cold Philadelphia night, the chill an immediate contrast to the heat of her fear. She left everything behind: her daughter, her love, her life.

She disappeared, a prisoner of her own choice — a choice made out of the most primal love and the deepest, most profound fear.

I lost myself to save my child. I hope she understands one day.

Sarah vanished into the night, but the impact of her decision didn't disappear with her. It would shape the life of a girl she left behind — and the woman now preparing to guide her.

In Fayetteville, Leha Harrington tugged a crumpled volunteer form from the printer. Her life often felt like that — wrinkled, pulled in too many directions, but still holding together. Every morning she ran three miles along the base perimeter, humidity clinging to her skin. Most mornings, after her run, she stopped by Simon Temple AME Zion Church — sometimes to pray, sometimes just to sit in the quiet before the day began. Running and those small moments of stillness were her release valves, her way of staying strong for everyone — her family, her community, and now a girl named Tyashia.

She called Safiya — her friend, her soft place to land, the warm voice behind The Gentle Ground Café where stories were held with tenderness and truth. Safiya was a few years older, but no one ever felt an age gap with her; she moved through the world with a calm, centered ease that made people feel seen, not managed. Her faith wasn't loud or performative. It lived in her principles, in the way she listened, in the way she held space without judgment.

"The Philly transplant," Safiya said, her tone thoughtful rather than gossipy. "Rough situation."

"Cancer. Aunt passed last week," Leha replied. "And Sylvia's her guardian."

Safiya let out a low, thoughtful note. "Sylvia operates on her own frequency. What's our approach?"

Leha hesitated. "What if I can't reach her? What if she's too broken?"

Safiya's voice softened, warm as the café she ran. "Faith isn't in a title. It's in what you do."

Leha breathed in. *Action is needed.*

Her mind drifted — not to strategy, but to the people who shaped her. Her sister Melina, her closest confidante, a registered nurse who poured herself into everyone else's healing while her own love life kept bruising her heart. Her father Sam, the quiet foundation she and Melina leaned on when their parents' twenty-five-year marriage cracked apart. And her mother — now in Charlotte — whose sudden distance still stung in ways Leha rarely admitted. Even as adults, the move had felt like abandonment, like a door closing without warning.

And then there was Ron — the guidance counselor who had been a constant presence in her work long before she built her program. A veteran who served ten years before returning home, his calm, matured wisdom written in the undisturbed steadiness of his face, the kind that made young people trust him without hesitation. He counseled students at Westover High and stepped in for her youth whenever she needed him, no questions asked. Her father had once been his First Sergeant in the Army, a connection neither of them talked about much, but one that lived quietly beneath their respect for each other.

He had always shown up for her community. For her family. For the youth who needed someone relentless.

She looked at the name again. *Tyashia.*

This one needed tenderness. And offering that meant lowering her guard — something she hadn't done in a long time.

While Tyashia lay awake in a house that didn't feel like hers, miles away Leha moved through her apartment with a heaviness she couldn't quite name. Two women, strangers for now, each carrying their own ache — one bracing for a new beginning, the other preparing to hold someone she had not yet met.

Chapter Four

The Day the Ground Shifted

The last bell had barely faded when the teacher's lounge filled with the soft clatter of microwaves and end-of-day exhaustion. Leha slipped in with a mentoring referral in her hand, hoping for a quiet corner. Instead, she walked into a pocket of laughter.

Mr. Jordan — tall, brown-skinned, locs pulled back — leaned against the counter. Mr. Ellis, with his warm, sun-kissed complexion and easy smile, stood beside him. Across from them was Connor, pale-skinned, sandy-haired, the kind of man who filled space without noticing he did.

Their banter bounced around the room, harmless on the surface. At the far table, Ms. Davenport ate her lunch in measured, unhurried bites. Silver coils framed her face. She wasn't part of the conversation, but she heard every word.

Jordan cracked a joke. Ellis doubled over laughing. Connor grinned, shaking his head like he was indulging children.

He pointed at Ellis.

"You better get yourself together…"

A pause.

Not playful. Not searching for a word. A choosing.

A small, deliberate silence opened in the room — just wide enough for history to step through.

Then Connor finished the sentence, releasing the word like he owned it.

"...boy."

It didn't ride the same breath. It arrived separate. Intentional. As if he had reached for it, weighed it, and decided he could.

The room reacted before anyone spoke.

Leha felt the air tighten, pulled into a thin, sharp line. Ms. Davenport's fork froze mid-air. Ellis's laughter died in his throat. Jordan blinked, the smile slipping from his face.

The silence wasn't empty. It was crowded. It was full of every ancestor who had ever been renamed, diminished, or commanded to shrink.

Leha felt them — heard them — whispering through the walls, resonating deep in her ribs. A warning. A witness. A memory older than the building itself.

Connor didn't notice. He grabbed his coffee, still smirking, and walked out.

The door clicked shut.

Ms. Davenport set her fork down with a soft, deliberate clink that sounded louder than it should have.

"Did you just let that man call you *boy*?" Her voice was calm, but her eyes burned with a heat that came from decades of watching the same scene play out in different rooms.

Jordan shrugged, uncomfortable. "It's not that deep, Ms. D. Connor's cool."

"Cool?" She leaned back, folding her arms. "Baby, I was grown before that man was born. I've seen 'cool' white folks call Black men 'boy' with a smile on their face and a whip in their tone. That pause he took? That was him deciding he could say it."

Ellis nodded slowly, the history of it pressing into him. "He shouldn't've said it," he murmured.

Ms. Davenport wasn't finished.

"That word ain't never been harmless," she said. "Not when it comes after a pause like that. That pause was the truth. That pause was the permission he thought he had."

Jordan looked down, shame creeping in around the edges. "I hear you," he said quietly.

Leha didn't speak, but she felt the truth vibrating in her bones. She thought of her grandfather, her uncles, the men who had taught her how language could bruise without ever raising a hand.

The room exhaled only when Ms. Davenport picked up her fork again.

Later that night, while she and Ron cleaned the kitchen, she told him what she'd witnessed.

"I heard," Ron said. "Ms. Davenport went straight to Connor. Told him exactly why that word — especially with that pause — wasn't okay."

Leha looked up. "How'd he take it?"

"He got defensive. Told her if she had a problem, she could file a complaint." Ron shook his head. "But later, after he sat with it, he realized what he'd done. He apologized to her. And to the guys."

Leha nodded, but the ache didn't leave her chest.

Because the apology mattered. But the pause mattered more.

It was proof that history wasn't past. It was present. It was alive. It was still shaping the air they breathed.

And Leha knew — deep in her spirit — that this was exactly why her work mattered. Why witnessing mattered. Why lineage mattered.

The world didn't change in grand speeches. It changed in rooms like that lounge. In pauses that revealed the truth. In elders who refused to let history slip by unnoticed.

By the time she got home, the heaviness of the day followed her inside. She needed grounding more than sleep.

The night before the workshop, Leha moved through her apartment in a hush that felt almost sacred. The day had been long, her thoughts heavier than she wanted to admit, and the silence pressed against her ribs like a truth she could no longer outrun.

She reached for her favorite candle from The Black Home — the one she saved for nights when she needed grounding more than rest. The matte black vessel felt cool in her hands, its presence deliberate, intentional, like something crafted to hold more than wax. On the shelf beside it sat a So Lit Candle Company tin, a soft lavender blend she burned on lighter days. Supporting Black woman–owned brands wasn't a trend for her; it was a practice, a way of honoring the hands that created what held her.

Tonight, she needed the depth of this one.

She lifted the lid, and the scent rose to meet her: warm amber, smoked cedar, and a whisper of something green and quiet, like the moment a leaf lets go of its branch.

She lit it with a slow breath. The flame caught, then came to rest — a small, unwavering presence in the room.

Leha sank to the floor, her Be Rooted journal open across her knees, the same brand she gifted to mentees when they were ready to name their truths. She didn't know that miles away, a girl she had yet to meet was hiding the same kind of journal at the bottom of a cardboard box, too hurt to open it.

The candle's fragrance unfolded around her, softening the edges of her thoughts. It smelled like stillness. Like truth. Like the kind of home she had never quite found after her parents' divorce but kept trying to build inside herself.

She wrote until the words blurred — about the youth she couldn't reach, the mentors she wished she'd had, the exhaustion that clung to her like a second skin, the fear that she was pouring from a cup cracked in places she refused to name.

The candle burned low, its flame reflecting in her eyes as though reminding her of something she had forgotten — that even a small flame can hold its own in the dark.

When she finally closed her journal, her chest felt a little less tight. Not healed. Not whole. But softened. Shifted. As if the scent itself had loosened something knotted deep inside her.

She whispered into the quiet, "Let me be ready." Then she cupped her hand around the flame and blew it out, watching the final curl of smoke rise like a blessing she didn't yet know she'd asked for.

The conference room at the Raleigh Community Leadership Institute buzzed with nervous energy that pressed lightly against the walls. Folding chairs scraped softly against the polished tile as people settled in. A projector flickered against a white screen, its faint whir blending with the murmur of early-morning conversation. The scent of burnt coffee drifted from a table in the back, mingling with the faint smell of dry-erase markers and the lingering chill of the building's overactive air conditioning.

Leha sat near the front, notebook open, pen poised, heart pounding harder than she wanted to admit.

She had driven up from Fayetteville before sunrise, the sky still a deep indigo when she eased onto I-95 — a strange choice for her. Leha was a back-roads girl, always had been. She called them the scenic routes, the roots, the ones that let her breathe. Her father and sister teased her for it, swearing she'd save half her life if she'd just take the highway like everybody else. But Leha liked the slow way. The winding way. The way that gave her space to think without having to keep pace with travelers racing toward the next exit.

This morning, though, she'd taken the highway because she needed to get there early — needed to be ready. She wasn't questioning her purpose; that part was clear. Her work was rooted in showing youth the beauty they owned, the kind they didn't always see in themselves. What weighed on her now was the responsibility of it all. The fear of failing someone who needed her dependable.

Even in the quiet, her thoughts pressed louder than the engine. She wanted to learn. She wanted to do right by the young people who trusted her. And she hoped — in that soft, private way she rarely admitted — that she was growing into the kind of mentor they deserved.

The workshop title sat bold on the screen:

"Trauma-Informed Mentoring: Building Safe, Sustainable Relationships."

A woman with silver braids and warm eyes stepped to the front. She wore a flowing teal blouse and sensible flats, but her presence filled the room like sunlight.

"Welcome," she said, her voice warm and inviting. "Today isn't about learning how to fix anyone. It's about learning how to hold space."

Hold space. The words found their way into Leha's chest like a stone and a balm at the same time — and for the briefest of a moment, she saw the teacher's lounge again. The pause. The way a single breath could reveal a wound older than the room itself.

The facilitator continued. "Mentors need nourishment too. You cannot pour from an empty cup."

Leha's pen froze mid-sentence.

She had spent years pouring — into work, into survival, into perfection. Into being the strong one. The reliable one. The one who didn't break. But she had never once considered what it meant to be held.

The workshop moved through modules:

- recognizing trauma responses
- building trust slowly
- setting boundaries
- understanding cultural context
- avoiding saviorism
- creating community-care systems

Leha scribbled notes furiously, her handwriting growing messier with each revelation. Her mind raced with possibilities — new ways to reach youth, new ways to support mentors, new ways to build something that mattered.

She thought of the youth who shut down when touched, the ones who flinched at raised voices, the ones who apologized for things that weren't their fault. Trauma wasn't always dramatic; sometimes it was quiet, patterned, predictable in its unpredictability. And it wasn't limited to one race or one neighborhood — poverty, instability, and loss had a way of crossing boundaries people pretended were fixed.

During a break, she stepped outside into the crisp morning air. The sun was rising over the Raleigh skyline, casting warm gold across the parking lot. Cars glinted like scattered coins. A breeze brought the faint scent of morning greenery and pavement slowly warming under the early light.

She leaned against her car, breathing deeply, letting the cool air settle her nerves.

A woman approached — tall, soft-spoken, wearing a navy cardigan and carrying a steaming cup of tea.

"You're taking a lot of notes," she said with a gentle smile.

Leha laughed nervously. "I'm trying to build something. I just don't know what yet."

The woman nodded knowingly. "That's how it starts. A feeling. A need. A spark."

Leha hesitated. "What if I'm not ready?"

"No one is ready," the woman said. "We grow into readiness."

Leha swallowed hard. "I want to help young people. But I don't want to hurt them by doing it wrong."

"That's why you're here," the woman said. "That's why you'll be good at this."

Later, during the final session, the facilitator dimmed the lights and asked everyone to write down one sentence:

"What kind of mentor do you want to be?"

Leha stared at the blank page for a long moment. Her hand trembled slightly. She thought of her father's even presence, her mother's distance, her sister's quiet strength. She thought of the youth she'd seen fall through cracks too wide for one person to fill. She thought of the moments in her own life when she'd had support — and the moments when she'd had to hold herself together alone.

And she thought of the lounge. The pause. The way silence could wound — or protect.

Then she wrote:

"I want to be the ground I needed when the world felt tilted."

She didn't know it yet, but that sentence would become the foundation of everything she would one day build — the mentoring work, the community partnerships, the leadership programs, the spaces where young people and mentors alike could breathe, grow, and belong. Even the global work that would eventually call her name had its roots in this moment.

As she drove back to Fayetteville, the sun warm on her face and the smooth, even glide of the road beneath her, she felt something she hadn't felt in years.

Promise — the ground shifting beneath her in the best possible way.

Chapter Five

Fruitbelt, Buffalo, New York, 1983

Every present moment is built on the foundations of the past — on promises whispered in community centers and sealed with shared laughter. Even then, Safiya felt something shifting inside her, like a leaf catching wind before it knows it's falling.

The Langston Hughes Center on High Street buzzed with life — not a gym, but a creative heartbeat for the neighborhood. All day, kids drifted in and out of workshops: jewelry making, woodcraft, photography, dance. By early evening, the tables were pushed back, the lights dimmed, and a DJ set up near the wall, wires snaking across the floor. Saturday nights belonged to the youth — a safe space, a joyful space, a place where Black kids could breathe.

Outside the neighborhood, people called kids from the East Side "trouble," "gang-bound," "unruly." But inside places like Langston Hughes and the Neighborhood House Association, the truth was different. These centers weren't just after-school programs — they were sanctuaries, training grounds, community classrooms. They taught discipline, creativity, leadership. They held the kind of structure the city never credited Black youth with wanting or mastering.

The space gripped the scent of floor wax, jerry curl activator, and the warm heat of bodies dancing — girls trying hard not to sweat out their perms — the unofficial perfume of the early '80s. A crowd gathered around the open floor, waiting for the breakdance competition to start. Most were spectators — cheering, clapping, hyping up their favorites. Breakdancing wasn't just moves; it was art, pride, and peace. No fights. No drama. Just rhythm and skill.

Lakena bounced beside Safiya, all energy and attitude, her bell-bottom jeans swishing with every step. Her gold hoop earrings swung wildly, catching every bit of her excitement.

"Yo, Saf! They 'bout to start!" she said, tugging Safiya's arm like she couldn't stand still another second.

Safiya laughed, smoothing her hair. "Girl, you are a trip."

Teens formed a circle as the DJ dropped a beat heavy enough to vibrate the floor. Kangol hats, windbreakers, fat laces — the whole Fruitbelt showed up. Someone shouted, "Ayyyye, go 'head!" and the crowd echoed back.

"I could do that," Lakena muttered, chin up, eyes gleaming.

Safiya giggled. "You can't even moonwalk straight."

"Watch me then."

Before Safiya could stop her, Lakena strutted into the center like she owned the whole East Side. She hit a move — full attitude, full flair — and the crowd erupted. It didn't matter that she wasn't one of the real competitors. It was the confidence that got them.

"That's my girl," Safiya whispered, pride swelling in her chest.

Later, they cooled off outside, leaning against the brick wall of the center. The Buffalo night air was crisp, a welcome break from the heat inside. Streetlights cast long shadows across the sidewalk, and the distant rumble of a bus echoed down High Street.

"High Spot run?" Lakena asked, rubbing her stomach. "I'm starving."

Safiya rolled her eyes. "You always starving."

"And you know it," Lakena shot back, popping her gum. "Come on. I want some pizza and wings. And yes — we gettin' blue cheese and celery sticks."

Safiya laughed. "Ain't nobody in Buffalo eatin' wings without blue cheese."

"Exactly," Lakena said, snapping her gum. "That's how you know we real."

Safiya nudged her. "We goin'?"

"Bet."

They had a little money left over from babysitting Lakena's nieces and nephews. In a family of eight, somebody was always having a baby, and being number seven meant Lakena was the built-in sitter. Safiya helped whenever she could — not just for the cash, but because that's how things worked in the Fruitbelt. Older sisters passed down responsibility, younger girls stepped up, and the neighborhood kept itself going long before the city ever bothered to.

Darling, Lakena's oldest sister, always paid them fair — not much, but enough for a slice, some wings, and the small pride of buying their own food with money they'd earned themselves.

They pushed open the High Spot door, the warm smell of grease and fresh pizza drifting out behind them as they stepped into the night. The Fruitbelt lay ahead — familiar, welcoming, home.

They crossed Mulberry, stepping around a pothole big enough to twist an ankle.

"Girl, watch it," Safiya said.

"It's Buffalo," Lakena shrugged. "Potholes got potholes."

They crossed Orange, the lamps blinking like they were tired too. A group of neighborhood kids were posted up on a porch, laughing loud.

"Hey Saf! Hey 'Kena!" one of them called.

Lakena clutched the pizza box tighter. "Don't let them see the wings," she whispered. "They gon' be askin' for some, and they ain't gettin' none of our food."

Safiya snickered. "You wrong."

"I'm hungry. Hunger make you honest."

They walked the last block toward Peach Street, where both their houses sat just a few doors apart. The fruit-named streets were more than a map; they were a language, a lineage, a neighborhood stitched together by families who'd lived there for generations.

"Saf..." Lakena's voice softened — rare, real. "No matter what... you know we good, right? Like... for life. Fruitbelt for life."

Safiya bumped her shoulder. "Fruitbelt for life. Always."

They kept walking toward Peach Street, pizza box warm in Safiya's hands, wings tucked under Lakena's arm, blue cheese containers clinking together like tiny promises.

Safiya's childhood taught her the power of community — not the kind written about in newspapers, but the kind built in drill team practices, summer camps, and Saturday night dance circles. She and Lakena had marched with the Neighborhood House Association Drill Team before they could spell "precision," wearing matching jeans and white T-shirts because uniforms were a dream they hadn't reached yet. They learned discipline, timing, pride — the kind of lessons people never credited Black girls with mastering.

The year they placed second at Drill-A-Rama, the whole Fruitbelt celebrated like they'd won the Super Bowl. A local artist even painted a mural of the drill team on the side of a building on Jefferson Street — bright colors, bold stances, the whole squad immortalized in motion. It stayed there for years, a testament to what the neighborhood built together, until a new owner painted over it, erasing a piece of history the community never forgot.

Across the ocean, another child was learning a different lesson: what it meant to survive without a net, and how that absence would one day shape the way he held others.

Chapter Six

The Soil That Shaped Him

The drought in Kenya had been relentless, a suffocating blanket of dust and despair that withered the maize and silenced the cattle. The earth cracked like old pottery. The riverbeds shrank into thin, muddy veins. Chemelu, barely a man, watched his village shrink with each passing month, the vibrant communal spirit draining away like water from cupped hands. Even the acacia leaves curled inward, as if bracing themselves against a world that had forgotten them.

The anger he carried was a bitter, scorching thing — a frustration with a world that could be so cruel, so indifferent. He remembered the sound of his mother's quiet prayers at night, the way his father stared at the sky as if demanding answers from a silent God. He remembered the hollowed faces of neighbors who had once been vibrant, the quiet resignation of elders who had seen too many seasons of loss. In his village, survival had always been collective — no one ate unless everyone ate — and watching that fabric fray taught him early how deeply communities depend on shared resources, shared labor, shared hope.

The student visa to the United States wasn't just an escape; it was a mission. A vow. A promise to himself that he would never again feel that helpless. He knew his journey wasn't unique — drought had pushed thousands of young people across borders, turning climate into a quiet migration force long before the world had language for it.

He arrived in North Carolina with little more than a suitcase, a worn leather journal, and a fierce resolve to build something better. That journal would one day sit beside a Be Rooted one — a pairing he could never have imagined then, two stories destined to intertwine. He pursued degrees in African Studies with a singular focus: to share the philosophy of Ubuntu — *I am because we are.* He vowed to build community wherever he landed.

He found a home, both geographically and spiritually, at Fayetteville State University. The campus buzzed with possibility — students from every background, faculty who believed in the power of education, and a community that felt familiar in its kindness. The rust-colored earth, the longleaf needles, the humid air — they reminded him of home in ways he hadn't expected. At the HBCU, he recognized a familiar rhythm — a community shaped by resilience, by history, by the unspoken understanding that education was never just personal advancement but a collective investment.

As a professor, his classroom became more than a lecture hall; it was a laboratory for connection. He saw his students not as pupils, but as future places of refuge for their own communities.

"We are not separate," he would tell them, his deep voice carrying a quiet certainty. "Fear is the illusion of separation. It makes you forget the God within us all."

He worked tirelessly to make his lessons matter beyond academia. His students were often out in the community, partnering with local organizations. He sent them to the same places Leha poured her heart into, believing that real-world application was as essential as theory.

He was already a respected partner of the Rooted & Rising program, having sent dozens of students to volunteer their time and skills. He loved watching them return changed — more complete, more compassionate, more aware of their own power.

His interest in the Rebuilding the Village Youth Initiative grew from this same philosophy. He saw modern city kids — disconnected from heritage, from community, from themselves — and he ached to offer them the foundation he had found in Ubuntu. He understood that disconnection wasn't a personal failing but a structural one — the result of fractured neighborhoods, overworked parents, underfunded schools, and a society that asked children to be resilient without giving them roots.

He recognized the same hollowed look he had seen in drought-stricken villages: the look of young people who had been asked to survive without being taught how to belong. It struck him that hardship wore the same expression everywhere — whether carved by hunger, violence, or neglect — proof that the conditions shaping young people's lives were different in form but not in impact.

So when he agreed to attend the meeting at The Gentle Ground Café, it wasn't just to pitch a mentorship program. It was to plant seeds of belonging, structure, and the unwavering belief that every child carried inherent worth.

He didn't know it yet, but the café's warm light and leaf-green walls would become a kind of sanctuary — a place where his past and future would finally meet. A place where the soil of his childhood and the soil of his purpose would merge.

He also didn't know it yet, but that meeting would change everything — for him, for Leha, and for the community they would one day build together.

Chapter Seven

A Mentor Who Saw the Unsaid

The scent of rich, dark soil and rosemary clung to Chemelu's hands as he finished tending his small garden. Dew still clung to the leaves, catching the early light like tiny shards of glass. A rare morning breeze drifted across the yard, stirring the magnolia leaves and cooling the North Carolina humidity that would soon settle like a heavy blanket. He brushed the dirt from his palms, grounding himself in the ritual that guided him each day. The rising sun warmed his back, a quiet reminder of the principles he lived by.

His world was shaped not by fear, but by the quiet certainty of connection. Gratitude was his prayer. Ubuntu — *I am because we are* — was his compass. Each sunrise affirmed the truth that rooted him: we are held together by something larger than ourselves.

He closed his eyes for a moment, inhaling the scent of rosemary, basil, and the faint sweetness of honeysuckle drifting from the neighbor's fence. In these moments, he felt closest to home — to the red earth of Kenya, to the elders who taught him that tending the land was a form of tending the soul. A single leaf drifted from the magnolia above him, landing softly at his feet — a quiet reminder that even falling things can land with grace.

Across town, Leha Harrington was preparing for the "Rebuilding the Village" Youth Initiative meeting at The Gentle

Ground Café. The event — a collaboration between her community-based mentoring work and several local partners — had drawn an impressive crowd. The room buzzed with purpose. This was what community looked like — showing up for the hard work of healing.

She scanned the attendees, her heart swelling with pride. Mayor Mitch Colvin stood near the front, deep in conversation with Veronica Jones, Vice Chairwoman of the Cumberland County Board of Commissioners. Judge Toni King, composed and unmistakably in command, spoke with volunteers about WORTH Court and Reclaiming Futures. Swan Davis of the Let's Make It Happen Together Youth Program was off to the side, laughing with a couple of teens he'd brought with him, his hand resting lightly on one boy's shoulder as he offered a few words of encouragement. Tracey Morrison from The Exclusive Press moved through the room with her notebook, capturing the energy of the night. A few teens from the mentoring program lingered near the back, watching the adults with a mix of curiosity and hope.

Fayetteville had shown up.

Later, after the meeting ended, the café slipped back into its familiar warmth — the scent of roasted coffee beans, a hint of cinnamon, soft jazz drifting through the air. Mismatched armchairs invited lingering, and curated books lined the exposed brick walls. A Be Rooted journal sat on the counter near the register, left behind by a mentee earlier that day — its gold-stamped affirmation catching the light. Leha made a mental note to return it.

She moved through the space with practiced efficiency, stacking chairs and wiping tables, her mind snagging on the rough edges of Tyashia's intake form. The room exhaled into stillness, the last traces of conversation fading as she worked. Soft jazz hummed low in the background, wrapping the café in a gentle hush.

Lost in her thoughts, Leha didn't notice the man approaching until he stepped into her peripheral vision — calm, composed, as if the room itself had opened to make space for him.

Chemelu's presence was quiet yet assured, commanding attention without demanding it. Tall, with rich chocolate-brown skin that held its depth even under the overhead lighting, he carried himself with a secure confidence. The crisp lines of his attire hinted at discipline; the subtle scent of sandalwood and shea evoked the motherland.

He looked almost regal.

"Forgive me for interrupting, Ms. Harrington," he said, his voice deep and soothing. "Your insights tonight about the importance of mentoring were a necessary reminder of the power of community."

Leha stilled, the damp cloth still in her hand. His directness, paired with the tenderness in his eyes, lowered her guard in a way she didn't expect. His appearance was striking, but it was his presence — strong — that drew her in.

"Please, call me Leha," she said, offering a gentle smile. "And thank you. My best friend Safiya owns this place. She believes in the power of stories and community. I just believe everyone has beauty within them — even when they can't see it, even when they make it hard to see."

A warm smile touched his lips. He picked up a stray napkin and dried a wet spot beside him.

"A bookstore and coffee shop is a powerful combination for community," he said. "Spaces like this... they become sanctuaries."

Leha nodded. "Safiya curates every shelf with intention. She says books are mirrors and windows — mirrors to see yourself, windows to see the world. She wants people to feel held when they walk in here."

"That is a ministry," he said softly. "Even if she doesn't call it one."

Leha's smile deepened. "She wouldn't. But she lives it."

He nodded, thoughtful. "The Creator works through people like that — those who build spaces where others can breathe."

Leha felt a spark — unguarded, unexpected.

"You're a man of faith, then?" she asked.

"A man of gratitude," he corrected gently. "I teach African Studies at FSU. The core of my heritage is Ubuntu — I am because we are. We are all connected, a living expression of the divine. My gratitude is my prayer, Leha. It is my daily practice."

"I love that," she said softly. "My best friend Safiya is like that. She's Muslim, follows her spiritual leader's teachings. We have different faiths, but she shows me every day that faith isn't in a title. It's in the principles you carry out — the kindness, the integrity, the support."

She paused, a memory surfacing.

"She grew up in Buffalo, in the Fruitbelt neighborhood. She once told me how she learned to see the 'God within' people — even the ones who struggle."

"Oh?" he encouraged.

"She remembers a neighbor, Bennie, who would get fall-down drunk on weekends. But when he wasn't drinking, he shoveled snow for elders, ran errands for seniors — he helped everyone. Safiya said Bennie taught her that everyone carries divinity, even when they're broken. We just have to choose to see it."

"A valuable lesson," Chemelu said, eyes warm with understanding. "It is the choice to look past the superficial damage and recognize the inherent worth of a soul."

They continued working, clearing the last of the clutter. The room seemed to quiet around them, the world narrowing to the space they shared.

"Sometimes we forget how deeply woven we are," he said softly. "Fear tricks us into believing we stand alone, when the divine thread runs through all of us."

A chill moved through Leha — one that had nothing to do with the air. His words struck something tender. Her carefully maintained guard. Her distant mother. Her fear of failing Tyashia. Her doubt during her morning run.

"That sounds like something I needed to hear today," she admitted. "I worry I'm too guarded sometimes."

"We all guard what is precious," he said gently. "The challenge is knowing when the guard is no longer needed."

He reached into his pocket and pulled out a small, elegant business card.

"I have a book I think you might appreciate — on Ubuntu and community psychology. I can bring it to you, or we can get coffee sometime."

Leha felt the spark again — quiet, warm, unexpected.

"Next week sounds perfect, Chemelu."

Later That Week

Leha stood in front of her open closet, debating outfits the way she always did when something — or someone — mattered. She wanted to look sophisticated, but with a gentle hint of intrigue — approachable, yet polished. After a few moments of consideration, she decided on dark-wash jeans, a crisp white blazer, beige pumps, and delicate gold jewelry. A high braided bun completed the look.

A short drive later, she sat across from Chemelu at a small corner table in The Gentle Ground Café. Afternoon glow streamed through the windows, catching dust motes that drifted lazily in the air. The scent of freshly ground coffee wrapped the room in comfort. A mellow neo-soul track hummed in the background.

The promise of their last encounter had become something tangible.

The front door chimed, and a young woman entered, trailed by two children who looked to be about eight and ten. The moment they spotted the owner behind the counter, the children — a boy and a girl — took off running.

"Safiya!" they shouted in unison.

Safiya looked up and beamed, catching each child in a quick hug as they swarmed her.

"Hi, Chloe and Carter, how are you doing?" she asked.

"Carter, I hear you won your school's spelling bee?" she added, giving him an enthusiastic high five.

"Yes!" Carter straightened proudly. "The last two words I spelled were *mosque* and *declaration.*"

"Wow, I am proud of you," Safiya said, her smile widening. "*Declaration* is a powerful word. Nice job."

Their mother, Neema, walked up slowly, carrying a small, flat cardboard box.

"Hey, Neema," Safiya greeted her warmly, taking the box. "Are these the lemon bars you mentioned?"

"They are," Neema replied, brushing a neat bundle of sisterlocks from her face. "Fresh from my bakery this morning. I saved you the best samples."

"Wonderful. I know exactly who I'm recommending these to," Safiya said with a laugh, already adding a price tag to the display case.

Leha watched the exchange, her heart tugging at the quiet space of the moment — a Black woman entrepreneur balancing business and motherhood in the same breath, children in tow because childcare was a luxury and community was the real safety net. Safiya didn't just buy Neema's baked goods; she amplified her, made space for her, folded her into the fabric of the café. It was the kind of everyday support that rarely made headlines but kept whole communities standing.

The small family found a spot at a nearby table. It was a simple moment — but it was everything Safiya believed in. Community. Opportunity. Dignity.

Chemelu followed Leha's gaze.

"It warms my heart," he said quietly.

Leha nodded. "It really does."

He reached into his bag and pulled out a slim volume with an African print cover.

"I found the book I mentioned."

"Thank you," she said, running her fingers over the textured surface. "This reminds me of my time in Kenya."

She told him about her trip — the Maasai elders, the dawn hot-air balloon ride, the raw beauty of the Mara. He listened with the same patient attention he had shown the night they met.

Their conversation deepened, moving past surface topics into shared values. Leha found herself opening up about her work with teens — the responsibility of guiding young people through a world that chipped at their spirits, especially Black boys carrying burdens too big for their age, and Black girls wrestling with their reflection in a society that prized straight hair over their own crowns.

"I have a new intake coming in this week," she said quietly. "A girl from Philly. I've only read her profile and spoken with her aunt, but… there's so much pain between the lines. You can feel it."

Chemelu nodded, listening with the same patient attention he had shown the night they met.

"Pain often shows itself before the person does," he said. "Sometimes through silence. Sometimes through anger. Sometimes through distance. But underneath, it is almost always fear."

He shared a memory of his youth in Kenya — of community rising together during impossible times. His story reminded Leha of the mobile mentoring bus, of the Community Anchor Initiative, of the people who showed up for one another.

"You challenge my idea of strength," she admitted.

A complaint erupted at the counter — a customer upset about a cold latte. Leha tensed, instinct flaring.

Chemelu gently placed his hand over hers. "One moment."

He approached the counter with calm authority, offering to pay for a fresh drink and a baked good. The tension dissolved.

When he returned, he resumed his seat and lightly touched the back of her hand.

"Strength isn't the absence of vulnerability," he said. "It's the capacity to be vulnerable and still move forward in love and connection."

Leha didn't pull away.

For a moment, the bustling coffee shop, the intake form waiting at her office, and the image of a girl she had yet to meet all faded.

In Chemelu's presence, she felt something she hadn't felt in a long time — possibility.

Not just for the work she did. For herself.

Chapter Eight

The Gentle Ground

The porch was quiet, wrapped in the thick stillness of a North Carolina evening. Fireflies blinked lazily over the yard, and the redbirds offered their endless chorus in the trees. A warm breeze drifted across the wooden planks, carrying the faint scent of jasmine from Safiya's garden. Two empty mugs sat between her and Leha on the small table, the last of the mint tea cooling in the day's leftover heat.

Leha had just ended her Sunday noon ritual — the weekly, carefully choreographed phone call with her mother in Charlotte.

"Amicable," she muttered, leaning back against the porch swing. She dragged a hand through her natural hair, the motion sharp with frustration. "We talked about the weather. My garden. Her church announcements. Fifty-eight minutes of avoiding anything real. It's an art form at this point."

She exhaled, the familiar pull of emotional distance settling over her like a shawl she never asked to wear.

"Sometimes I just want to scream at her," she whispered. "Why the distance? Why the wall?"

Safiya listened, her expression softening. She reached across the small table and placed her hand over Leha's, her touch warm and grounding.

"I know you want to fix it, L," she said gently. "You want to mediate the peace, organize the feeling, make the relationship make sense. But I need to tell you something I don't talk about much."

The night seemed to hold still. Even the redbirds softened.

Safiya took a slow breath, her eyes glazing with a sorrow that had lived inside her for decades.

"My mother… she took her last breath in my arms," she said quietly. "Right here in Fayetteville. I cared for her those last few months — day in, day out."

Her gaze drifted toward the dark yard, unfocused, lost in memory.

"It was December 22nd. I remember the exact date because it was the day the world stopped making sense."

Leha stilled, her own frustration shrinking in the shadow of her friend's grief.

"I was holding her hand," Safiya continued. "A hand that had worked tirelessly — raising five children, keeping our home afloat in Buffalo, wiping my tears when I fell off my skates." Her voice trembled. "I remember the smell of the room. Peppermint oil from her diffuser… mixed with that faint, metallic scent of sickness. I remember the oxygen machine — hiss, hiss, click."

She swallowed hard.

"And then the machine kept going, but she didn't. One minute there was breath, warmth, life… and the next there was just stillness. Silence. That foundational warmth just… vanished."

Leha's eyes burned. She saw her friend — her strong, balanced, faith-rooted friend — laid bare.

"There's an ache when you lose a mother that only someone who has lost a mother understands," Safiya whispered. "It's a specific kind of wound. A foundational piece of yourself that disappears."

Leha inhaled shakily. Her mother's face rose in her mind — cinnamon highlights, bright smile, guarded heart. She thought of her own walls, built to protect a tenderness she rarely acknowledged.

Safiya squeezed her hand.

"Cherish the presence, Leha. Fix what you can. Hold the peace where you can't. But do it while she's here. While she's still on this earth."

The certainty of those words draped over Leha like both a blessing and a warning. Something in her chest loosened — not relief, but recognition. Safiya wasn't telling her to force closeness or pretend the ache wasn't real. She was reminding her that time was a fragile thing, and that distance, once permanent, could never be bridged.

Tomorrow morning's pre-dawn run would carry a new purpose — not escape, but intention.

Chapter Nine

Hope in Motion

Safiya's words about the ache of maternal loss lingered in Leha's chest long after their conversation ended. They clung to her like a shadow that refused to step back — quiet, insistent, filling the places she tried to keep closed. What had once been an abstract fear — her mother's mortality — now felt painfully real, like a bruise she kept pressing without meaning to. The reminder pressed her toward presence, toward cherishing the complicated, imperfect people who made up her family. It was as if a page had shifted inside her — small, but unmistakable.

That conviction guided her movements as she prepared for the evening.

The community hall buzzed with a quiet urgency, the kind that made the air feel charged. Folding chairs scraped against the floor, volunteers whispered instructions, and the faint scent of coffee drifted from a table near the entrance. Flyers for the **Strength in Solidarity Suicide Prevention Event** lined the walls, their bold lettering a reminder of the gravity of the night.

Tonight wasn't just another community gathering. It was a lifeline.

Leha adjusted her name tag, smoothing the edges as if that small act could quiet her nerves. She stood beside her father, Sam, and her sister, Melina. Sam had driven them, his posture rigid in the quiet car, explaining that the event — hosted by Retired Command Sergeant Major Wesley Jackson, Director of the Sandhills Valor Network — was vital for the veterans he worked with and for his own ongoing awareness of PTSD after multiple combat deployments.

"A full house," Melina murmured, smoothing her Womack Army Medical Center uniform. Her voice held a mix of pride and apprehension.

"It is," Leha said, scanning the crowd.

The room was a mosaic of faces — Soldiers in uniform, veterans in unit ball caps, military spouses with tired but determined eyes, teenagers, elders, and Gold Star families. People who had lost someone. People who feared losing someone. People who were fighting to stay alive themselves.

Military life had its own sociology — a world where families shouldered the burden of repeated separations, where spouses became both shelter and guide, where children learned resilience before they learned multiplication. The uniforms in the room told one story; the eyes of the families told another.

This was community — showing up for the hard things, the heavy things, the things that required courage just to name.

A ripple moved through the room as the Fort Bragg Garrison Commander, Colonel Ramirez, entered with his senior enlisted advisor. They broke stride to shake Wesley's hand — a gesture of respect between leaders who understood the cost of service.

Wesley stood tall, his presence unmistakable. Even out of uniform, he held the quiet authority of a man who had spent decades leading Soldiers. His service record was etched into the lines of his face — Desert Storm, Iraq, Afghanistan, Korea, Germany, and countless stateside assignments. A lifetime of service, sacrifice, and leadership.

Leaders like Wesley bore more than their résumés revealed — the moral injuries, the impossible decisions, the memories they never spoke aloud. The Army taught them to lead Soldiers, but it didn't always teach them how to manage what followed.

Sam found them a seat toward the middle of the hall, near the back, his eyes scanning the room even as he guided his daughters. Leha had grown up watching that vigilance — the way Soldiers never fully relaxed in public spaces, the way trauma taught the body to stay ready. It was a kind of hyper-awareness passed down like an heirloom in military households, unspoken but ever present.

A small tension she hadn't realized she'd been holding eased slightly as her father sat beside them; he was "on duty," yes, but they were safe.

The speaker at the podium began to talk about finding calm not in the absence of chaos, but within it. Leha nudged her father gently.

"Wesley's philosophy," she whispered.

Sam nodded, a faint smile tugging at the corner of his mouth. "We learned that the hard way at the Sergeants Major Academy."

"Class 54," he added, pride and memory threading through his voice. "Fort Bliss. Long days, longer nights. We were just two senior NCOs trying to make sense of the world and lead Soldiers the right way."

He exhaled slowly, the breath leaving him like something he'd been holding for years.

"Wesley's the real deal," Sam said. "He's shouldered more than most. And he still shows up for people."

Leha felt the full force of that. The room, the event, the community — it all made more sense now.

The speaker continued — a tall man with a calm voice and eyes that held too many stories. He talked about finding calm not in the absence of chaos, but within it. About learning to breathe through the storms instead of waiting for them to pass.

Sam nodded slowly. "For a long time, peace meant the end of a deployment. Quiet. Safety." His gaze drifted to the stage. "Here… it feels different. Like it's a choice, not just a condition."

She knew what he meant. In military families, peace was often temporary — a wait between orders, a breath between storms. The rhythm of their lives was shaped by rotations, relocations, and the quiet recalibration that came every time someone returned home changed in ways they couldn't yet name.

Melina placed a gentle hand on his arm. The gesture was small, but it gathered decades of shared history — moves, deployments, homecomings, silences. Leha felt pride swell in her chest. This was resilience — choosing to engage with the hard things rather than hide from them.

As the speaker talked about foundations and tides, Leha's thoughts drifted to Tyashia. The girl's anger. Her grief. Her walls. A young soul trying to stay afloat in waters she never asked to swim. She realized suddenly that Tyashia wasn't the only one navigating invisible battles. Military kids grew up in the shadow of deployments, goodbyes, and the quiet grief of watching parents carry burdens they couldn't explain.

How do I reach her? she wondered. *How do I help her find something to hold onto when she's lost so much?*

When the event ended, Wesley stepped forward to address the crowd, his voice carrying the calm command of a man who had led people his entire life.

"To every Soldier, veteran, spouse, and family member here tonight," he said, "thank you for your service — not just the service you gave in uniform, but the service you give every day by choosing to stay, to heal, to show up for one another. This community is our rally point. We hold the line together."

The room erupted in applause — not loud, but deep. A sound of recognition. A sound of belonging. It wasn't applause for a speech. It was a collective exhale from people who understood that service didn't end when the uniform came off, and neither did the wounds.

Later, back at Leha's apartment, she and Melina sat around her small dining table, sipping iced tea. A woven straw tray from Jamaica rested between them, its sun-bleached edges carrying the feel of markets and morning laughter. The heaviness of the event lingered, but so did a sense of closeness.

Leha's phone buzzed.

She glanced at the screen. "Mom's going back to school."

Melina nearly choked on her tea. "Good for her. What's the major? Basket weaving?"

"GeoSpatial Studies," Leha read, disbelief coloring her voice.

Melina giggled. "GeoSpatial what now? Does she even know what that is?"

Leha dialed their mother before she could overthink it. Martha answered on the second ring, her voice bright and polished.

"Oh, daughter, it's fascinating! Mapping and data analysis of the earth's surface. And between that and dating after twenty-five years of marriage, I figured I needed a challenge!"

Leha blinked. Dating? School? Her mother was full of surprises.

After they hung up, Melina wiped a tear of laughter from her eye. "She's something else."

"She is," Leha said softly. "Always navigating the twists and turns."

The amusement faded, leaving the familiar thrum of unresolved tension — but also the enduring truth that family, however imperfect, was still worth showing up for.

Leha leaned back in her chair, letting the moment settle. The ache Safiya had described earlier — the ache of losing a mother — echoed faintly in her chest. She wasn't ready for that ache. Not yet. Not ever.

But tonight, surrounded by her father and sister, she felt something she hadn't felt in a long time.

Hope in motion — quiet, sure, like a leaf finally catching the wind.

Later, lying in bed, Safiya's words still echoed in her chest. The ache of losing a mother — the ache of almost losing one — pressed against her ribs like a memory she hadn't touched in years. She stared at the ceiling, her gaze drifting to the papyrus print of

Egyptian hieroglyphics she'd brought back from Cairo, the familiar symbols offering a kind of calm she hadn't expected.

Some wounds didn't start in adulthood. Some began long before you had the language to name them.

And as the house fell into its nighttime quiet, another memory rose — uninvited, but insistent.

A younger version of herself. A moment she had never fully unpacked. A truth she had learned too early.

She closed her eyes.

And the past opened.

Chapter Ten

The Day She Learned What Love Can Hide

Leha was nine the first time something in her family shifted — not loudly, not dramatically, but quietly, like a picture frame tilting on the wall without anyone noticing.

She adored her father. Everyone knew it. Sam Harrington was her hero — the constant force who lifted her onto his shoulders after long field exercises, who taught her how to lace her sneakers tight for morning runs, who always seemed to bring the scent of sweat, sun-baked fabric, and the faint trace of Army gear. When he walked into a room, the air changed. He was gravity.

Her mother knew that. And she protected it.

Martha kept her own emotions tucked away like folded linens — neat, pressed, hidden behind the closet door. She never wanted her daughters to lose sight of their father's goodness, even when the demands of military life pressed hard against her ribs.

Melina saw more than she should have. Even at six, she watched their mother with wide, perceptive eyes — eyes that caught the tremble in Martha's hands when Sam packed for deployment, the way she lingered in the doorway after he left, the way she smoothed the tablecloth twice when once would have been enough.

Leha didn't see it. Or she didn't remember seeing it.

To her, their family was perfect — a tight, unbreakable unit moving from base to base, held together by Sam's strength and Martha's quiet efficiency. She didn't notice the silences that stretched too long. She didn't notice the way her mother's smile sometimes faltered when Sam walked out of the room. She didn't notice the exhaustion in Martha's eyes after another night of waiting for a phone call that didn't come.

She only noticed the good. She only saw her father.

One Saturday morning, the illusion wavered — just for a moment.

Sam had returned from a field exercise, boots dusty, uniform creased. He kissed Martha's cheek, kissed Leha's forehead, and dropped his rucksack by the door. Everything looked normal.

But Melina tugged on Leha's sleeve and whispered, "Mama's sad."

Leha frowned. "No she's not."

But when she looked — really looked — she saw it. A quiver. A shadow. A tightness around Martha's mouth as she flipped pancakes. The second batch burned. Martha never burned pancakes.

Sam stepped outside to "check the car," though the engine wasn't even warm. The screen door slammed behind him.

Martha stood at the stove, spatula in hand, staring at the ruined pancakes as if they were a sign.

Leha approached. "Mama?"

Martha blinked, then smiled — too quickly, too brightly. "I'm fine, baby. Go play."

But Melina stayed rooted in the doorway, watching their mother with a seriousness far beyond her years.

Later that afternoon, Leha found her mother sitting on the edge of the bed, hands clasped tightly in her lap. The sunlight had shifted, casting long shadows across the room.

"Mama?" Leha whispered.

Martha looked up, eyes soft but tired. "Sometimes grown-ups go through things, Leha. Hard things. But we keep going. We keep the house running. We keep the girls safe. That's what matters."

Leha nodded, believing her.

Melina stood behind her, silent, watching.

Years later, when the separation finally came, Leha realized that her mother had been holding the family together with quiet, invisible threads — threads she never wanted her daughters to see.

She had hidden her ache so they could keep loving their father without question. She had swallowed her fear so they could feel safe. She had shouldered the emotional load so they wouldn't have to.

And Leha — the observant one, the strong one — had missed it entirely.

Now, lying in bed after the suicide prevention event, Safiya's words echoing in her chest, Leha understood something she hadn't before:

Her mother's silence wasn't distance. It was devotion. A sacrifice made in the shadows.

Tomorrow, she would reach for Tyashia differently. Not as a mentor. Not as a fixer. But as someone who knew what it meant to love a parent so deeply that you missed their pain.

Some wounds were inherited. Some silences were learned. And some bonds were forged in the spaces between what was said and what was swallowed.

There are stories mothers never mean to pass down — stories stitched into silence, into sacrifice, into the quiet corners of a life lived for everyone else. And there are stories daughters inherit without knowing, carrying them like folded notes in the lining of their hearts.

But there is also the moment — the sacred, trembling moment — when a mother finally speaks her truth aloud. And a daughter finally hears it. Not as a wound. Not as a heaviness. But as a doorway.

Healing begins there.

In the soft unraveling of perfection. In the courage to say, "I was afraid." In the grace to answer, "Me too." In the recognition that strength is not the absence of breaking, but the willingness to rebuild.

Mothers are not monuments. They are women — shifting, unlearning, remembering, choosing. And daughters are not just witnesses to that evolution; they are shaped by it, freed by it, softened by it.

This is the lineage that matters. Not the uniform. Not the roles. Not the years spent holding breath.

But the moment the breath is finally released.

The moment a mother chooses herself. The moment a daughter sees her clearly. The moment both realize that healing is not a destination, but a shared inheritance — passed down not through perfection, but through truth.

And in that truth, something ancient and tender is restored. A lineage made whole. A love made honest. A future made possible.

At The Gentle Ground Café, a slim book sat on the highest shelf behind the counter — a place Safiya called "the altar." Its spine was a soft, weathered green, the title embossed in gold script:

The Weight of Quiet Women *by Amara Ellison*

The cover showed a simple line drawing of a woman's hands — one open, one closed — as if holding something fragile and letting something go at the same time.

Safiya kept it there on purpose. "Some books," she liked to say, "wait for the right reader."

Leha had noticed it once, in passing — the way the gold lettering seemed to glint, the way the cover felt both tender and strong. She hadn't reached for it.

Not yet.

But one day, she would. One day, the words inside — stories of mothers who held the world together quietly, daughters who learned too late what that love had cost — would land in her hands at the exact moment she was ready to understand them.

For now, the book simply waited. Patient. Composed. Like lineage itself.

Chapter Eleven

Melina's Kitchen

Fayetteville felt different now — not because Leha had gone anywhere, but because her mother's first visit home after the separation had shifted something inside her. Martha had moved through Leha's apartment with a new kind of ease, wearing a honeysuckle-and-lemon perfume the girls had never smelled on her before, laughing in a way that didn't sound rehearsed. Even the crooked picture frame in the guest room had made her smile instead of reach for a tool kit. It was the first time Leha truly saw her mother as a woman rebuilding, not a wife holding everything together. That quiet shift lingered with her now — a reminder that even the strongest women deserved room to lean.

As she stepped out of the car, her foot hovered over a small ant pile near the edge of the driveway — one she hadn't noticed before. The mound looked harmless, almost neat, but a few disturbed grains of sand revealed the frantic movement beneath. She held there, watching the tiny bodies surge and scatter.

Something about their restless, hidden labor reminded her of her mother — always shifting, always in motion, always moving toward a life Leha couldn't quite see.

The image of Martha walking into the airport lingered in Leha's mind — a woman stepping into her own life at last. It contrasted sharply with the image of her hyper-vigilant father, a man who found his footing in structure and a quiet pastor. Relationships were messy, complicated things.

And soon, she would be sitting across from a girl who was already learning that lesson too early.

Leha hadn't met Tyashia yet — only read her file, heard the whispers, seen the patterns that echoed too closely the ones she'd watched unravel her own family. A girl walking a dangerous line, trading one form of control for another. A girl who needed someone to reach her before the pattern hardened into permanence.

Leha hoped she would be enough.

A few hours later, Leha stood in Melina's bright, modern kitchen, sipping coffee from a mug that read *Nurse: Healing Hands, Caring Heart.* The space smelled of onion, garlic, and fresh herbs — sharp, grounding scents that filled the room with life.

Melina — tall, gorgeous, with smooth yellow-brown skin and striking brown eyes — chopped vegetables with rhythmic precision. Her knife hit the cutting board in a steady cadence, like a heartbeat trying to find its balance.

"He's serious this time, Mel," Leha said, setting her mug down. "Dad wants our blessing."

Melina didn't stop chopping. "He's wanted our blessing for the last three women, Leha. Dad's a serial blesser."

"This is different," Leha insisted. "Sandy is… quiet. Not loud and flashy like the others. She understands him — the military stuff, the trauma."

Melina set the knife down softly. "Are you saying that because you like her? Because she's not Candace?"

"No," Leha sighed. "I genuinely think she's good for him. He's calmer. And Dad seems to actually trust her."

Melina exhaled slowly, looking out the window. A leaf drifted past the glass, caught in a lazy spiral before settling on the porch. Her eyes followed it, her expression tightening.

"Dad's opinion counts for a lot. But a blessing is a big deal, L. It means we accept this person as our new stepmother. Potentially forever. We've been burned before."

"I know," Leha said softly. "But Dad's happy, Melina. Genuinely happy."

A small, sad smile touched Melina's lips. She picked up the knife again but didn't resume chopping. "Happy is good. I just don't want to see him hurt again. Or us."

She stared at the blade, her beautiful features tightening. "It's easy for us to give Dad advice, to see his patterns. But my life..." She trailed off.

Leha straightened. "What's up, Mel?"

Melina set the knife down again — this time with a definitive clatter. "I'm tired, Leha. I feel like I'm stuck in this cycle. I keep finding men I have to fix, and it's draining. I give great advice to everyone else, but I can't seem to use it myself."

"Like the mailman?" Leha asked gently.

"Yeah. The lying, married, father-of-three mailman," Melina said, rolling her eyes. "Or the guy Dad tried to hook me up with — the one who was more interested in impressing the retired Command Sergeant Major than dating me."

She leaned forward, her voice cracking. "I'm scared, Leha. I'm terrified I'm going to end up alone. A spinster nurse handing out bandages and bad advice."

The confession hung in the air — raw, honest, heavy.

Leha moved closer, placing a comforting hand on her sister's arm. "You're not going to end up alone, Mel. You're just tired of men who don't 'get' you. Someone will see you for who you are — not a project."

"Maybe I already have," Melina murmured, a thin shadow of vulnerability crossing her eyes — a moment Leha didn't catch.

Leha smiled. "Okay. I'll reserve judgment on Sandy. For now. But I want to meet her. A proper interrogation."

"You got it," Melina said, lifting her mug. "I'll coordinate the dinner."

As Leha turned to leave the kitchen, Melina stayed leaning against the counter, her hand drifting subconsciously to her stomach. Her smile faded into a private, anxious thought — one she wasn't ready to share.

As Leha drove home, the sun dipped low, casting long shadows across the road. The quiet stretch of evening felt like an intermission — a breath between the day she'd lived and the one waiting for her tomorrow. She thought about the crooked frame in her mother's loft — a symbol of a life finally allowed to lean, shift, and breathe.

Everyone in her family seemed to be rebuilding something: her mother's independence, Melina's confidence, her own sense of purpose.

And somewhere across town, she knew her father was doing the same — searching for a peace he had never quite learned to claim.

The kind of peace that asked for a place to rest, not a uniform.

And soon, she would meet a girl who needed that same kind of presence — someone calm, someone patient, someone who understood what it meant to grow up loving a parent so deeply that you missed their pain.

Leha didn't know Tyashia yet. But she could already feel the shadow of what was coming.

Chapter Twelve

The Blueprint of Possibility

The memory lingered long after the moment passed — her mother's quiet ache, the silence she once mistook for strength, the realization that even the most solid foundations could shift without warning. It stayed with her like a soft pressure beneath her ribs, not painful but present. A reminder that the work she did with youth wasn't separate from her own story. It was shaped by it.

By the time she reached her office, dusk settling into indigo outside the windows, that awareness stayed with her — a tenderness she hadn't expected, a clarity she didn't know she needed.

The rhythmic scratch of her pen against her planner was the only sound in the quiet room. The building had long since emptied, leaving behind the faint glimmer of the hallway light and the low hum of passing cars outside. Inside, Leha was in her element — surrounded by optimism, purpose, and an overflow of motivation.

Spread across her desk were detailed calendars, color-coded sticky notes, and whiteboards mapping out the Sandhills Community Initiative's upcoming workshop series: **The Saturday Blueprint**. These all-day sessions, held on the last Saturday of each month, were the cornerstone of SCI's outreach — equal parts education, empowerment, and community healing.

She leaned back in her chair, rubbing her temples. Planning these events required a delicate balance of engagement and depth. They had to be relevant, sticky, and real. They had to meet youth where they were, not where adults wished they would be. She knew too well that young people weren't struggling in isolation — they were navigating the ripple effects of underfunded schools, overworked parents, unstable housing, and the quiet griefs that came with growing up in communities worn at the seams but still holding together. The Blueprint wasn't just programming; it was a response to the gaps society left behind.

Her planner lay open to a page filled with carefully written topics:

- Self Esteem
- Critical & Creative Thinking
- Values & Beliefs
- Healthy Habits
- Money Matters
- Self Expression
- Personal Growth

Each word held power. Each topic represented a gap she had seen in the lives of the youth she served — gaps she was determined to fill. Not because the youth were broken, but because the systems around them often were.

Her eyes drifted to the intake folder at the edge of her desk — the one with **Tyashia Harrington** printed neatly across the tab. The folder seemed to pulse with its own gravity, tugging at something tender inside her — the same place her mother's confession had shaken loose earlier. She knew now, more than ever, that silence had a cost. She didn't want this girl to carry hers alone.

Will she even show up? Will she trust me enough to try? Can I reach her before the world hardens her completely?

The questions lingered, heavy and unresolved.

She let the quiet settle into her bones. One step at a time. One child at a time. One blueprint at a time.

Her fingers drifted to the beaded bracelet on her wrist — the one she'd bought during her trip with Sampton Safaris Ltd. in Kenya. Sam, her guide, had slipped it onto her arm on the last day and said, *"These beads carry stories. Wear them when you need to remember your own."* She hadn't thought about the bracelet in a while — not until Chemelu stepped into her life and its stories began to stir again.

Tonight, as she stared at Tyashia's intake folder and felt the responsibility press gently across her shoulders, she traced the smooth beads with her thumb. The bracelet drew back to herself, reminding her of the red earth beneath her feet in Nairobi, the quiet courage she'd found there, and the truth the experience taught her — that growth was a winding path, never a fixed point. And that lineage — even the painful parts — could be rewritten with intention.

She made a note to contact **Jermecka Hamilton-Jackson**. The recent news release announcing Hamilton-Jackson's election as Director at Large for the North Carolina Nurses Association had caught her attention. A woman of color in a leadership role in the health sector was the perfect touchstone for the Healthy Habits workshop.

Highlight resilience and leadership, Leha wrote, circling the topic. *She'll inspire them.*

Her phone buzzed, breaking the quiet. A missed call notification glowed on the screen — one she didn't have the energy to return tonight. She set the phone aside, exhaled, and dialed **Melodie**, co-leader of the Rooted & Rising program. Melodie was her go-to collaborator for the Saturday events; her program's reach into the neighborhoods was invaluable.

As the call connected, a soft coo drifted through the receiver — little Ahli, her one-year-old grandson, adding his own gentle soundtrack to the moment.

"Hey, Melodie," Leha said, smiling at the sound. "Oh my goodness, he sounds adorable."

"Hey, Leha," Melodie replied, a tired laugh threading through her words. "He's my little shadow today. What are you doing still working?"

"Always planning, never stopping," Leha chuckled. "I'm mapping out the Blueprint series. We need volunteers for the Money Matters session. Can you help coordinate some parents to share their experiences with overcoming financial hardship?"

"Consider it done," Melodie said. "The parents need that conversation as much as the kids. And we'll get the Blue Anchor ready for transportation. We're in this together, remember?"

"Ubuntu," Leha said softly. "I am because we are."

Melodie exhaled — the kind of nod you could hear through the phone. "We've been living that long before we had a name for it."

After the call, Leha stared at the blank line beside *Critical & Creative Thinking*. She needed someone who could make abstract thought engaging. Someone who could connect philosophy to lived experience. Someone who could speak to the "divine within" and the power of thought.

Chemelu's name surfaced immediately.

Just as she reached for her phone, it buzzed.

A text from him: **Are you still mapping out the world in that office of yours? The Gentle Ground is closing soon. Come for a coffee and fresh air.**

A genuine smile warmed her face. Perfect timing.

Later that evening, The Gentle Ground Café was settling into its final moments of the day, the last of the customers trickling out as Safiya wiped down the counter. A thriving pothos sat near the register in a ceramic pot shaped like an open book, its trailing vines spilling over the edges as if reaching for conversation. The scent of espresso and cinnamon lingered, weaving itself into the room the way it always did at closing time.

Leha slipped inside, her shoulders relaxing the moment she crossed the threshold. This place always felt like a sanctuary — part coffee shop, part community hub, part sacred ground.

Chemelu sat in their usual corner, a book open in front of him. He looked up as she approached, his expression softening.

"You made it," he said.

"Barely," she laughed, sinking into the chair across from him. "My planner tried to hold me hostage."

"I suspected as much," he said, closing the book. "Your mind is always building something."

As she settled across from him, the beads on her wrist caught the light. Chemelu's gaze drifted toward them — curious, gentle.

"That bracelet," he said quietly. "It's Kenyan."

Leha glanced down, surprised he'd noticed. The band was unmistakable — rows of tiny red, black, green, and white beads woven in the colors of the Kenyan flag, finished with two small wooden beads at each end. It was the kind nearly everyone wore in Nairobi — handmade, humble, full of story.

"Yes," she said softly. "I bought it on my trip to Kenya. I wanted to surprise you by wearing it today."

A slow smile spread across his face, something tender gleaming in his eyes.

"Then you're carrying a piece of home," he said. "And a piece of my childhood."

The moment rested between them — quiet, certain, undeniable.

Leha cleared her throat gently, something brightening within her. "Well… tonight I'm building a workshop series. And I need a philosopher."

His eyebrows lifted. "A philosopher?"

"A professor," she corrected, smirking. "Someone who can teach critical thinking to high schoolers. Someone who can make it feel… alive."

Chemelu leaned back, considering her. "Alive," he repeated. "That is a worthy challenge."

"You might be a little too formal for them," she teased lightly.

His smile deepened, a rare spark of excitement lighting his eyes. "My classroom is about connection, not formality, Leha. And yes, I would be honored. To teach the youth to think critically, to see the connections between their lives and the wider world — that is the highest form of community action."

He leaned in slightly, his voice taking on that resonant tone that always seemed to settle her spirit. "I will teach them to question the illusion of separation. To understand that their thoughts have power. That they can use their minds to build, not merely survive."

Leha felt a wave of certainty wash over her. *This is the work,* she thought — the work her mother never had the space or support to do for herself. The work she now understood with new clarity.

"It's settled then," she said softly. "You're on for the third Saturday in March. Resilience is the assignment."

Chemelu's eyes softened, lingering on her a moment longer than necessary. "Then resilience," he said, "will be our shared lesson."

A small flutter rose in her chest — unexpected, but not unwelcome.

The future softened, no longer a solitary burden but something held in gentle company.

It felt like a blueprint she was building with rooted hands… and an assured heart.

When Leha finally stepped out of Gentle Ground, the night air wrapped around her like a cooler, sharper version of the café's comfort. The bracelet on her wrist glinted — a small echo of Kenya, of home, of purpose. Chemelu's words moved through her like a change in weather, subtle, insistent, impossible to ignore.

Leha unlocked her car, exhaling slowly.

Tomorrow, she would meet **Tyashia Harrington**.

And Tyashia's world was already beginning to crack.

Chapter Thirteen

The Small Openings

Across town, while Leha sifted through the quiet truths of her own childhood, another girl was learning how to navigate a house full of strangers and expectations she never asked for. Different stories. Different wounds. But the same ache of trying to find firm ground in a world that kept shifting beneath her feet.

Tyashia sat on the edge of the bed, flipping through the stack of school forms Sylvia had left on the desk. Westover High. New classes. New teachers. New people staring at her like she was the new problem in the room. She didn't bother filling anything out. The papers felt heavy in her hands, like expectations she never agreed to carry.

Her phone buzzed — a notification from a group chat she wasn't part of anymore. She swiped it away. The screen felt like a reminder of everything she'd lost: her friends, her routines, the familiar rhythm of Philly sidewalks. Here, even the silence felt different.

A sharp knock sounded, followed by the door cracking open just enough for Tasha to lean in.

"You got the forms?" Tasha asked, her tone clipped, like she was checking a box.

Tyashia nodded but didn't speak.

Tasha's eyes flicked to the untouched papers, then to the half-unpacked duffel bag in the corner. "School starts Tuesday. Don't be late. Westover don't play about tardies."

Tyashia kept her face blank.

Tasha lingered a second longer, arms crossed, thumb tapping her phone screen. A faint TikTok sound leaked from the hallway — some trending audio Tyashia didn't recognize yet.

"And… don't be weird," Tasha added, lowering her voice. "People already askin' who you are."

There was no malice in it — just the sharp edge of a girl who understood the rules of her terrain. The hallway. The cafeteria. The For You Page. The group chats that could turn someone into a joke before lunch.

Tyashia's stomach tightened. "I'm not trying to be anything."

"Good," Tasha said, shrugging one shoulder. "Just… stay in your lane. I got my own stuff."

She closed the door before Tyashia could respond.

Silence crept back in — thick, unfamiliar, too neat. Tyashia stared at the forms in her lap, her throat tight. She wasn't trying to be anyone's sister. She wasn't trying to take up space in a house that already felt full. She just wanted to survive the week.

Another knock — softer this time.

The door opened a few inches, and a small face peeked in.

"Um… can I show you something?"

Simon. Ten years old. Wide-eyed. Unbothered by anything, including his older sister's attitude.

Tyashia hesitated, then nodded.

Simon slipped inside, holding a massive LEGO build with both hands — a spaceship with moving wings, tiny compartments, and a level of detail that made her blink.

"I finished it today," he said proudly. "It took me three weeks. Wanna see how the engine opens?"

Tyashia leaned forward despite herself. "You built all that?"

"Yep." He pressed a hidden button, and a panel slid open. "I like science stuff. And basketball. And dinosaurs. But mostly science."

A small smile tugged at her mouth. "This is… actually really cool."

Simon beamed. "Thanks! Did Aunt Asiah used to like stuff like this? I heard you say she was fun. How come I never really knew her?"

The question hit her like a soft punch. She swallowed. "She… she lived in Philly. And things were just… complicated."

Simon nodded, accepting her answer without pushing. "Well… I wish I knew her. She sounds nice."

Tyashia's chest tightened — but in a different way this time. Softer. Sadder. Seen.

A knock interrupted them.

Cassidy, the middle sibling, twelve years old and already a comedian, poked her head in.

"Can I come in? Or is this the 'new cousin no entrance' zone?"

Tyashia huffed a laugh — the first real one since she arrived.

Cassidy stepped inside dramatically, hands on her hips. "Just wanted to tell you not to pay Tasha any mind. She acts like she runs the house, but she don't even run her own laundry schedule."

Simon giggled.

Cassidy straightened her posture, deepened her voice, and mimicked their father perfectly: "Welcome to Camp No Return, Troop. You will learn to like it here, Troop."

Even Tyashia laughed — a small, startled sound she didn't expect.

Cassidy grinned. "See? You'll be alright."

For a moment, the room felt less foreign. Less sharp. Less like a place she was intruding on.

Later, when the house finally quieted, Tyashia slipped downstairs for a glass of water. The pale glow of a tablet screen pulsed from the living room — Sylvia scrolling through Facebook reels, Leonard half asleep beside her. Their voices drifted low but clear enough to catch.

"What kind of mother leaves her child and never returns?" Sylvia whispered.

The softness Tyashia had felt upstairs vanished in an instant. Her throat closed. A slow pressure gathered behind her ribs, like a truth insisting on space. The ache she lived with — the one she never named — flared hot and sharp.

She stood frozen in the hallway, the cool glass in her hand suddenly too heavy.

Upstairs, Simon's spaceship still sat on her bed — wings open, compartments waiting, a tiny world built piece by piece. Down here, one whispered sentence shattered the small opening she'd felt.

She turned away from the kitchen, moving quietly back up the stairs, the ache settling into her bones like something inherited. Something she didn't ask for. Something she didn't know how to carry.

Something she would have to face — whether she wanted to or not.

Chapter Fourteen

The Unforgiving Glow

Westover High buzzed with the kind of energy she used to love — loud, messy, alive. But today it scraped against her nerves like sandpaper.

Even the drive in had felt wrong. Turning off Bonanza Drive, she'd caught sight of the cemetery sitting right at the edge of the campus — rows of quiet stones watching the school like silent witnesses. And just beyond it, Westover Middle School sat tucked beside the high school, close enough that she could imagine her little cousin walking those halls. The whole layout felt strange, too close, too exposed. Life and death sharing the same stretch of road.

By the time she stepped inside, her shoulders were already tight, resentment wrapped around her like a second skin, guarding the part of her that still felt cracked and unfinished.

She needed air.

Pushing past a knot of gossiping girls, she slipped into the nearest restroom. The door swung shut behind her, muting the chaos to a distant, underwater roar. Inside, the silence felt too sharp. A slow drip from one of the sinks echoed in the corner — a small, irritating reminder of how nothing here seemed to fit quite right.

Tyashia walked to the long bank of mirrors and splashed cold water onto her face, hoping to rinse off the displacement clinging to her like dust.

She looked up.

And for a heartbeat, the girl staring back wasn't her.

The reflection felt like a stranger — hollow-eyed, stripped of the attitude she used to wear like armor. Her braids, usually a crown she wore with pride, hung heavy, as if even they were tired. She stepped closer, earbuds already in, the mauve pink T-shirt peeking out beneath her jacket — white letters declaring *Built for This.* She let the bass thrum against her ribs like armor.

A wave of grief rose, hot and sudden, tightening her throat. Moisture gathered, stubborn and hot, forcing the tears back down where they belonged.

Not here. Not in this place. Not in front of mirrors that showed too much.

She straightened her spine, rebuilt her mask piece by piece, and walked out — leaving the stranger in the glass behind her.

The hallway smelled of gym socks, floor wax, and the cheap sweetness of a hundred body sprays. Wolverine pawprints dotted the floor. Blue and silver banners shouted *Wolverine Pride* from the rafters.

Clusters of students leaned against lockers, phones angled just right — recording dances, retaking selfies, checking who had viewed their stories. A group of boys huddled around someone's screen, laughing at a viral clip. A girl walked by with a ring light clipped to her phone case, filming a *Get Ready With Me: First Day Back* vlog as if the hallway were her studio.

Tyashia clutched her crumpled schedule in one hand and the signed mentoring forms in the other — the ones Sylvia had practically shoved at her that morning.

Mandatory, Sylvia had said. *Non-negotiable.*

Tyashia had dropped them off in the front office before first period, the receptionist sliding them into a tray labeled **SCI / After**

School Mentoring. Seeing her name on that list had made her stomach twist.

Now, as she searched for Room 204, she kept reminding herself:

Just get through the day. Then the meeting. Then home.

Rounding a corner, she nearly collided with a girl whose edges were perfectly laid and whose makeup was too precise for a Monday morning.

Tasha.

Her cousin's eyes flicked over her — hoodie, braids, guarded expression — and something sharp flashed across her face.

"Watch where you going," Tasha snapped, then caught herself. "Oh. It's you."

Tyashia stepped aside. "My bad."

"You lost?" Tasha asked, popping her gum. "Room 204 isn't down this hall."

"I'm figuring it out."

"Well, figure faster." Tasha lowered her voice. "People already asking who you are. Don't make it weird."

Behind her, a girl held up her phone, whispering, "That's her?" A notification pinged on Tasha's screen. She glanced down, smirked, and tucked the phone away.

A small, stubborn tension gathered beneath Tyashia's cheekbones. "I'm not trying to make anything weird."

Tasha shrugged, but her eyes softened for half a second. "Just… don't bring Philly drama here. Westover don't do all that."

Tyashia didn't respond.

She just wanted to disappear.

By the time the dismissal bell rang, her head throbbed. She stepped outside, the late-afternoon sun too bright, the air too thick. She followed the sidewalk toward the community center — the place Sylvia had circled on her schedule, the place the receptionist had pointed to when she turned in her forms.

The building sat between the playground and the basketball court, painted a warm beige with navy trim. Kids played outside. Parents chatted. A few Soldiers in PT gear jogged past.

Tyashia tugged her hoodie tighter.

A basketball thudded against the pavement — rhythmic, alive. A group of boys were running a half-court game, their laughter rising above the bounce of the ball. One of them called out, "Aye, new girl! You hoop?"

Tyashia shook her head, but the corner of her mouth twitched — the smallest, reluctant almost-smile she'd managed all day.

"Good," the boy said, grinning. "We full anyway."

Their laughter followed her as she walked toward the entrance — a tiny, unexpected mercy that loosened something tight in her chest.

Inside, the air smelled faintly of coffee and lemon cleaner. Flyers lined the bulletin board — tutoring schedules, community events, a candle-making workshop, something called *The Saturday Blueprint*.

She didn't care.

She just wanted to get this over with.

A few minutes later, Leha stepped into the lobby.

Tyashia glanced up.

The woman was put together — natural hair healthy and styled, a simple but elegant dress that fit perfectly. She looked like someone who belonged in warm cafés where people talked about futures instead of survival.

Leha smiled warmly. "Tyashia Harrington? Hi, I'm Leha. Come on back — we'll talk in my office."

Tyashia pulled out one earbud. "Okay."

The small office was bright and welcoming, painted a cheerful yellow. Posters of global landscapes — Paris, Kenya, Jamaica — adorned the walls. A carved wooden bowl from Kenya sat on the desk. An alabaster vase bearing the image of an Egyptian queen rested on a shelf. The faint scent of Kenyan coffee lingered in the air.

It was clean, warm, and everything Tyashia was predisposed to hate.

"Take a seat," Leha said, gesturing to a comfortable chair near the window.

Tyashia ignored it and chose a stiff metal chair by the wall.

Leha didn't push.

"So," Leha began, folding her hands calmly. "I heard you've had a tough time recently. I'm sorry about your aunt."

"It is what it is," Tyashia muttered.

"Sometimes," Leha said softly, "that's what we say when the truth hurts too much to touch."

Tyashia's jaw clenched.

"My aunt signed me up," she muttered. "It's mandatory."

"It may be mandatory to show up," Leha replied, "but what you do here is your choice. I'm not here to fix you. I'm here to walk with you."

Tyashia didn't believe her. But she didn't leave either.

"I'd like to connect you with Ron," Leha continued. "He's the school counselor — but he also has an office here after school. He's grounded. He listens. And I think he could be a quiet place to land for you."

Tyashia hesitated. "Will he try to fix me?"

"No," Leha said. "He'll meet you where you are."

Something in Tyashia shifted — not much, just a small loosening, like a knot pulled one thread at a time. She didn't believe everything Leha said, but she didn't feel the urge to bolt either.

She had to start somewhere.

And the idea of beginning again didn't feel like a threat anymore. Not easy. Not hopeful. But possible — like one of Simon's LEGO sets she'd seen him working on at Sylvia's house. A thousand scattered pieces, overwhelming at first glance… but somehow, in his small, patient hands, they always became something whole.

Maybe she could learn to build like that too. One piece at a time. One breath at a time. One fragile, trembling step toward something that didn't hurt.

Chapter Fifteen

Between Two Worlds

The next morning, Tyashia stood at the end of Shortridge Road, watching the man across the street wrestle a trash bin down his driveway. He spotted her and offered a polite wave — the kind of neighborly gesture she never knew how to return. It only made her feel more like she'd wandered into someone else's life.

Cottonade — or "the 'Nade," as she'd heard people call it — was quiet at this hour. Neat houses sat beneath tall, mature trees, the kind of aggressively suburban calm that made her feel even more out of place. Everything here felt too still, too manicured, too polite.

She adjusted the hem of her T-shirt — soft lavender, with the words **Keep Rolling** printed across the front in looping script. Asiah had bought it for her last summer, insisting she needed "something gentle to wear on hard days." Today, it felt like a whisper she wasn't ready to hear.

Over it, she wore a lightweight black bomber jacket, the kind with ribbed cuffs and a silver zipper she could fidget with when her nerves got loud. It wasn't a hoodie — it was sharper, cleaner, something that made her feel a little more put together without trying too hard. She paired it with dark jeans and her favorite black sneakers with the worn-in soles.

When the large yellow bus finally groaned to a stop, smelling of diesel and old vinyl, she climbed the steps and headed straight for an empty seat near the back. She shoved her earbuds in before she even sat down, letting the music that refused to lie to her drown out the world.

The bus rumbled forward, picking up more students along the way. Tyashia kept her gaze fixed on the window, watching the green blur of Fayetteville roll past — nothing like the cracked sidewalks and brick rowhomes of Philly. For a moment, she could almost hear the wheels of her skates hitting the uneven pavement back home. The memory tightened her throat.

At the next stop, two students climbed aboard with a kind of presence that shifted the air.

Vince — tall, broad-shouldered, dressed in black cargo joggers and a fitted long-sleeve graphic tee — swaggered down the aisle as if the bus belonged to him. His phone lit with a half-finished TikTok draft. Meja followed, her expression carved from stone, eyes sharp and scanning, taking in everything and trusting nothing. She wore wired headphones — a quiet rebellion in a world obsessed with Bluetooth.

They slid into a seat near the front, already deep in conversation. Their voices carried just enough for Tyashia to catch fragments — bitterness, frustration, something jagged beneath the surface. She didn't know them, but she recognized the energy instantly.

People who'd been disappointed too many times. People who built walls because they had to. People who survived by staying hard.

A thin pulse of recognition tugged at her chest before she shoved it down.

A few stops later, a girl with bright, curious eyes and a cascade of neat braids hovered beside Tyashia's row. Tyashia ignored her, staring harder at the passing trees.

But the girl didn't move on.

She slid into the seat across the aisle and flashed a wide, genuine smile — the kind that felt suspiciously bright.

Tyashia turned up her music.

The girl tapped her arm.

Tyashia yanked out an earbud. "What?"

"Hi!" the girl chirped, unfazed. "I'm Kendra. I haven't seen you on the bus before. You new to the 'Nade?"

"The what?"

"Cottonade," Kendra laughed. "Everybody calls it the 'Nade."

Tyashia shrugged. "Yeah. I'm new."

Kendra leaned in, undeterred. "I live on Shortridge too — number 1204. What number are you?"

"I don't know," Tyashia muttered. "It's just a house."

Kendra didn't miss a beat. "Anyway, welcome. It's a pretty cool area. I go to Westover too." She eyed the earbuds. "So… you a music person?"

Tyashia put her earbud back in and turned toward the window again.

A few minutes later, Kendra tapped her again.

Tyashia sighed. "What now?"

Kendra pointed to her backpack. Dangling from the zipper was Tyashia's roller-skate-shaped bag charm — bright blue and white, with tiny stitched pom-poms and the words **Roll, Bounce, Skate** embroidered across the side.

"Oh my gosh!" Kendra squealed. "Is that a skate charm? You skate?"

Tyashia blinked, caught off guard. "Yeah. I skate."

"That's what's up! I go to the rink every Friday night," Kendra said, excitement bubbling. "Skating helps me think. It's like therapy on wheels, you know?"

"No," Tyashia muttered — but the mention of skating pierced a tiny hole in her armor.

She sealed it shut immediately.

"Bet," Kendra said cheerfully. She pulled on her headphones and let the music guide her — a tap of her foot, a tilt of her head, a bright little beat only she could hear. She scrolled through her phone, liking videos, sending streaks, tapping through stories with the ease of someone who lived half her life online.

Tyashia shoved her earbud back in, letting the raw, honest lines fill her head again. She glanced at Kendra across the aisle. The girl seemed so open, so willing to connect. Too willing.

It had to be a performance. Nobody was that nice without wanting something.

Still… something about her voice tugged at a place Tyashia didn't want to acknowledge. A place Leha had poked at yesterday. A place that remembered what it felt like to have a friend.

She turned back to the window, jaw tight.

Up front, Vince glanced over his shoulder — just once — eyes lingering on her with a small shift of recognition. Meja followed his gaze, her expression unreadable.

Tyashia looked away quickly.

Trust led to abandonment. She wouldn't make that mistake again.

Saturday morning came too quickly.

Tyashia had successfully avoided Leonard all week, but Sylvia cornered her in the kitchen.

"Tasha has a JROTC event on base this morning — a drill competition," Sylvia said, voice edged. "Leonard is running the show, and I'm volunteering at the sign-in tent. You're coming with us. It counts toward your SCI mentoring portfolio."

Mandatory. The word hit like a punch.

An hour later, they were packed into the family's large SUV, which smelled of the same aggressive lemon polish Sylvia used on every surface in the house. Tasha sat in the passenger seat, fidgeting with her tablet, recording a quick *Come with me to my drill comp* video for her followers. Tyashia was wedged in the back, arms crossed, headphones ready.

Today she wore a charcoal zip-up track jacket — sleek, fitted, with white piping down the sleeves — over her **Made of More** shirt. It wasn't armor, but it felt like something she could hide inside without disappearing completely.

As they approached the Yadkin Road Gate, the air inside the SUV shifted. Even Sylvia's posture straightened. A line of cars crawled forward beneath the giant **Home of the Airborne and Special Operations Forces** sign. The American flag snapped sharply in the wind.

The SUV ahead of them rolled up to the guard shack. The MP scanned the driver's military ID, handed it back, and snapped to attention with crisp precision.

"Airborne, Sergeant Major," he said, voice sharp enough to slice the air.

Tyashia's eyes widened. She'd never seen anything like that — a stranger recognizing rank with that much certainty, that much consequence.

Sylvia eased their SUV forward next.

The Soldier's posture softened the moment he saw the civilian IDs. No salute. No sharp greeting. Just a polite, "Have a great day, ma'am," as he handed Sylvia's ID back through the window.

The difference landed hard.

Inside Fort Bragg, everything felt too big, too controlled. They passed rows of identical barracks, Soldiers jogging in formation, cadence echoing across the road. A Blackhawk thudded overhead, its shadow sweeping across the SUV. Signs pointed toward Womack Army Medical Center, Range 37, and training areas Tyashia couldn't pronounce.

Every other vehicle seemed to be a dark SUV like theirs. Everyone moved with purpose — the kind of precision Leha admired and that Tyashia instantly hated.

They arrived at a sprawling parade field buzzing with activity. Hundreds of teenagers in perfect ROTC uniforms stood in rigid formations. Drill instructors barked commands. Boots hit pavement in sharp, synchronized clacks. The smell of cut grass mixed with sweat and metal.

"See? This is what we train for," Tasha said proudly, adjusting her uniform with practiced pride.

Tyashia watched her cousin hop out of the SUV, adjusting her uniform with a confidence Tyashia couldn't imagine feeling anywhere.

She was assigned to hand out water bottles. She stood at the edge of the field, feeling like an alien anthropologist observing a strange, disciplined culture. Leonard strode past in his own sharp uniform, barking orders, eyes scanning the field but never landing on her long enough to acknowledge her presence.

This rigid structure — the rules, the hierarchy, the discipline — was their hold in the world. Their identity. Their comfort.

It was everything she resented.

A sudden roar split the air. A massive C-17 transport plane thundered overhead, low and loud. Tyashia jumped, her whole body reacting before her mind caught up. She stared up at the gray belly of the plane, a wave of displacement washing over her so strong it made her dizzy.

This is their world, she thought. *I don't belong here.*

A small ache unfurled beneath her ribs. She looked down at her hands, the lavender **Made of More** shirt hidden beneath her track jacket. Today, it felt like a taunt.

She scowled at the ground. A bright red pine needle lay at her feet — out of place, like her. She picked it up, rolled it between her fingers, then flicked it away.

"Not today," she muttered.

She went back to handing out water bottles, the culture of the military world pressing down on her shoulders like a pack she wasn't ready to carry.

Chapter Sixteen

Between Two Currents

A distant artillery boom cracked through the morning, sharp enough to jolt something in Tyashia as she crossed the courtyard. The drill competition on Fort Bragg still clung to her, the echo of boots and commands replaying in her chest. She'd tried to shake it off, but the memory followed her like a shadow.

Leha's voice lingered too — soft, grounding, threading through the noise in her head.

She cut across the back courtyard, hoping to avoid the hallway chaos.

But the courtyard wasn't empty.

A cluster of students stood near the picnic tables — not loud, not chaotic, but intense in a way that made the air feel charged. Tyashia recognized them instantly.

Vince. Meja.

They weren't talking so much as igniting — low voices, sharp gestures, the kind of conversation that radiated heat even when you couldn't hear the words.

Vince leaned against the table, broad-shouldered and confident, wearing gray Nike tech sweats and a crisp graphic tee with bold lettering across the chest. His chain caught the morning light.

Meja stood beside him in black cargo pants and a fitted crop hoodie, arms crossed, eyes scanning the courtyard with practiced suspicion. Her nails were long, almond-shaped, painted a deep metallic blue — the kind of detail that said she noticed everything.

Tyashia slowed.

She didn't want to be near them. But she couldn't look away.

People with walls always recognized each other.

Meja's gaze flicked up first. Sharp. Assessing. Then Vince's. Calculating. Curious.

Tyashia's stomach tightened.

Before she could turn, a familiar voice called from behind her.

"Tyashia?"

She spun around.

Leha stood near the walkway, a stack of folders in her arms, her expression warm but not intrusive. She looked out of place in the courtyard — too calm, too centered, too… sure in herself.

"I was hoping to catch you," Leha said. "I wanted to check in — things have felt heavy lately."

Tyashia swallowed. "I'm fine."

Leha nodded, not pushing. "Just remember — you don't have to carry everything by yourself."

A muscle in Tyashia's jaw twitched. She hated how much she needed to hear that. She hated even more that Leha could see it.

Behind her, Vince murmured something to Meja. Meja smirked. Tyashia felt their eyes on her back like heat.

Leha followed her gaze, noticing the pair without reacting. "If you ever need a quiet space before school, my office is open."

Tyashia shrugged. "Maybe."

Leha offered a small, patient smile — the kind that didn't demand anything — and headed toward the main building.

As she walked, Chemelu appeared from the opposite direction, a travel mug in hand. He greeted Leha with a warm nod.

"You look troubled," he said gently.

"Just checking on one of my students," Leha replied.

Chemelu took a thoughtful sip of his tea. "Ah. The youth were… how do you say it… 'giving very much attitude' today."

Leha blinked. "Chemelu. Please don't ever say that again."

He paused mid-sip, genuinely confused. "Is that not correct?"

"It is," she said, laughing despite herself, "but it's also… not for you."

He nodded slowly, as if filing the information away with academic seriousness. "Understood. I will retire the phrase."

"Immediately," she added, still smiling.

A small warmth settled between them — a brief, human moment that softened the morning's heaviness.

The moment passed, and Leha continued toward the building.

The instant she disappeared inside, Vince and Meja approached.

Not close. Not threatening. Just… present.

Vince nodded at her. "You're the new girl from Philly, right?"

Tyashia stiffened. "Yeah."

Meja tilted her head, studying her like a puzzle. "You look like somebody who's seen some things."

Tyashia didn't answer.

Vince smirked. "We get it. Westover's loud. Fake. People smiling like their lives perfect."

Meja added, "But some of us see through it."

Their words hit a place she didn't want touched.

A place that remembered pain. A place that recognized it in others. A place that felt safer in shadows than in sunlight.

From the hallway entrance, Kendra's bright voice echoed — calling someone's name, laughing at something on her phone. Tyashia didn't turn.

Vince's eyes flicked toward the building. "You ever wanna sit with people who don't pretend? We're around."

Meja's gaze softened — barely. "Just saying."

They walked off, leaving Tyashia standing in the courtyard, heart thudding, caught between two worlds:

Leha's gentle calm. Vince and Meja's familiar darkness.

She didn't move for a long moment.

Chapter Seventeen

Preparing the Ground

The bell rang, snapping the courtyard back into motion. Students spilled into the hallways, laughter and footsteps ricocheting off the brick walls. Vince and Meja drifted toward the main building, their voices low, their energy electric. Kendra nearly jogged past Tyashia, waving at someone, her brightness slicing through the morning like a neon streak.

Tyashia stood still for a moment, suspended between the three of them — Kendra's soft radiance, Vince and Meja's familiar shadows, and Leha's calm, unsettling hope.

Her breath snagged, thin and startled.

She didn't know which pull scared her more.

A notification buzzed on her phone. **Reminder: SCI Mentoring — Session with Ron.**

Of course. Another adult. Another conversation she wasn't sure she could survive.

But her feet moved anyway.

She slipped into the hallway, letting the tide of students carry her forward. The noise rose around her — slamming lockers, shouted greetings, the squeak of sneakers on waxed floors, the click of acrylic nails on phone screens. A girl filmed a quick hallway TikTok. Someone yelled, "Send me that clip!" A boy brushed past her, hoodie up, blasting drill music through a tiny speaker.

It all felt distant, muffled, like she was underwater.

She passed Vince and Meja near the stairwell. Vince gave her a nod — subtle, knowing. Meja's eyes flicked over her, unreadable.

Tyashia looked away quickly.

By the time she reached the counseling wing, her pulse had finally eased, but the morning's heaviness clung to her like dust she couldn't brush off. She waited outside Ron's door, hand hovering over the handle.

Leha's voice echoed in her mind. *You don't have to carry everything alone.*

She wasn't sure she believed that.

But she opened the door anyway.

Ron sat alone in his office, the early morning shine filtering through the blinds in soft stripes. The building was quiet — that sacred, fleeting stillness before the first bell, when the halls hadn't yet filled with teenage noise and unspoken stories.

His desk was neat, save for the file in front of him.

Harrington, Tyashia.

He opened it slowly.

Aunt deceased. Mother absent. Relocation from Philadelphia. Signs of grief, anger, withdrawal.

He exhaled — a long, grounding breath that came from somewhere deeper than his lungs.

He'd seen this kind of pain before. The kind that didn't shout. The kind that hardened into silence if no one reached it in time.

He stood and walked to the small sink in the corner of his office. Warm water ran over his fingers as he washed his hands — a ritual shaped by both his Army years and his faith. The discipline of one, the reverence of the other. A symbolic cleansing before stepping into someone else's storm.

"Lord," he murmured, drying his hands, "help me meet this young lady where she is. Help me hear what she can't say yet."

He straightened the chairs, placed a box of tissues within reach — not centered, but off to the side, where it wouldn't feel like an expectation — and whispered a final prayer.

"Let her know she's not alone."

A soft knock sounded at the door.

"Come in," he said.

Tyashia stepped inside, the air smelling faintly of paper, wood polish, and the clean bite of hand sanitizer. Ron sat behind his desk, exactly as Leha had described him — a quiet presence. His neatly trimmed beard framed a face that radiated calm, and his eyes held the kind of unwavering grace that made people feel seen even when they didn't want to be.

A framed photograph sat on his desk: a family group smiling with unguarded joy. The image made something twist inside her — a reminder of what she'd lost, what she'd never had, what she didn't trust anymore.

She chose the stiff metal chair by the window — the same kind she gravitated toward in Leha's office. Hard edges. No comfort. No softness. A chair that didn't ask anything of her.

Ron didn't comment. He simply nodded, giving her space.

"Leha tells me you're new to Fayetteville," he said, his voice low and even. He didn't push. Didn't pry. He just let the silence settle between them like a soft blanket.

But silence had presence. And eventually, it pressed too hard.

"Everyone just wants me to get over it," she snapped, arms crossing tightly over her chest. "Get over my aunt dying. Get over my mom leaving."

Ron leaned forward slightly, his large hands folding on the desk. "Grief has its own timeline, Tyashia. You don't 'get over' a loss like that. You learn how to carry it."

He gave the words room to land.

"It's like an overloaded backpack. When you first put it on, it feels impossible. But piece by piece, we can take some of what's inside it out. First, though, we have to name what's in it."

Her voice thinned to a thread. "I'm tired of carrying it," she whispered.

The tears came fast — hot, sudden, unstoppable. The ones she'd swallowed since the funeral. The ones she'd buried under anger and silence.

Ron slid a box of tissues toward her, but he didn't speak. He didn't fill the space. He just stayed present.

She cried for Asiah — for the good days, the laughter, the joy she brought into every room. She cried for the unfairness of cancer. She cried for her mother, for the abandonment that still stung like a fresh wound. She cried for the girl she used to be.

When the sobs finally slowed, Ron spoke gently.

"You know, anger is just the protector. It's like a bouncer at a club — keeping the real, scary emotions out. What's the scariest emotion you're protecting right now?"

She hesitated. The wall she'd built — brick by brick — cracked under the pressure of his patience.

"That everyone always leaves," she said, barely audible.

Ron nodded, his expression soft. "That's a heavy thing to carry. But we can work on that."

He let the silence breathe again before continuing.

"Leha mentioned she gave you a small assignment — to find one good thing in Fayetteville."

Tyashia stiffened. "I haven't."

"Not yet," he corrected gently. "But that's your homework for next time. One thing. Anything. A tree. A song. A moment. A person."

She didn't argue. She didn't trust her voice.

She stood, feeling unburdened and terrified at the same time — like she'd set something down but wasn't sure she could walk away from it. The office felt quieter now, the ticking clock less sharp, the air less suffocating.

She stepped into the hallway.

The noise hit her immediately — laughter, footsteps, the slam of lockers — but it didn't swallow her whole this time.

Up ahead, Kendra stood at her locker, her pink headphones around her neck. A mirror was taped inside, ringed with tiny stick-on rhinestones like a makeshift studio setup. She'd even labeled the corner *Kendra Live.* She spotted Tyashia and lifted a hand in a small, hopeful wave.

Tyashia didn't wave back. But she didn't look away either.

Further down the hall, Vince leaned against the water fountain, Meja beside him. They weren't smiling, but their eyes tracked her with a quiet recognition — the kind that said *we see you* in a way that felt both comforting and dangerous.

Three currents. Three possible paths. Three versions of who she could become.

She pushed open the side door and stepped outside.

A single magnolia leaf drifted down from the tree above her, spinning lazily before landing at her feet. She stared at it — simple, soft, unbothered by the weight she carried. For a moment, she let herself breathe.

As she headed toward the exit, Sylvia's voice drifted from the main office. She stood with Leha near the front counter, arms crossed, expression tight in that way adults get when they're trying not to show worry.

"...she's been quiet," Sylvia was saying. "More than usual. I don't know what to do with that."

Leha nodded, listening with the same sturdy presence she offered Tyashia. "Quiet can mean many things. Sometimes it's protection. Sometimes it's exhaustion. Sometimes it's just... grief settling in."

Sylvia exhaled sharply. "She won't talk to me. Not really."

"She doesn't have to talk yet," Leha said gently. "But she does need consistency. And options."

Sylvia hesitated. "Is she making any progress?"

Leha didn't sugarcoat it. "She's hurting. But she's showing up. That matters more than you think."

Sylvia looked down at her hands. "I just want to do right by her."

"You are," Leha said. "And I'd like to support that. SCI is doing a small service project this Saturday — nothing overwhelming. Just assembling hygiene kits for students who need them. I think it could give her a sense of purpose. A place to breathe."

Sylvia considered this, then nodded. "If you think it'll help... she can go."

"I'll pick her up at nine," Leha said.

They parted ways, and Sylvia stepped outside — just as Tyashia approached. Sylvia opened her mouth to say something, but Tyashia brushed past her, jacket collar up, earbuds in.

Sylvia watched her go, worry tightening her jaw.

Leha watched too — but with something softer. Something patient.

A moment later, Leha caught up to her near the doors.

"Oh — Tyashia," she said, rebalancing a stack of folders. "I was hoping to catch you."

Tyashia stiffened. "Why?"

Leha offered a small, warm smile. "SCI is doing a service project this Saturday. Nothing big — just assembling hygiene kits for students who need them. I think it could be a good fit for you."

Tyashia opened her mouth to refuse, but the words stuck. Ron's voice echoed in her mind.

One good thing.

She swallowed. "Do I have to?"

"No," Leha said gently. "But I'd like you there. And I think you might like you there too."

Tyashia didn't answer. But she didn't say no.

Leha nodded, as if that was enough. "I'll pick you up at nine."

As Leha walked away, Tyashia felt eyes on her. Vince and Meja stood near the trophy case again — watching, assessing, recognizing something in her she wasn't ready to name.

She folded her arms across her ribs and stepped outside into the cold air.

Saturday was coming.

And something in her — small, trembling, stubborn — was beginning to shift.

Chapter Eighteen

The Weight of Compassion

The air inside the mentoring outreach van smelled faintly of disinfectant and old floor mats — the scent of places where people waited, hoped, or tried to start over. Tyashia sat in the back seat, headphones clamped over her ears, watching the Cumberland County scenery blur past the window. Tall Carolina evergreens. Brick houses. A sky too open, too bright.

Saturday mornings used to mean roller skating through Philly streets with Asiah cheering from the stoop. Now she was being hauled to Westover Middle School for "volunteer work" — Leha's latest attempt at what she called community action.

Leha drove with her usual calm focus, hands relaxed on the wheel. The compact van moved down the road, Foxy 99 playing low on the radio — the kind of smooth Fayetteville R&B mix that made the morning feel softer than Tyashia wanted it to.

In the passenger seat sat a boy about her age, wiry and quiet, posture stiff with the same discomfort she felt.

Kaymon.

Leha had introduced him briefly when he climbed in — a soft-spoken kid from Westover High who'd been in the program longer than she had. He hadn't said a word since they left.

Great, she thought. A field trip for the emotionally damaged.

She pushed her earbuds in tighter, letting the bass drown out her thoughts.

Leha parked near the school's side entrance. "Okay, team," she said brightly, turning in her seat. "Today we're focusing on dignity and hygiene. The school received a grant for a washer and dryer, but they need hygiene kits to go with it. SCI is filling the gap."

Tyashia shrugged and grabbed a cardboard box from the back. She didn't want to care. Caring hurt.

Inside the gym, a long table was already set up with bulk supplies — soap, toothpaste, deodorant, sanitary products, socks, combs, and small laundry pods. A rolling cart of folded hand towels sat off to the side, its wheels squeaking every time someone brushed past it, the sound cutting through the wide, echoing space.

"Tyashia, you take the sanitary products. Kaymon, you're on soap and toothpaste," Leha said, already arranging items into neat assembly lines.

Tyashia moved to her station, working quickly and mechanically. She tore open a bulk pack of maxi pads and began stacking the smaller packages into tidy piles. The repetitive motion soothed her — something to do with her hands, something that didn't require talking or feeling.

Crinkle.

The sound froze her.

The plastic in her hand — that soft, familiar crinkle — pulled her backward in time.

Suddenly she was in Asiah's tiny Philly laundry room, the smell of Tide thick in the air. She remembered folding clothes that didn't belong to them — uniforms, mismatched socks, shirts in sizes too small for her.

Because some kids don't have clean clothes to wear to school, Tye, Asiah had said gently. *Everyone deserves a clean start.*

Asiah had kept a locked cabinet in her classroom filled with spare clothes, underwear, toothbrushes, combs, and those same little boxes of pads. She never made a show of it. She never asked for recognition. She just quietly made sure kids had what they needed.

That was community action.

The memory hit like a soft punch — grief and admiration tangled together. Silence pressed against her windpipe. She forced the sting back with a slow inhale and kept stacking.

But something had shifted.

This wasn't busy work. It mattered.

She sped up her pace, hands moving with new purpose, her breath evening out as she worked.

Across the table, Kaymon glanced at her — just once — as if he recognized the shift. He didn't speak, but his hands moved faster too.

Two kids who didn't want to feel anything… feeling something anyway.

Later, Leha approached with a small frown. "We seem to be short on deodorant sticks. We may need to adjust the numbers."

Tyashia glanced at her pile. She had already added a few extras she'd found in the main supply bin.

"Oh," Leha said, noticing. "Looks like you already fixed it. Good thinking."

Heat rose in Tyashia's cheeks. "Just wanted to finish faster," she muttered.

But she didn't meet Leha's eyes.

She kept her expression flat for the rest of the project, even as she quietly slipped a few extra bundles of socks into the final boxes.

When they finished loading the van, Leha locked the door and smiled. "Great work today, team. We made fifty kits."

Kaymon offered a tiny smile — the first she'd seen from him.

Leha stretched her back, then glanced at the two of them. "You know," she said lightly, "if y'all keep working this fast, I'm going to have to start bribing you with Bojangles biscuits."

Kaymon snorted — an unexpected, soft laugh he tried to hide.

Tyashia blinked. She hadn't expected that sound from him. She hadn't expected it from herself either — the small, reluctant tug at the corner of her mouth.

Leha grinned. "See? I knew food would break the silence eventually."

Kaymon shook his head, embarrassed but smiling now. "I mean… if you're offering biscuits…"

Leha gasped dramatically. "Oh, so *now* you talk."

The moment was small, but it cracked something open — a sliver of warmth in the cool morning air.

Tyashia shoved her hands into the pockets of her black cargo joggers, the fabric soft from wear. She wore a cropped windbreaker today — black with a silver zipper and a subtle reflective stripe across the chest. It wasn't flashy, but it felt like armor she could move in.

She walked toward the van without a word.

She was still grieving. Still angry. Still lost.

But something inside her — something small and fragile — had shifted.

She didn't have a name for it yet. But it was there.

Chapter Nineteen

The Divine in the Everyday

Leha was reviewing the Sandhills Community Initiative (SCI) program budget when her phone rang. It was Safiya.

"As salaam alaikum, my friend," Safiya's warm voice greeted her.

"Wa alaikum as salam, Safiya," Leha replied, smiling as she put the call on speaker. She could hear the faint clatter of ceramic and imagined Safiya in her kitchen, surrounded by spices and the two wooden plaques she loved — *Start with Bismillah* and *End with Alhamdulillah* — hanging from a simple burlap rope.

"How are things?"

"Busy, but good. Ramadan is approaching, so we're prepping a bit differently."

"Ramadan," Leha echoed. "I know the basics, but not the rhythm of it."

Safiya chuckled softly. "Most people only see the fasting. But Ramadan is a whole reset. A cleansing. A month where everything slows down and sharpens at the same time."

Leha's fingers stilled, listening.

"I start with meal planning," Safiya continued. "Suhoor — the pre-dawn meal — has to be light but sustaining. Oats, dates, fruit, lots of water. And for iftar, I always break fast with dates and water, then something warm. My navy bean soup is a staple."

Leha smiled. "You and that soup."

"You'll thank me one day," Safiya teased. "But it's not just food. I map out my prayer times. Fajr before sunrise, Dhuhr at midday, Asr in the afternoon, Maghrib at sunset, Isha at night. During Ramadan, I add Taraweeh — the night prayers. It's a beautiful exhaustion."

Leha imagined the discipline, the devotion, the intentionality. "That sounds… centering."

"It is," Safiya said. "And before each prayer, we perform Wudu — a ritual washing. Hands, mouth, nose, face, arms, head, ears, feet. It's physical, yes, but it's also a spiritual cleansing. A way of washing off the world before entering a moment with God."

Leha leaned back, absorbing the quiet wisdom. "A form of resilience."

"Exactly," Safiya replied. "It's choosing to look past the superficial damage and recognize the inherent worth of a soul — including your own."

They lingered in the hush before Safiya's voice softened again.

"Thank you," she said. "For letting me talk about my faith without shrinking myself."

"You never have to shrink around me," Leha said gently.

"I know," Safiya replied. "But that's rare here. You give me space to breathe."

When the call ended, Leha stayed still for a moment, letting Safiya's words settle. Something in her chest felt clearer — not louder, not brighter, just aligned. She needed space to carry that feeling forward, so she grabbed her keys and drove toward The Gentle Ground Café, craving the subtle warmth of Safiya's space before the gallery event.

The café was in its late-afternoon lull — intimate chatter floating from a couple by the window, their shared smiles and quiet laughter filling the space more than the speakers ever could. Sunlight spilled across the wooden floor in warm rectangles.

Behind the counter, Safiya was rearranging the bookstore display — her quiet ritual whenever the café felt too still. She moved with intention, fingertips brushing the spines of books as if greeting old friends.

She paused at a pair of titles she'd been debating all week:

How to Eat to Live — Elijah Muhammad Message to the Black Man — Elijah Muhammad

She held them for a moment, weighing their presence. Not because she doubted their place here — but because she understood what they carried. The history. The tension. The pride. The questions.

A college student wandered in, ordered a chai latte, and drifted toward the shelves. He rested at the two books Safiya had just placed, reading the back covers with quiet curiosity. He didn't buy them. He didn't ask questions. He simply let the moment take him — a moment of recognition, a moment of inheritance.

Safiya watched him with a softening in her eyes. She didn't interrupt. She didn't explain. She simply let the moment exist.

Leha watched from across the room, something warm blooming in her chest. Faith in the everyday. Culture in the open. Curiosity without shame.

Her phone buzzed.

A text from Chemelu: **Looking forward to the gallery opening tonight. Hope your day has been kind to you.**

Leha smiled — a genuine, unguarded smile that reached her eyes. She slipped her phone into her bag, thanked Safiya for the space, and stepped back into the bright afternoon.

The comfort of the café lingered as she drove toward the downtown arts district. The late-afternoon sun stretched long across the pavement, and something in her eased — clear in her purpose, softened by connection, ready for whatever the evening held.

That evening, the gallery stirred with life — a brushed snare whispering through the speakers, a sax line curling lazily around the murmur of conversation and the clink of glasses. The scent of perfume mingled with wine and the earthy aroma of clay and canvas.

Chemelu didn't just look at the art; he interpreted it.

"This artist," he said, pausing before a vibrant abstract piece streaked with Fayetteville red clay, "is showing the 'God within' the earth itself. They see divinity in the ground we walk on."

Leha found herself captivated — not just by the art, but by him. His gratitude for life was infectious. She watched how he navigated the crowd, how people leaned in when he spoke.

"You have a way of seeing the world that's truly unique," she said softly.

"We all do," he replied. "We just have to choose to open our eyes."

Their hands brushed — a small, unplanned moment — but it carried a quiet certainty that startled her. Not fear. Not hesitation. Just… recognition.

"But what about the kind of fear that doesn't move when you push it?" she asked, thinking of Tyashia. "The kind that settles in your bones."

"When fear grows too heavy for one person to carry," he said gently, "community becomes the hands that lift it. No one heals alone, Leha. Not truly."

She felt something shift — not a dramatic revelation, but a quiet alignment, as if his words named a truth she had always known but never spoken aloud.

"Did you always believe that?" she asked.

"My father taught me," he said. "During the drought in Kenya, our community nearly broke. But we shared everything we had. We prayed together. Faith is practical. It's sharing your last cup of water. It's telling a story to keep hope alive."

Leha exhaled, the truth of his words settling into her chest.

"Safiya says faith isn't a title," she murmured. "It's the principles you carry out."

He nodded. "Ubuntu is simple. Your well-being is linked to mine. When I help you, I help myself."

A colleague stopped them briefly. They responded with practiced poise, then slipped back into their shared space.

He reached out and rested his fingers lightly against the back of her hand — not asking, not assuming, simply offering presence. She didn't brace herself. She let the moment land.

As they moved through the gallery, weaving past a few students from Fayetteville State University, Leha felt a tug of purpose. Even in the middle of art and soft jazz and the coziness of Chemelu's presence, Tyashia lingered in her thoughts — not as a worry, but as a calling.

Ubuntu. I am because we are.

Looking at Chemelu, she realized she was building her own network of deep connections — her father's strength, Melina's laughter, Safiya's quiet faith, the community leaders she partnered with, and now Chemelu's quiet divinity.

Faith over fear.

The pieces of her life were forming a stronger whole. The walls she had carried for so long — the ones she thought kept her safe — felt suddenly unnecessary in the ease of his presence.

Later that night, when she returned to her office to grab a forgotten folder, she stood at her desk, feeling the echo of the evening settle into her. She reached out to Safiya to coordinate schedules for the week ahead, her mind already turning toward the youth she served — especially Tyashia.

The future held challenges, yes. But it also held glimmers of hope.

Chapter Twenty

The Circle That Holds Us

Leha's home in Fayetteville always welcomed you before you even stepped inside — a wreath of eucalyptus and dried lavender hanging on the door, and a welcome mat stitched with *Leave Your Worries at the Door*, its edges softened by years of women crossing that threshold with stories they weren't ready to say out loud. On Sister Circle night, the house felt prepared, expectant, arranged with the kind of intention that made every woman who entered feel held.

The living room had been transformed: chairs pulled into a wide arc, soft blankets draped over the couch, candles flickering on the coffee table, sending soft gold across the room.

The air was fragrant with the feast Leha had spent the afternoon preparing — lemon chicken roasted with herbs, creamy macaroni and cheese bubbling under a golden crust, bright salads tossed with citrus dressing, and decadent desserts that promised comfort. Cooking for the Circle was her offering of Ubuntu — nourishment as love, food as fellowship.

The Sister Circle Book Club was more than a gathering. It was a force.

There was Maya, the sharp-witted attorney whose opinions could slice through any argument with surgical precision. Brenda, the kindhearted nurse whose laughter filled every room like a burst of summer air. Sarah, the perpetually optimistic teacher who believed every problem had a solution if you just breathed through it. Aisha, the quiet powerhouse who ran her own catering business and carried wisdom in her silence. And Natalie, the introspective social worker who always surprised them with her depth.

Their opinions often clashed — sometimes loudly — but the ritual of food and fellowship always stitched them back together.

Safiya sat near the window, grounding as always. She'd brought a fresh bag of BLK & Bold specialty beans from The Gentle Ground Café — a gesture Leha never took for granted. The rich, roasted aroma drifted through the room, mingling with the scent of lemon chicken and warm spices. It added a subtle depth to the air, a quiet nod to Black craftsmanship and community care.

Leha smiled as she set the beans beside the coffee maker. "You always bring the good stuff."

Safiya shrugged lightly, her eyes gleaming. "We support who supports us."

Leha, usually the pragmatic organizer, felt a flutter of nerves tonight. She had more than literature to share. Something inside her had shifted — something tender, something hopeful — and she wasn't sure she was ready to name it aloud.

Once the room gathered itself, she opened the meeting. "Welcome, ladies. Tonight's discussion: *The Best of Everything* by Kimberla Lawson Roby."

The debate ignited instantly.

"I found Alicia utterly frustrating," Maya declared. "She had everything — stability, a good husband — and she nearly threw it all away chasing a superficial dream."

"Relatable," Sarah countered. "Stability can feel like a trap. The book captured that tension between gratitude and ambition."

Natalie surprised them. "It wasn't about wanting everything. It was about redefining fulfillment. Sometimes you have to break things down to rebuild what truly matters."

The conversation swelled — career versus family, ambition versus contentment, gratitude versus longing. Leha moderated with practiced ease, guiding the dialogue through its natural peaks and valleys. She loved watching these women think, challenge, soften, and expand.

After an hour, Brenda stretched. "Alright, enough deep thoughts. Leha, that chicken smells divine. Let's eat and talk about real life."

The transition was seamless. The women filled their plates and circled around the dining table. Conversation shifted to job promotions, children's milestones, and local gossip. Leha felt the familiar sincerity of belonging settle over her — a pull she hadn't realized she'd been craving.

It was Safiya who finally turned to her, eyes narrowed with affectionate suspicion. "Leha, you've been quiet tonight — for you, anyway. You've got a whole vibe happening. Something's up. Tell us about this art gallery outing."

A blush crept up Leha's neck. "It was just an evening at the gallery, exploring local artists."

"With a handsome stranger, apparently," Maya teased.

Twelve pairs of eyes turned toward Leha.

Taking a breath, she recounted her evening with Chemelu — the way he interpreted art through the lens of heritage and spirituality, his philosophy on community and gratitude, the subtle charisma he carried without effort. She spoke of the warmth of his touch, the way he saw divinity in the everyday.

When she said his name, a ripple of laughter moved around the table.

"Chemelu?" Aisha grinned. "That's a powerful name. You usually go for the Johns and Mikes, Leha."

"I know," Leha admitted, smiling. "It's different. He's different."

She told them about his stories of Kenya, his father's practical faith, and how he challenged her worldview in ways that felt both unsettling and deeply right.

"He sounds remarkable," Brenda said.

"He uses vulnerability as a strength," Leha murmured. "It's disarming. He sees divinity everywhere."

"Ubuntu," Safiya said softly. "Your well-being is linked to mine."

The meal became a space of connection — advice offered, cautious optimism shared, and a collective celebration of the budding romance that had clearly shifted something inside their usually guarded friend.

Hours later, after dishes were cleared and final hugs exchanged, Leha stood at her front door, waving goodbye to the last car pulling away. The house was quiet now, but the echo of laughter, debate, and shared stories lingered like a warm after-evening haze.

She closed the door and leaned against it, feeling a profound sense of peace.

She had fought fear with action for so long. But tonight, surrounded by her community, she understood Chemelu's point perfectly:

Sometimes, the community *is* the action.

Something in her shifted, and the future felt less like a duty to fulfill and more like a story she was finally ready to live — and eventually share at the next Sister Circle Book Club meeting.

The next morning air was cool against Leha's skin as she ran along the quiet streets near her apartment, her breath even, her mind clearer than it had been in weeks. Running had become her ritual — a moving meditation, a way to shake loose the heaviness she carried from work, from family, from the quiet ache she rarely named.

But lately, something else had been stirring in her. A desire for release. For clarity. For a body that felt as strong as the community she was trying to build.

Safiya's words about fasting and intention lingered in her mind.

What we put in our bodies is sacred.

By the time she finished her run, sweat cooling on her skin, she found herself wondering — not for the first time — whether she needed to change the way she nourished herself. Whether her morning runs were asking her to choose differently.

That evening, she and Chemelu met at Tandoori Bites. The moment she stepped inside, she felt it — the elegance, the intention, the way the room seemed to hold its own sense of welcome. Along the far wall, rows of wine bottles were arranged with deliberate care, their deep reds and amber tones adding richness to the space. The scent of cardamom, cumin, ginger, and roasted vegetables rose around her like an invitation.

"This place is beautiful," she murmured.

Chemelu smiled. "It's one of my favorites. The owner believes food is a form of gratitude."

They were seated at a small table along the wall, the wood polished smooth beneath her fingertips. The owner himself stopped by, greeting them with a warm-heartedness that felt like family.

"We're honored to have you," he said, eyes bright. "Let me bring you something special — our vegan favorites."

Leha felt a flutter of anticipation.

When the dishes arrived — chana masala simmered in rich tomato gravy, aloo gobi fragrant with turmeric, a creamy coconut-based vegetable korma — she felt her breath catch.

"This is… beautiful," she whispered.

"Food should be," Chemelu said softly. "It should honor the body."

She took her first bite. Warm. Comforting. Alive with flavor. It felt like nourishment in a way she hadn't expected.

"I could get used to this," she said, surprised by her own honesty.

Chemelu's smile deepened. "Your body is asking for something. You're listening."

She thought of her morning runs. Her desire for clarity. Her need for grounding. Her longing for a life that felt intentional.

"Maybe I'm becoming a vegetarian," she said, half teasing, half serious.

"Or maybe," he said gently, "you're stepping into yourself."

The words moved through her gently, landing where she needed them the most.

As they lingered over warm naan and spiced tea, Leha felt something shift — a quiet alignment between her body, her spirit, and the life she was building.

Healing wasn't just emotional. It was physical. It was spiritual. It was choosing, again and again, to honor the God within.

And tonight, at Tandoori Bites, she felt that choice settling into her bones.

Chapter Twenty-One

Crosswinds Rising

The morning began with the familiar clatter of dishes and the soft spill of Sylvia's radio — a Leela James slow burn drifting through the kitchen, her voice rising and falling like someone trying to love their way through a hard season. The melody wrapped itself around the room, warm and aching, smoothing the edges of a tense house. The scent of turkey bacon and cinnamon oatmeal lingered in the air, grounding and familiar.

Leonard was already gone. He'd slipped out before sunrise, still operating on military time even in retirement, heading to Westover High to prep the JROTC drill team for their early practice. His absence left the house quieter, but not calmer.

Tyashia sat at the table picking at a bowl of cereal that had long surrendered its crunch. Across from her, Simon was building a tiny LEGO structure between bites of toast, his low-top fade sharp and freshly lined — the kind of cut Sylvia insisted on every two weeks.

"Mom, look," he said, holding up a miniature tower. "If I add this piece, it won't fall even if you shake it."

Sylvia leaned in just enough to inspect it, careful not to disturb his hair. "Baby, that's impressive. You're gonna build something big one day."

Cassidy slid into the seat beside Tyashia, stealing a grape off her plate. "You look tired," she said, not unkindly. "Like… extra tired."

Tyashia shrugged. "Didn't sleep much."

Cassidy nodded knowingly. "Yeah. This house is loud even when it's quiet."

Before Tyashia could respond, Tasha swept into the kitchen, ponytail tight, JROTC jacket crisp, energy sharp as ever. She moved with the precision of someone who lived by routine — Leonard's influence stamped into her posture.

"You ready?" she asked, grabbing her backpack. "Bus comes in five."

Her tone wasn't rude — just short, guarded, like she was still deciding how much space Tyashia was allowed to take up in her world.

Sylvia placed a hand on Tasha's arm — a gentle, grounding touch. "Be kind," she murmured.

Tasha didn't answer, but her jaw loosened a fraction.

Simon held up his LEGO tower again. "Tyashia, look! It didn't fall."

She managed a small smile. "That's dope, Si."

His grin widened, bright and unfiltered — the kind of smile that made something warm stir in her chest.

Cassidy bumped her shoulder playfully. "See? There you are."

Tyashia rolled her eyes, but the corner of her mouth twitched.

As they headed out the door, a sharp gust of morning air swept across the porch — brisk enough to sting, brisk enough to wake. The elementary bus groaned to a stop at the corner, and Simon and Cassidy jogged toward it, backpacks bouncing. A minute later, the high school bus rumbled up the street, brakes squealing. Tasha climbed on first — rare for her, with ROTC — and Tyashia followed, tugging her jacket tighter around her.

She didn't know why, but the moment she stepped onto the bus, the kitchen's sense of safety felt a thousand miles away.

By lunchtime, the cafeteria roared with the kind of noise that made thoughts scatter — trays clattering, chairs scraping, voices rising and crashing like waves against tile walls. The air smelled of reheated pizza, orange cleaner, and the faint cafeteria scent every school seemed to carry.

Tyashia stepped inside, earbuds already in, letting the bass thrum against her ribs like armor. She scanned the room the way a newcomer learns to — quick, cautious, calculating. Every table had its own little universe: athletes clustered around protein shakes and bravado, JROTC cadets in crisp lines, anime kids trading stickers, the quiet ones reading with their heads down.

Her conversation with Ron earlier in the week had cracked something open inside her — a small valve releasing pressure she didn't know she'd been holding. It left her feeling raw, exposed, and desperate to seal herself back up.

Everyone looks so normal. Like their worlds haven't shattered.

She slid her tray onto an empty table near the wall, choosing the seat with her back protected. Old habits. Necessary ones.

That's when she saw them.

Meja sat at a table near the center, posture stiff with practiced indifference. She picked at her fries like she was daring them to disappoint her. Her eyes were sharp, scanning the room with the vigilance of someone who'd learned early that safety was a myth.

Beside her, Vince leaned back in his chair, legs stretched out, commanding space without asking. He wore black cargo joggers and a fitted long-sleeve tee with a bold graphic across the chest — the kind of outfit that said he cared about style but would never admit it. Every movement radiated a restless confidence, the kind that demanded attention even when he wasn't speaking.

Tyashia didn't want to be anywhere near them. But she watched anyway, drawn to the strength of their walls.

Easier to be angry than scared.

Meja's gaze flicked toward her — quick, assessing, familiar. Vince followed her line of sight, his eyes landing on Tyashia with a slow, knowing recognition.

Tyashia looked away, but her pulse quickened.

Across the room, Kendra waved enthusiastically from a table decorated with pink notebooks and glitter pens. She patted the seat beside her, beaming like she'd been waiting all morning for Tyashia to walk in.

Too bright. Too hopeful. Too much.

Tyashia pretended not to see her.

A slight ripple of unease tightened her stomach — a familiar warning she ignored.

Later that week, Ron stood at the window of his office, watching the cafeteria empty into the hallway below. A student asked him for directions, but his attention drifted back to the trio — Tyashia, Meja, and Vince — orbiting each other with the gravitational pull of shared wounds.

He had seen the referral notes on Tyashia's intake form: anger, resentment, abandonment. He had seen the same pattern in Vince for months — the need to dominate conversations, the constant posturing, the desperate attempts to be seen after feeling replaced by a younger sibling. And Meja... she was a fortress built from betrayal.

Ron had worked with kids like this for decades. They were magnets for each other — drawn together by a shared vacuum of unmet needs.

Outside his window, a yellow pencil rolled across the courtyard — bumped loose from someone's backpack, wobbling along the concrete as the cross draft from slamming doors nudged it in unpredictable directions. It spun, stalled, then drifted again, like a kid searching for a hand steady enough to pick it up.

The next morning on the bus, Tyashia sat in her usual seat, earbuds in, watching the familiar houses of the Cottonade subdivision roll by. The emotional vulnerability she'd shown with Ron still clung to her like a bruise — tender, exposed. She reinforced her shield of indifference, letting the conscious rap pulse through her ears like armor.

Kendra slid into the seat across the aisle, bright and cheerful as always.

"Hey, Tyashia! Settling into the 'Nade yet?"

Tyashia yanked out an earbud. "Not really."

"Dang, for real?" Kendra pulled out her oversized pink headphones. "Give it time. It grows on people."

Her optimism felt aggressive. Nobody is that happy for real.

Up front, Vince and Meja sat together, their heads bent in conversation — a synchronized storm of bitterness.

"He just doesn't get it," Vince muttered. "My stepdad acts like I'm an afterthought. Everything's about my sister now."

Meja nodded, lips twisting. "Family is overrated. They always disappoint you eventually."

She glanced toward the back of the bus, her eyes landing on Tyashia. "That new girl — she's got the look. She knows what's up."

Vince followed her gaze, studying Tyashia with calculating interest. A small smile tugged at his lips.

"Maybe we should invite her to hang out."

Meja shrugged. "Bet. She could use a dose of reality."

Back in her seat, Tyashia watched Kendra bob her head to bright pop music, completely absorbed in her own world. The contrast made Tyashia's chest tighten — too much cheer, too much hope.

She looked toward the front of the bus and caught Vince's eye. He offered a slight nod, a silent acknowledgment. Tyashia didn't smile back, but the attention — the shared understanding of pain — felt more familiar than Kendra's sunshine.

It was an easy connection. A dangerous one. But it felt like something she could hold onto.

A few days later on the ride home, Kendra tapped her arm before her stop.

"Hey, you listen to a lot of conscious rap, right? Check out this local guy — Ahmad Latif. His album *Ville Promises* is fire. Real lyrics about the struggle here."

She hopped off the bus, leaving the faint scent of coconut hair oil behind.

Tyashia stared at the empty seat, the pink headphones resting where Kendra had been. A hint of curiosity cut through her suspicion.

Music had always been her escape. Maybe — just maybe — it could be her lifeline here too.

Outside the window, a scrap of notebook paper clung stubbornly to the bus frame, fluttering wildly in the wind — refusing to let go.

Tyashia didn't know whether she admired it… or feared she was just like it.

Chapter Twenty-Two

The Quiet Shift

The late afternoon sun slanted across Fayetteville, stretching long shadows across the pavement like quiet reminders of everything the day had borne. A wandering breeze swept through the parking lot of Westover High, stirring loose gravel that skittered across the asphalt in restless zigzags — tiny stones pushed into motion by forces they couldn't control.

Leha stood outside the school building, waiting for the last of her mentees to be picked up. Her phone buzzed with a text from her father.

Dinner soon? Want you and Mel to meet Sandy properly.

A small brightness stirred in her as she typed back a quick yes. But the feeling dimmed when she looked toward the bus loop.

Tyashia wasn't there.

She usually lingered — hovering near the curb until the last possible moment, pretending she didn't want company even as she waited for it. Today, she had vanished the moment the bell rang.

A scrap of lined paper tumbled toward Leha's feet, flipping and twisting before catching against her shoe. Someone had doodled a half-finished heart in the corner, the ink smudged as if the artist changed their mind mid-stroke.

Caught between wanting connection and running from it, she thought.

She slipped the paper into her notebook and headed inside.

Ron was in his office, sorting through a stack of student files. He looked up when she knocked.

"You seen Tyashia?" she asked.

Ron leaned back in his chair, rubbing the bridge of his nose. "Not since this morning. She seemed… guarded. More than usual."

Leha sank into the chair across from him. "I'm worried. She's opening up, but it's like every step forward scares her into taking two steps back."

Ron nodded slowly. "Kids like her don't trust calm. They trust patterns — even the painful ones."

A hush formed between them, familiar and heavy.

"You ever feel like we're trying to catch something that doesn't want to be held?" Leha asked softly.

Ron huffed a tired laugh. "Every day."

"Some of them land," he said. "Some don't. But we keep reaching."

Leha exhaled, the long day settling into her shoulders. "I'm meeting Dad and Sandy for dinner soon. Melina's coming too."

Ron's eyebrows lifted. "Big night."

"Yeah," she said, smiling faintly. "Feels like everyone in my family is shifting. Mom's rebuilding. Dad's softening. Melina's… unraveling a little."

Ron's voice gentled. "And you?"

Leha hesitated. "I'm trying to stay secure. But sometimes I feel like I'm balancing on a thread."

Ron's expression softened. "Threads can hold more than people think."

She nodded, letting the words settle.

As she stood to leave, Ron added casually, "Tell Melina I said hello. Haven't seen her around lately."

Leha's expression relaxed — just a beat. "I will."

Something unspoken moved between them. Not romantic. But familiar. Curious. A recognition of two people who understood the emotional labor of holding other people's worlds.

Earlier that morning, the cafeteria buzzed with early-morning noise — trays clattering, sneakers squeaking, the smell of syrup-soaked waffles and reheated sausage drifting through the air. Tyashia slipped into an empty table near the wall, earbuds already in, staring at nothing in particular. The vulnerability she'd shown with Ron still clung to her like a bruise — tender, exposed. She rebuilt her armor piece by piece, letting the bass-heavy, truth-telling lyrics pulse through her ears like a shield.

She kept her gaze fixed on the far wall, letting the movement around her blur. Students drifted in clusters — laughing too loud, dragging their feet, performing versions of themselves they hoped would hold.

Across the room, Vince and Meja were laughing — sharp, brittle laughter that didn't reach their eyes. Vince wore dark jeans and a clean white tee layered under a black puffer vest, the kind of outfit that made him look older than he was. Meja had on glitter-rimmed eyeliner and a cropped denim jacket with rhinestones along the seams — her version of armor.

Their voices projected just enough for Tyashia to catch the tone, familiar in a way that made her stomach twist.

Kendra spotted her and slid into the seat across from her, bright as ever. "Hey! I found another song for you—"

But Tyashia turned up her music, shutting her out.

Kendra's smile faltered for a moment. Then she adjusted her pink headphones and began tracing little shapes on the table with her fingertips — soft, absent-minded motions, unaware she was the only person in Tyashia's world still trying to reach her.

The final bell released the building in a rush of noise and bodies. Students spilled into the parking lot, some heading to sports, some to after-school programs, some straight home. Tyashia walked alone, backpack slung over one shoulder, the late-afternoon sun low and hazy.

Leha stood near the front entrance, talking with another teacher, her tote bag at her feet. She caught Tyashia's eye and offered a small, warm nod — not intrusive, just present.

Tyashia looked away first.

She wasn't ready for that kind of closeness. Not today.

She cut across the sidewalk and headed toward the neighborhood, the air cooling as the sun dipped lower.

A few blocks from school, Vince's beat-up sedan rolled to a slow crawl beside her. The headlights shimmered in the thinning daylight, catching dust and leaves swirling across the pavement.

Meja leaned out the passenger window, smoke curling from her lips. "Yo, Philly," she called. "You walking home by yourself again?"

Tyashia froze.

Vince tapped the side of the car, smirking. "You coming or what?"

Her heart thudded. She didn't know why she'd stopped walking. She didn't know what she was looking for.

But she knew what she was running from.

She opened the back door and slid in.

The car smelled like cheap cologne, fast-food wrappers, and something sweet-burnt lingering in the air — the unmistakable scent of loud. A vape pen pulsed blue in Meja's hand, the tip glowing each time she inhaled.

"Relax," Meja said, exhaling a cloud that drifted toward Tyashia. "It's just a little something to take the edge off."

Vince passed her a second vape, the metal cool against her palm. "Try it. Helps you forget all the fake stuff."

Tyashia stared at the vape. Her fingers tightened around the device, her pulse thudding in her ears.

She thought of Ron's office. She thought of Sylvia's kitchen. She thought of Simon's LEGO tower — upright because someone believed it could be. She thought of Kendra's pink headphones and coconut-scented hair oil. She thought of her aunt's voice:

Baby, don't let the world choose for you.

Meja nudged her. "Come on. Don't be scared."

Tyashia lifted the vape halfway to her lips.

Her hand shook.

Then she set it down on the seat beside her.

"No," she said quietly. "Not today."

Vince raised an eyebrow. "You sure?"

She nodded, jaw tight. "Yeah."

Meja shrugged and took another hit. "Suit yourself."

The car rolled on, music thumping low, the air thick with smoke and unspoken choices.

Tyashia stared out the window, her reflection faint in the glass — a girl caught between two worlds, choosing neither, choosing something else entirely.

When the car finally slowed near her street, she slipped out without a word.

"Next time," Vince called after her.

But Tyashia wasn't sure there would be a next time.

She walked the rest of the way home, the evening air cool against her face, her lungs filling with something that felt almost like clarity.

She didn't step into the storm. Not tonight.

But she had walked close enough to feel its pull — and close enough to know she didn't want to drown in it.

Chapter Twenty-Three

Gathering the We

The evening air drifted through the open windows of Sam's dining room, carrying the faint scent of something simmering in the kitchen. As Leha and Chemelu stepped inside, the house greeted them with the unmistakable imprint of Sam's life in uniform — a wall lined with framed commendations, a polished coin display catching the light, and a carved wooden soldier standing guard on the sideboard, rifle in hand and cavalry hat tilted just so.

A shadow box hung above it, the folded American flag resting beside his Command Sergeant Major rank and the plaque honoring his thirty-one years of service. On the shelf below, a black mug stamped with the Army emblem and the word *Retired* sat proudly among family photos.

The space felt alive with enthusiasm — the kind born from years of family dinners, quiet reconciliations, and the undeniable presence of a man who had led Soldiers, raised daughters, and built a home that held all of it.

On the table sat a spread of comforting classics: baked chicken with crisp golden skin, creamy macaroni and cheese bubbling under a toasted crust, collard greens simmered low and slow, and warm cornbread perfuming the room with butter and memory.

Sandy stepped forward with a smile. "I made a vegetarian plate for you and Chemelu," she said gently. "Just like we talked about."

Sam froze mid-reach, fork hovering over the chicken. "Vegetarian plate?" he repeated, squinting at Leha. "Now hold on. Since when you a vegan?"

Leha laughed, already bracing herself. "I'm working on it, Daddy. Trying to eat cleaner."

Sam leaned back, eyes wide with mock disbelief. "A vegan," he said slowly. "So what — you just gon' eat plants now? Leaves and twigs? That's your whole diet?"

Leha rolled her eyes, smiling. "It's not leaves and twigs."

Sam pointed his fork at her, grinning. "Now you know you love chicken too much to be a vegan. I have seen you tear up a wing plate like it owed you money."

Even Chemelu chuckled, trying — and failing — to hide it behind his hand.

Sandy swatted Sam lightly. "Leave her be. She's trying something new."

Sam held up both hands. "I'm just saying — if she makes it a whole week without fried chicken, I'll be impressed."

Leha shook her head, laughing. "Y'all are impossible."

But the teasing — the laughter — loosened something in her chest. It felt like family again. Like ease. Like home.

Sam greeted Chemelu with a firm handshake and a reserved, appraising nod. But as the meal unfolded, his posture softened. He leaned back in his chair, sharing stories and laughter, a genuine smile replacing his earlier caution. The clink of silverware and the soft chorus of crickets outside blended into a soundtrack of home.

Melina arrived late, slipping through the door with a bright smile that didn't quite reach her eyes. Her silk-pressed bob framed her face perfectly, every strand in place — but Leha caught the tightness in her shoulders, the way she gripped her purse strap as if bracing for impact.

"Sorry I'm late," she said, kissing Sam on the cheek before hugging Sandy. "Traffic was a mess."

Leha knew better. It wasn't traffic. It was everything Melina wasn't saying. But tonight wasn't the night to push.

Melina took the seat beside Leha, offering a small, curious smile toward Chemelu. "So this is the man I've been hearing about."

Chemelu returned the smile warmly. "It's an honor to finally meet you."

Something in Melina's expression softened — the first genuine ease Leha had seen on her face in weeks.

Sam cleared his throat, gesturing toward Chemelu with his fork. "This man here knows a thing or two about integrity."

Leha felt her chest warm. Sam didn't hand out compliments easily. His approval — silently granted through his engaged listening and the respect in his gaze — meant more to her than she expected. It was a seal of legitimacy she hadn't realized she was seeking.

She watched the two men talk, their laughter weaving together with an ease that made her chest expand.

Two parts of my life finally meeting without friction, she thought. *This — this sense of belonging — is what I've always longed for.*

Later, with the dishes cleared and the men tucked in the living room, Leha and Melina found themselves alone in the kitchen, rinsing plates in a quiet rhythm.

"You seem… different. In a good way," Melina said softly, not looking up from the sink.

Leha paused. "Do I?"

Melina nodded. "Yeah. Like something finally clicked into place."

Leha hesitated, then spoke. "I'm trying to build something real. For the kids. For myself. For all of us."

Melina's hands stilled in the dishwater. "I'm glad. I'm trying too. Some days it feels like I'm holding everything together with tape."

Leha touched her sister's arm. "You're allowed to lean, Melina. Even on me."

Melina swallowed hard, blinking back something she didn't want to name. "I know. I'm working on believing that."

Before Leha could respond, Chemelu stepped into the doorway, his presence warm and grounding. "May I borrow you for a moment?"

Melina smirked. "Go. I'll finish up."

As Leha followed him to the porch, she caught a brief glance at her phone — Ron's name lit up with a missed call. Melina's eyes flicked toward it, then away, a tiny spark of something unspoken passing between them.

Outside, the evening breeze moved across the porch, stirring the wind chimes and lifting the edges of the welcome mat. It carried a faint saltiness — the kind of inland drift that sometimes rode up from the coast when the weather shifted — and it brushed past Leha with a coolness that reminded her of evenings spent near the water, even though the ocean was more than an hour away.

She found herself confiding in Chemelu about Tyashia — the cafeteria tension, the withdrawal, the near-spiral with Vince and Meja.

"It's a classic case of fear shaping behavior," Chemelu said, his tone shifting to thoughtful seriousness. "She lost control of her life when her mother left and her aunt died. Now she gravitates toward people who project control — mistaking dominance for safety."

Leha nodded, her heart tightening. "Ron is helping her see that. But the pull of the toxic relationship is strong."

"We must give something to return to," Chemelu said gently. "Show her the strength within herself. You are building a community around her — you, Ron, her aunt, Simon Temple AME Zion Church. The support is there if she chooses to accept it."

His words passed through her like revelation. A wave of clarity washed through her.

Chemelu wasn't just offering advice — he was holding up a mirror, reflecting the purpose she was finally embracing.

She wasn't just helping Tyashia. She was building something. A network. A foundation. A living embodiment of Ubuntu — *I am because we are.*

She wasn't just fixing a printer jam anymore. She was rerouting an entire life. Something in her aligned, and she felt the full force — and the full beauty — of that calling.

Later, the multipurpose room at SCI buzzed with quiet anticipation as Leha arranged the last stack of mentor folders on the table. The late afternoon sun poured through the tall windows, casting warm rectangles of gold across the polished floor. Every small sound — a shifting chair, a tapped pen, a cleared throat — echoed just enough to remind everyone they were in a room built for everything and nothing at once.

Tonight was the quarterly mentor orientation — a gathering of new volunteers, community partners, and youth advocates. It was the kind of evening that always made Leha's heart beat with purpose.

Safiya slipped in beside her, carrying a tray of spiced tea from The Gentle Ground Café. "You've got a look about you," she said, nudging her gently. "What's stirring in that mind of yours?"

Leha smiled, smoothing the edge of a folder. "Just thinking about something Susan L. Taylor always said."

Safiya raised an eyebrow, already knowing the answer.

"'We are the ones we've been waiting for,'" Leha recited softly. "Every time I prepare for these orientations, I hear her voice. She built a whole movement around healing our communities from the inside out."

Safiya's expression softened. "And you're carrying that torch beautifully."

Before Leha could respond, the door opened and a tall woman with a warm, easy smile stepped inside. Melodie's presence was calm and unruffled — the kind of energy that filled a room without ever demanding it. She carried a canvas tote with the Rooted & Rising logo stitched across the front.

"Melodie!" Leha called, crossing the room to greet her.

Melodie pulled her into a hug — the kind that said *I'm here, and I've got you.* Behind her, two teens from her program wheeled in boxes of school supplies and hygiene kits.

"Thought we'd bring a little extra support," Melodie said, tapping one of the boxes. "The kids insisted. They said SCI held them down, so it's only right they give back."

Leha felt her throat tighten — the good kind of ache. "You always show up."

Melodie shrugged lightly. "That's the work. We rise by lifting others."

The words landed with the same depth and grace as Susan L. Taylor's wisdom — a lineage of service stretching across generations.

As volunteers filtered in, Leha stepped to the front of the room. She glanced at the faces before her — teachers, retirees, college students, community leaders, and the teens from Melodie's program who stood proudly beside the Blue Anchor banner.

She took a breath.

"Thank you all for being here," she began, her voice moving with a calm, gathered strength. "Tonight isn't just about training. It's about community. It's about Ubuntu — *I am because we are.* Susan L. Taylor once said, 'We are the ones we've been waiting for.' And she was right. Every one of you is part of the village our young people need."

She gestured toward Melodie. "And we're honored to partner with leaders like Melodie Jackson and the Rooted & Rising team — people who show our youth that hope isn't abstract. It's active. It's present. It's us."

Melodie dipped her head humbly, the teens beside her beaming.

In the back of the room, Tyashia stood with her arms crossed, trying to look unimpressed. But something in her chest shifted — a small, unfamiliar lift. She watched the teens from Melodie's program laugh and unload supplies, watched the mentors greet one another with genuine care, watched Leha speak with conviction that felt like truth.

Maybe community wasn't just a word. Maybe it was a lifeline. Maybe it was something she could reach for — someday.

For now, she stayed in the doorway, listening.

But while Leha was building a circle of support, Tyashia was learning that not every harbor is safe — and not every hold endures.

Chapter Twenty-Four

The Harbor That Isn't Safe

In the days after the mentor orientation, something in Tyashia felt off-balance — like a door had cracked open inside her, letting in something she wasn't sure she wanted. She kept her head down, did her work, showed up to mentoring with Leha even when she didn't feel like talking.

Mostly, she listened. Mostly, she tried not to feel anything.

Ron's office, tucked away at the quiet end of Westover High, felt like the only calm pocket in a building that never stopped buzzing. A hush drifted through the room, shaped by the steady tap of rain against the window, turning the woods beyond the courtyard into a watercolor of shifting greens and browns.

Tyashia sat curled in the armchair across from Ron, her oversized flannel bunched around her fists.

The room smelled faintly of cedar, warm coffee, and Ron's aftershave — a grounding mix that eased the tightness in her chest.

She needed grounding. The storm inside her was getting louder.

The almost-moment with Vince — the idling car, Meja's smirk, the vape pen blinking blue in the dark — had left her shaken. She hadn't stepped fully into their world, but she'd felt the pull. And the pull was real.

"He tells me what to wear," she said quietly, picking at a loose thread on the chair. "He says the stuff I like isn't 'high school material.'"

Ron nodded, expression calm and open. He leaned forward, elbows resting on his desk.

"That's control, Tyashia. Not care. Control is rooted in fear. Love is rooted in freedom." His voice was gentle, centered. "Ask yourself this — does Vince's script feel like something you chose, or something you were handed? Real love lets you choose your own outfit."

Tyashia swallowed. "But he's so strong."

Strong people didn't leave you. Strong people commanded the room. Strong people didn't get replaced.

She thought of Aunt Asiah's old white leather skates, the colorful pom-poms bouncing with every stride. Asiah's message had always been simple: *keep rolling.* Strength was movement, not domination.

Vince's strength felt different — rigid, heavy, like Aunt Sylvia's military-tight routines. It felt impossible to match.

Ron looked toward the rain-blurred window. "Strength is not dominance, Tyashia."

He turned back to her, thoughtful. "A lot of young people who act controlling… they're usually carrying something heavy underneath. Sometimes it's fear. Sometimes it's insecurity. Sometimes it's feeling like they don't matter unless they take up space."

He didn't say Vince's name. He didn't have to.

"When someone grows up feeling overlooked or unsure of their place," Ron continued, "they can start believing that control equals safety. That if they don't hold tight, everything will fall apart."

Tyashia's breath caught. She knew that feeling. She knew it too well.

Ron held her gaze, warm and steady. "That fear you mentioned? It makes control feel like a safe harbor. But real safety comes from recognizing your own worth — not someone else's script."

Something clicked inside her — not loud, but clear.

She began to see the pattern: Fear of abandonment made her cling to control, even if the control belonged to someone else.

So she started resisting in small, quiet ways — wearing her favorite blue T-shirt under the blouse Vince picked out, answering Meja's texts later than usual. Tiny rebellions. Early signs of her Quiet Courage.

She also put on Ahmad Latif's *Ville Promises* album, letting the music's honesty settle into her bones. The lyrics about surviving the struggle — a gift from Kendra — made her feel seen. One line echoed in her mind like a mantra:

Promise yourself you will not fold.

It reminded her of Asiah's message to keep rolling.

Ron asked gently, "Did you find your 'one thing,' Tyashia?"

She hesitated, then nodded. "The park near my house. It's quiet. The trees are old."

It was where she and Kendra had started skating. A place that smelled of sun-baked earth and honeysuckle. A place that felt like breathing.

Ron smiled. "That's a good thing. A very good thing. A real turning point."

The session ended, and Tyashia stepped into the mild drizzle. The air felt fresh, almost new. A small brown baby bird hopped across the sidewalk, its damp feathers puffed against the drizzle. It danced at her sneaker, blinking up at her before fluttering clumsily toward a puddle.

She watched it wobble, something in her chest loosening with it.

A small plan formed in her mind.

The next time Vince told her what to do, she would voice her own opinion — even if it was just about grabbing fries from Cook Out instead of wherever he demanded they go.

A tiny act of defiance. But a beginning.

That night, after her session with Ron, Tyashia lay on her bed staring at the ceiling. The room was still new, but she'd worked hard to make it feel a little like Aunt Asiah's — affirmation posters taped neatly along the wall, a small stack of books from their trips to Harriet's Bookstore arranged beside the lamp, and a worn SEPTA token resting on her nightstand like a quiet anchor to home. A photo of her mother sat propped against a jewelry box, close enough to reach for, not yet framed.

She opened *Ville Promises* again, scrolling until her thumb hovered over a track she hadn't played yet.

"Northside Lullaby."

She pressed play.

A slow, unbroken beat filled the room — not loud, not aggressive, but solid in a way that felt like footsteps on familiar pavement. Then Ahmad's voice came in, low and honest, carrying the kind of history of someone who had learned to survive without losing himself.

Halfway through the song, a line rose through the melody — not shouted, not dramatic, but offered like a quiet truth:

Find the rhythm that brings you home.

Her breath caught.

It wasn't about toughness. It wasn't about dominance. It wasn't about running.

It was about returning — to herself, to her strength, to the parts of her she'd been taught to tuck away.

She closed her eyes, letting the words settle into the places she'd been avoiding.

This wasn't just a song. It was a compass. A mirror. A reminder that she didn't have to fold — didn't have to shrink to fit someone else's shadow.

Outside her window, the wind brushed against the old oak tree, tapping a loose branch gently against the glass — a soft rhythm that matched the beat in her headphones.

A quiet signal of a girl beginning to find her way back to herself.

From that night on, whenever the world felt too loud or Vince's voice pressed too close, she put in her earbuds and let "Northside Lullaby" guide her back to center.

It became her song — the one that held her when everything else felt off-balance.

Chapter Twenty-Five

When Maro Hale Came Home

In the days after her session with Ron, Tyashia moved through Westover with a different kind of awareness — not freer, not healed, but more awake to the parts of herself she had been avoiding. She still showed up to mentoring, but now she found herself listening differently, noticing things she hadn't let herself notice before.

On Thursday afternoon, as she was packing up her things, Leha tapped on her classroom door.

"Got a minute?"

Tyashia shrugged. "I guess."

Leha smiled — the kind of smile that didn't push. "Judge Lawson is hosting a youth circle this weekend. Small group. Invitation only. I think it would be good for you."

"Why me?" Tyashia asked, suspicion rising like a reflex.

"Because you showed up," Leha said simply. "And because sometimes the right room can shift something inside you, even if you don't realize it yet."

Tyashia didn't agree. But she didn't say no either.

The flyer sat on her bed like it was waiting for her to make a decision.

Youth Circle — Community Center — Saturday at 2 PM.

Simon was on the floor, building a LEGO spaceship with the kind of focus she wished she could borrow. He didn't look up when he said, "You going?"

"No," she snapped too quickly.

He clicked another piece into place. "Leha said it's important."

"Leha says everything is important."

Simon shrugged. "Not like this."

Tyashia glared at the flyer. "It's probably some boring workshop. Or a lecture. Or one of those 'tell me your goals' things."

Her phone buzzed.

Malik: You going tomorrow? Ms. Leha said it's mandatory-ish. **Jalen:** She said snacks. I'm going.

Tyashia rolled her eyes. "Snacks. Wow. Life changing."

Simon finally looked up. "You scared?"

She sat up fast. "What? No."

He shrugged again, smaller this time. "You look like it."

Her chest tightened. "I'm not scared. I just… don't feel like it."

Simon snapped a LEGO wing into place. "Sometimes you don't feel like going somewhere," he said, eyes still on his build, "and it ends up being good anyway."

She hated that he was right. She hated that he sounded like Asiah. She hated that she suddenly felt like she might cry.

She grabbed the flyer off the bed. "Fine," she muttered. "I'll go. But only because Leha will bug me if I don't."

Simon smirked. "Okay."

She threw a pillow at him.

Later that night, when she set her alarm, she did it gently — like she already knew something was waiting for her. Something she wasn't ready for. Something she needed anyway.

The rain had stopped an hour before the youth arrived, leaving the pavement outside the community center shining like a fresh promise. Thin puddles reflected the streetlights, trembling whenever someone walked past.

Inside, the multipurpose room buzzed with the restless energy of teenagers who had learned to expect disappointment but still hoped for something different. Leha stood near the back, clipboard in hand, watching them settle in. She noticed a faint streak of dried mud on Tyashia's sneaker — evidence of her rushing, of her choosing to come — and smiled at the quiet truth of it.

Judge Renée Lawson stepped to the front, her presence commanding without raising her voice. She wore her signature navy blazer — the one the youth joked she must sleep in — and a smile that held both authority and affection.

"Alright," she said, clapping her hands once. "I need everyone's attention."

The room quieted, but not by much.

"Phones," she said, raising an eyebrow.

A collective groan rolled through the room.

"All of them. Off. Away. And no posting until I say so."

Tyashia muttered something about "doing too much," but she slid her phone into her pocket. Malik tucked his into his sock. Jalen held his up like a white flag before surrendering it to his backpack.

When the last phone disappeared, Judge Lawson nodded. "Good. Now settle."

The room stilled. Not silent — never silent — but attentive enough.

Then the side door opened.

A man stepped inside, hood up, hands in his pockets, moving with the quiet confidence of someone who didn't need to announce himself. For a heartbeat, no one recognized him. He looked like any young man from the neighborhood — tall, lean, unassuming.

Then Malik's eyes widened. "No way," he whispered.

Tyashia sat up straighter. Jalen's mouth fell open. The room inhaled as one.

"Maro Hale?" someone breathed.

And just like that, the air shifted — charged, electric, reverent.

Tyashia's heart kicked once — sharp, unexpected. For a split second, she couldn't place why he looked familiar.

Then it hit her.

The mural. The one Sylvia pointed out downtown near the Market House. The one she pretended not to care about. The one whose eyes seemed to follow her as the car rolled past.

She hadn't wanted to admit it then, but something about that face — calm, grounded, knowing — had stayed with her.

And now here he was. Real. Present. Home.

A strange rhythm in her chest, something like recognition… or a quiet opening she hadn't dared name yet.

Maro lifted a hand, a soft smile tugging at the corner of his mouth. "Y'all good?"

The room erupted — chairs scraping, voices rising — but he laughed and motioned for them to settle.

"Come on now," he said. "Let's just talk. No performance. No cameras. Just us."

He walked to the edge of the stage and sat, feet dangling like he was back in middle school. As he sat, a faint shimmer of water slid from his cuff — leftover rain — falling away before the floor absorbed it.

For nearly two hours, he talked with them. Not at them — **with** them.

He asked their names like he was collecting verses. Their dreams like he was building a hook. Their fears like he already knew the bridge.

He told them about growing up on the east side, writing lyrics in the margins of his notebooks, feeling invisible until someone finally saw him. He talked about messing up, starting over, losing himself, finding himself again.

"You don't gotta come in here polished," he said, voice low and honest. "Life ain't about shining every day. It's about showing up — even when you feel cracked. Even when you feel unseen."

Someone in the back whispered, "He really came home… again," and the whole row nodded like it was gospel.

Leha watched Tyashia's shoulders drop, Malik's foot stop tapping, Jalen lean forward like he didn't want to miss a single word. She watched the room soften — not because a celebrity had walked in, but because someone who understood them had. Someone who remembered.

When Maro finally stood, the room held its breath. He nodded once — a quiet blessing — and slipped out the same door he came in. A faint trail of damp footprints faded behind him as the youth surged to their feet.

For three seconds, there was silence.

Then everything broke open.

Phones flew out of pockets. Malik shouted. Jalen paced in circles, hands on his head, repeating, "Ain't no way, ain't no way."

A girl wiped her eyes. "He said he used to write lyrics in the margins of his homework. I do that. I do that exact thing."

Someone else whispered, "He didn't have to come back. But he did."

Judge Lawson just smiled, arms crossed, satisfied.

Leha moved through the room slowly, letting the youth orbit around her. She didn't interrupt. She didn't redirect. She just listened.

Tyashia sat in her chair, knees pulled up, arms wrapped around them. She wasn't talking. She wasn't screaming. She wasn't pacing.

She was thinking.

Leha crouched beside her. "You okay?"

Tyashia nodded slowly. "He… he listened."

"Yes," Leha said softly. "He always does."

Tyashia swallowed hard. "He said you don't have to be perfect. Just present."

Leha smiled. "That's truth."

Tyashia looked at the faint damp mark on the floor where Maro had stood — already drying, already fading, but still there if you knew where to look.

"I didn't want to come," she whispered.

"I know," Leha said. "But I'm glad you did."

Around them, the youth kept talking — louder, freer, looser — like someone had cracked open a window and let a new horizon in.

Judge Lawson stepped forward. "Alright, circle up. Five minutes. Let's breathe this in before you run off and tell the whole city."

They gathered — messy, loud, imperfect — but together.

Tyashia found herself between Malik and Jalen, their shoulders brushing hers. She didn't pull away.

Judge Lawson looked around the circle, eyes soft. "What happened today wasn't about fame. It was about home. About someone who remembers where he came from and believes in where you're going."

The room quieted. She nodded once. "Carry that."

Tyashia felt something settle in her chest — not heavy, not painful.

Open. Unlocked.

As they filed out, she glanced once more at the spot where Maro had stood. The floor was dry now, but she could still feel the moment lingering in the air — a quiet truth dropped in a room full of kids who needed it:

You can start again. You can rise again. You can become.

And something in her finally believed it.

Chapter Twenty-Six

A Different Kind of Anchor

The morning after the youth circle, Leha felt the shift before she even reached her office. Something in the air felt changed — not fixed, not healed, but open. Maro Hale had walked into that room like a quiet storm, and the youth were still carrying the electricity of it.

Tyashia most of all.

She hadn't said much when the event ended, but Leha had seen the way the girl held her journal differently — not like a burden, but like a new shape of hope. A door had cracked open. And Leha knew better than to let an open door close without offering the next step.

Tyashia needed a space where her hands could move while her heart caught up. She needed something warm, intentional, creative. A different kind of center.

Leha closed the door to her office, her thoughts settling around her like a heavy shawl. The girl was a fortress of anger, but Leha had seen it — the brief spark of curiosity, the smallest crack in the armor. A moment of softness, brief but real.

Before she could sit, her phone buzzed.

Melina: You free later? Just… need to talk. **Leha:** Yes. Anytime.

Her sister rarely asked for help directly. Leha tucked the phone away, heart tightening. All of them were changing. All of them were trying to find their footing. Healing wasn't linear. It was communal.

She pulled out her phone again, this time to call Alexis Lee'nese, the vibrant owner of So Lit. As the phone rang, she heard footsteps in the hallway — slow, familiar, confident. The kind of footsteps that made the air shift before the person even appeared.

Chemelu approached, leaning against the doorframe, arms crossed loosely, eyes soft with concern.

"How did it go with the young warrior?" he asked, his voice a calm murmur that softened the edges of her fatigue.

Leha exhaled, offering him a tired smile. "Challenging. But something opened yesterday. Maro's visit… it stirred something in her. I'm trying to arrange her first candle-making class with Alexis. You know how much intention Alexis pours into those workshops — it's less a class and more an experience. I'm hoping it's the right kind of place for her spirit to catch its breath."

Chemelu nodded slowly, studying her face with quiet attentiveness. "It sounds powerful. I've always admired the way scent and light can shift a person's spirit." His voice dipped, warm and intimate. "Maybe I could join you for a class sometime."

Leha's breath caught — a subtle, unexpected hitch. A shared activity. A date in everything but name. Her pulse fluttered.

"I think that can be arranged," she said, her voice softer than she intended.

Saturday afternoon found Leha and Chemelu pulling into a small, stylish strip center in Fayetteville. So Lit wasn't just a store; it was a modern, chic studio space with a tender brightness spilling through its large glass windows. The kind of place that felt alive with creativity.

Inside, the air wrapped around them like a hug — a layered blend of essential oils, warm wax, and a faint hint of coffee. The studio buzzed with quiet energy. People mingled at a long communal table lined with clear white bottles, beakers, and tiny wooden spoons.

A tall, lean high schooler with an easy smile greeted them. "Welcome to So Lit! Do you have a reservation?"

"Hi, Elijah," Leha said warmly. "It's Leha. I'm here to see your mom, Alexis. And this is Chemelu."

Elijah's eyes widened. "Oh! Ms. Leha! Mom's in the back — she'll be right out. How are you?"

"I'm great. And how's track going at the high school? I saw your results from the last meet — impressive."

Elijah beamed. "Coach thinks I might make regionals if I keep my pace up. Thanks for checking in at the workshops."

"Keep it up," Leha said. "We're cheering for you."

As Elijah disappeared into the back, Chemelu turned to her with an appreciative look — one that lingered a moment too long.

"You have a gift for connecting with people," he said. "You don't just see them — you *see* them."

A slow heat unfurled inside her, deeper than the warmth from the wax warmers. "Just applying a little of that community action you taught me," she teased, though the air between them thickened with an unspoken pull neither of them could ignore.

He stepped a little closer, voice dropping. "You give people a sense of belonging, Leha. That is a rare gift."

Her breath stilled. Something inside her shifted — quiet, warm, and deeply seen.

A moment later, Alexis Lee'nese emerged — vibrant, energetic, her eyes sparkling with creative fire.

"Leha! Wonderful to see you. And you must be the famous Chemelu."

Leha flushed. Her Sister Circle friends had clearly been talking.

She explained the situation with Tyashia — the grief, the anger, the need for a grounding outlet.

"I love the idea," Alexis said, sweeping her hand around the aromatic studio. "Creating something with intention — focusing on scent, light, and presence — it's therapy in a jar. We'll get her signed up. She can start next week."

Relief washed through Leha. "Thank you, Alexis."

"And actually," Chemelu added smoothly, resting a gentle hand at the small of Leha's back, "we were just discussing joining a class ourselves. A little self-discovery date."

Leha blinked, surprised by the boldness — and by how right it felt. His hand was warm, reassuring. A touch that didn't demand anything, but offered everything.

Alexis grinned. "A date! Perfect. I have an opening for a couple's session next Friday night. Wine, music, custom scents. You two are officially signed up."

She turned to Leha with a playful wag of her finger. "Oh — and tell Safiya I finally made that Maple Walnut scent. Inspired by the ice cream she swears by. The one she has to get every time she goes home to Buffalo because nobody sells it down here."

As they left the studio, the promise of Friday night lingered in the air like a warm fragrance. The guard Leha had lugged for so long felt lighter, less necessary. Chemelu didn't just see the divine in the earth — he saw the divine possibilities in her life too.

A new sense of anticipation stirred in her — one custom-scented candle at a time.

Friday night arrived like a soft invitation, carrying with it the promise of scent, light, and something new unfolding between them.

So Lit held a soft wash of low light, gentle R&B drifting through the speakers like a warm breeze. The quiet bubbling of warm wax filled the room with a soothing rhythm. It felt less like a studio and more like a sanctuary — honeyed light, quiet laughter, the soft clink of glass jars.

Chemelu mixed a blend of sandalwood and oud with practiced ease, leaning close as Leha debated between vanilla and plum.

"Go with the plum," he murmured, his breath warm against her ear. "It suits the softness you hold."

Her breath caught. She laughed — a sound unburdened, genuine, rare.

Around them, the studio glowed with amber tones. Essential oils lined the tables like tiny vials of memory. Wax melted in silver pitchers, releasing soft ribbons of fragrance into the air.

It wasn't just a workshop; it was a sanctuary of scent and intention.

There, surrounded by customizable jars and quiet music, the guard she'd held around her heart for years began to dissolve. It wasn't about the candles. It was about the easy intimacy, the shared laughter, the quiet understanding that flowed between them like a warm current.

As they poured their finished creations into clear white jars with elegant black lids, the future felt less like a duty and more like a story she was finally ready to live — one shared moment at a time.

The candles would need time to cure. But the connection between them was already taking shape.

Chapter Twenty-Seven

Through the Cracks

Sylvia woke before dawn, as she always did. Coffee. Shower. Blazer and dress pants. Precision.

Order was her ritual, her armor, her proof that she had outrun the chaos of her childhood. She moved through the house quietly, the way she had learned to move through every space — controlled, composed, unshakeable. The kind of woman who never let the world see her sweat.

But that morning, something felt off. A heaviness she couldn't name pressed against her ribs.

She paused at the kitchen table, smoothing the edge of a placemat that didn't need smoothing. The house was still — too still — and in the silence she felt the familiar ache of a life she had built on discipline, not ease.

Upstairs, Tyashia stirred. Sylvia heard the soft creak of the floorboards, the shuffle of a teenager trying not to disturb anyone. That carefulness — that shrinking — unsettled her more than she'd ever admit.

Tyashia sat on the edge of the guest bed, wearing the T-shirt Asiah had given her the year before she died. Across the front, in soft, faded lettering, were the words:

Still Rising

She was supposed to be working on her English assignment — a paper on family legacy — but the blank page stared back at her. Every time she tried to write, memories rose instead. Not the polished ones teachers liked. The real ones. The ones that stung.

A breeze slipped through the cracked window, lifting the corner of her notebook. She closed her eyes, letting the air settle her. And just like that, she was back in Aunt Sylvia's kitchen on Thanksgiving prep day.

The air in the kitchen had been thick with aromas — onions sizzling in butter, collard greens soaking in cold water, yams waiting in a metal bowl. It should have felt familiar. It didn't.

Back in Philly, Asiah's tiny kitchen would already be alive with music, laughter, and the clatter of mismatched pots. Here, everything was crisp, controlled, and quiet.

Sylvia looked up from a stainless-steel pot. "There you are, Tyashia. Come on in, we're making the list." Her tone was brisk, but her eyes softened for a moment — a rare crack in her polished exterior.

"We've got the turkey marinating, the pies cooling. Leonard's outside prepping the smoker. We're doing a full spread — turkey, dressing, mac and cheese, candied yams, potato salad, green beans, cornbread. You have to tell me what kind of cakes you like."

Each dish was a map of past Thanksgivings — memories of Asiah's table, Asiah's hands, Asiah's love.

"It sounds like a lot," Tyashia murmured. "Aunt Asiah used to make everything from scratch, too."

Sylvia froze. A shadow of sadness crossed her face before she tightened her expression back into something composed.

"Well, that's the spirit of the holiday, isn't it? Carrying on the traditions." She pointed to a giant pot of greens. "I need help getting these started. You up for cleaning a few more?"

Tyashia hesitated. The image of Asiah soaking greens in the sink made her eyes sting. She swallowed the emotion down. "Sure."

She moved to the sink. The cold, vinegary water shocked her hands, grounding her.

"Um... Aunt Sylvia?" she asked quietly. "Do you put pork in your greens?"

Sylvia stopped stirring the macaroni base, briefly offended before letting out a short laugh. "What are you, a Muslim or something?" she teased. "We're not that strict with our food, girl."

"I just... I don't eat pork," Tyashia said. It wasn't religious — just a choice she'd made after Asiah switched for health reasons.

Sylvia waved a hand. "Well, you don't have to worry about that here. We don't eat pork either. I make the greens with smoked turkey."

A small sigh of relief escaped Tyashia.

It wasn't Asiah's kitchen. The rhythm was different. But the task was the same.

For a moment, she didn't feel alone.

Later that evening, Sylvia sat in the living room, the house finally quiet except for the tick of the clock inside her curio cabinet. The scent of Leonard's spaghetti sauce lingered in the air. The house smelled like clean laundry and freshly vacuumed carpet — the kind of tidy that came from habit, not comfort.

From the outside, they looked like the picture of a stable military family. But Sylvia knew better.

Her gaze drifted to the framed photo on the mantle — Leonard in his dress blues, smiling that proud, practiced smile.

But that foundation had a crack. A deep fissure that took years of silent, agonizing work to repair.

She remembered the night it happened — the night everything she believed about marriage, loyalty, and military life shifted.

Leonard had come home from downrange unexpectedly. She'd been excited — she'd cleaned the house, cooked his favorite meal, even ironed his uniform for the next day.

But he wasn't alone.

A woman from his unit had driven him home. Pretty. Polished. Too familiar.

Sylvia had stood in the doorway, apron still on, heart pounding. She didn't scream. She didn't cry. She simply watched the way the woman looked at her husband — like she knew a version of him Sylvia didn't.

Leonard had never told her everything. He'd confessed the part he could live with, not the part she couldn't. Sylvia hadn't asked for the rest — she couldn't. The emotional betrayal was already a wound; she refused to give her mind the images that would make it bleed.

He apologized for months. Years. He retired early. He deferred to her now — a quiet acknowledgment of the trust he had to rebuild.

Order became her salvation. Control became her shield. Silence became their peace treaty.

And now she was raising a grieving teenager who reminded her of everything she'd lost and everything she'd fought to keep.

That afternoon, Tyashia sat in the back seat of Vince's beat-up sedan, parked near the Fort Bragg perimeter. The air smelled of damp earth and the faint, sweet smoke curling from Meja's cigarette.

Vince kicked a loose rock. "He grounded me for a week," he muttered. "Just because I was fifteen minutes late. My sister can do whatever she wants, but I miss one curfew and I'm locked down."

Meja blew a perfect smoke ring. "Typical. They always disappoint you eventually."

Tyashia listened quietly. Vince's bitterness resonated with her own feelings of powerlessness in Sylvia's structured house.

Her phone buzzed. A message from Kendra:

Hey! Simon Temple has a youth event tonight. Free food. Bishop Thompson is speaking. Want to come? We could skate after.

A tiny spark of hope stirred.

"So Kendra texted me," Tyashia said casually. "There's some youth thing tonight at Simon Temple."

Vince scoffed. "A church event? Seriously? That stuff is corny."

The words hit harder than he knew.

"It sounded kinda cool," she murmured.

"Nah," Vince said sharply. "We're going to the bowling alley. Me and you are a team tonight."

He didn't ask. He told.

The spark dimmed.

But even as the car lurched forward, one name stuck in her mind like a whisper:

Bishop Brian R. Thompson.

A whisper of a different kind of strength — one that felt, strangely, like freedom.

Tyashia looked out the window, the cracked sidewalks and leaning fences blurring into landscape she recognized.

Something inside her shifted — quiet, but unmistakable.

She wasn't rising yet. But she was lifting her head.

The next morning, Sylvia opened her phone and the headline hit her like a blow:

FEDERAL GOVERNMENT SHUTS DOWN — EFFECTIVE IMMEDIATELY. NON-ESSENTIAL EMPLOYEES FURLOUGHED. ESSENTIAL STAFF TO REPORT WITHOUT PAY.

Her breath stalled.

She read it again. And again.

Her hands trembled — barely, but enough for her to notice.

She dressed anyway — muscle memory, denial, pride — and drove toward the base. The roads were eerily empty. The usual morning traffic of GS workers, contractors, and military families had thinned to a trickle.

At the gate, the guard shook his head.

"Ma'am… you're on the list. Non-essential."

The word stung.

Non-essential.

She forced a tight smile. "I'll wait for the official email."

But she didn't wait. She drove off base, pulled into a quiet parking lot, and turned off the engine to save gas.

She turned on the radio for noise, but the voice that filled the car made her still.

Akila Davis, the Black anchor who had become a trusted voice across the Carolinas, spoke with a calm that relayed truth like a blade wrapped in velvet.

"Good morning," Akila said. "We're continuing our coverage of the federal shutdown. And while officials in Washington describe this as a 'temporary inconvenience,' the reality on the ground tells a different story — especially for Black federal employees and military-adjacent families here in Fayetteville."

Sylvia's throat tightened.

"Black workers make up a significant portion of the federal workforce in this region," Akila continued. "Shutdowns don't just disrupt routines — they destabilize households. They interrupt childcare, delay medical appointments, and force families to choose between gas and groceries."

Sylvia turned off the radio, but Akila's words stayed with her — not as commentary, but as recognition.

She watched the city shift around her. The barbershop near the base had only one car in the lot. The nail salon's OPEN sign waved in the window, but no one walked in. The diner that fed half the GS workforce sat nearly empty, waitresses wiping down spotless counters just to keep their hands busy. The daycare center had fewer children — parents keeping them home to save money. Even the gas station felt hollow without the usual morning rush of uniforms and ID badges.

On Murchison Road, the dry cleaner had taped a handwritten sign to the door:

TEMPORARILY CLOSED — SHUTDOWN IMPACT.

Fayetteville sat in suspension, held in place by uncertainty.

Her phone buzzed — a bank alert, a reminder that bills did not care about congressional gridlock.

She closed her eyes.

She thought of her coworkers during the last furlough — the ones who had chosen between gas and groceries, who had called creditors with shaking voices, who had cried in bathroom stalls and worked without pay because "essential" meant "exploited." She remembered the women who skipped lunch to stretch food, the men who sat in their cars to avoid wasting fuel on the drive home.

She had judged them then. Quietly. Harshly.

Now she understood.

She wasn't above them. She was them.

A tear slipped down her cheek — the first she'd allowed in years.

She wiped it quickly, as if someone might see.

That evening, the house was quiet. Too quiet. Sylvia sat at the kitchen table, hands folded, staring at nothing. The shutdown had stripped her of her armor, leaving her raw in a way she didn't recognize.

Tyashia lingered in the doorway, notebook pressed to her chest.

"Aunt Sylvia?" she asked softly.

Sylvia looked up, eyes tired but open. "Yes, baby?"

Tyashia stepped closer. "Can I ask you something? About my mom?"

The question landed like a stone. Sylvia's breath stuttered — small, but unmistakable.

"What about her?" she asked, steadying her voice.

Tyashia swallowed. "What was she like? Before everything. Before she left."

Sylvia's gaze drifted toward the window, toward a past she had locked away. When she spoke, her voice was softer than Tyashia had ever heard it.

"Your mother was tender," Sylvia said. "Tender in a world that wasn't. She felt things deeply. She loved deeply. Sometimes too deeply."

Tyashia waited.

"And she had Ashia," Sylvia continued. "Those two… they were a pair. Thick as thieves. They understood each other in ways I couldn't. They didn't need me." A small, brittle laugh escaped her. "They didn't listen to me either."

Tyashia frowned. "Why not?"

Sylvia's jaw tightened. "Because I was the one always trying to keep the rules. Keep the peace. Keep us safe. And they…" She shook her head. "They lived from the heart. I lived from fear."

She paused, choosing her next words carefully.

"There were things happening back then," she said. "Things I tried to protect Sarah from. Things I didn't protect her from." Her voice thinned. "And when I failed… I thought distance would keep everyone safe."

Tyashia stepped closer. "What things?"

Sylvia's eyes shifted — fear, guilt, memory — then shuttered.

"Not now," she whispered. "I can't… not yet."

Tyashia's disappointment was immediate, but so was something else — a strange tenderness. Sylvia wasn't shutting her out. She was holding something back because it hurt.

"Do you know where she is?" Tyashia asked quietly.

Sylvia froze.

Just for a breath. Just long enough for the truth to cross her face.

Then she blinked it away.

"I know she's somewhere trying to survive," Sylvia said. "That's all I can say."

It wasn't an answer. It wasn't a lie either.

"You're not telling me everything," Tyashia said softly.

Sylvia's voice cracked. "I'm telling you what I can."

A long silence stretched between them — not empty, but full of everything unsaid.

Finally, Sylvia reached out, her hand hovering before she let it rest on Tyashia's.

"One day," she murmured, "I'll tell you the rest. When I can say it without breaking you. Or myself."

Tyashia nodded, even though her throat burned.

"Okay," she whispered.

It wasn't closure. It wasn't truth. But it was the closest they had ever come to meeting each other in the middle.

And it was enough — for now.

Later that night, Sylvia sat at the kitchen table again — no bills this time, just silence. Leonard hovered in the doorway, unsure whether to comfort her or give her space.

"You okay?" he asked softly.

She didn't look up. "I'm fine."

But her voice cracked.

He stepped closer. "We'll get through this. If I have to work a second job, we will get through this."

She wanted to believe him. She wanted to believe in something.

But the truth pressed against her ribs:

She had built her identity on a system that could collapse with a signature. She had built her pride on a job that could vanish overnight. She had built her superiority on a paycheck that wasn't coming.

And now she was raising a grieving teenager who saw right through her.

For once in her life, Sylvia felt small. Human. Breakable.

"I don't know how to do this," she whispered.

Leonard placed a hand on her shoulder — gentle, enduring, unfamiliar.

"We are in this together."

She closed her eyes.

Maybe that was the lesson. Maybe that was the beginning.

Over the next week, Sylvia saw the shutdown everywhere. Commissary shelves thinned. The childcare center shortened its hours. The barber on Murchison Road started offering "shutdown cuts" for ten dollars. At the gas station, a woman counted change with trembling fingers. A young Soldier bought ramen and nothing else. A civilian contractor sat in her car, shoulders shaking, trying to gather herself before going home.

Sylvia saw herself in all of them.

And in that moment, she understood what Asiah had always tried to teach her: that community was not weakness, that dependence was not failure, and that order was not the same as stability.

Her world had cracked open. And through the crack, something new was trying to grow.

One evening, Tyashia found Sylvia sitting at the kitchen table again — no bills this time, just silence.

"You okay?" Tyashia asked, hesitant.

Sylvia opened her mouth to lie. To say she was fine. To say everything was under control.

But the shutdown had stripped her of the illusion of control.

She looked at the girl — this child who had lost everything and still kept moving — and something inside her softened.

"I'm… figuring things out," Sylvia said quietly.

It wasn't much. But it was honest.

Tyashia nodded, surprised. "Me too."

They weren't standing on opposite sides anymore. They were just two people trying to survive a system that had failed them both.

And that was the beginning of something neither of them had words for yet.

Chapter Twenty-Eight

Where the Diaspora Meets

They met at The Gentle Ground Café to finalize details for the youth initiative, then drifted naturally to dinner at The Taste of West Africa — a Fayetteville gem tucked between a barber shop and a tax service office. The moment they stepped inside, the room greeted them like a velvety embrace. The air clutched the scent of jollof simmering low, ginger and garlic blooming in hot oil, and the earthy sweetness of plantains caramelizing on the grill.

Soft highlife music floated through the speakers, and the walls were painted in deep golds and reds — colors that felt like memory.

Sena, the owner, spotted them immediately. "Ah, Chemelu!" she called, her Ghanaian lilt bright and melodic. "You brought someone special today."

Leha flushed, but Sena's smile was too warm to be embarrassing.

"This is Leha," Chemelu said, his voice carrying a quiet pride. "She's family to the community here."

Sena clasped Leha's hands. "Welcome, my dear. You must try our vegetarian waakye plate. And the kontomire stew — it will bless your spirit."

From the kitchen, Mama Abena peeked out, her headwrap tied in a perfect knot. "Tell them to save room for sweet plantains," she called. "A little sweetness is good for the heart."

Chemelu laughed, the sound soft and familiar. "Mama Abena believes every problem can be solved with something sweet."

Mama Abena shrugged. "Has it ever failed?"

They chose a small table near the window, the wood worn smooth by years of stories. A woven kente runner stretched across the center, its colors deepening against the worn wood.

Over steaming plates — waakye, kelewele, kontomire stew, and a bright mango-ginger drink — Leha found herself opening up more than she expected.

She told him about Sam's military retirement, Melina's long shifts at the hospital, the delicate truce she maintained with her mother. She spoke of the divorce — the quiet ache it left behind, the way it made her cautious.

"It makes you wonder if anything truly lasts," she admitted.

Chemelu reached across the table, covering her hand gently. His touch was warm, intentional. "Trust is hard when you've seen foundations crumble. But your story is yours to write, Leha. Trust in that 'God within' you, and you will attract the lasting connection you deserve."

His words poured into her like oil.

She asked about his own journey — leaving Kenya, leaving his village, leaving the familiar.

"It was challenging," he said. "But community is not just geography. My father always said holding onto bitterness is like drinking poison and expecting the other person to suffer."

Before she could respond, Sena returned with a small plate of caramelized sweet plantains. "On the house," she said. "For joy."

Then she looked at Chemelu with a knowing tilt of her head. "East Africa, yes? Kenya?"

He nodded.

"My mother is always saying the diaspora is a big house," Sena said. "Different rooms, same foundation."

Mama Abena, overhearing, added, "And when we meet each other in new places, we remember the house is still standing."

Chemelu's eyes softened. "That is true."

Leha felt something warm bloom in her chest — a sense of belonging that reached beyond Fayetteville, beyond the moment, beyond herself.

She shared the story of her great-grandmother Macie, a nurse who graduated in 1950 from the Kate Bitting Nursing School in Winston-Salem — one of the few options available to Black women barred from white institutions.

"She lived in the nurses' residence, studied with enough light to see her notes, did her clinicals at the colored hospital," Leha said, pride swelling. "She graduated top of her class. The newspaper article about her is in a safe box at home."

Mama Abena nodded slowly. "Women like her built bridges we are still walking across."

The legacy of resilience pulsed through Leha's words.

Their conversation shifted to Sam.

"After he retired as a Command Sergeant Major, he couldn't sit still," Leha said. "He works with the Sandhills Valor Network now — helping unhoused veterans get off the street."

"That is noble work," Chemelu said.

Leha opened up even more — about her travels, her safari in Kenya, the peace of Jamaica. "Sometimes my work here makes me forget the world is bigger."

"Then we will have to make sure you remember," Chemelu replied, eyes warm.

When they finally stepped outside, the night air felt soft, almost tender. He walked her to her car, smiling as she pulled away. The evening had been everything he hoped for. Leha was brilliant, compassionate, beautiful — a rare combination of strength and grace.

A future he could claim finally felt real. He opened the car door and lowered himself into the driver's seat, his long frame folding in with practiced ease. The last traces of conversation and clinking dishes from The Taste of West Africa drifted out behind him as the door closed. His shoulders relaxed, the faint sheen of the restaurant's glow still on his skin.

Then his phone lit up.

Delilah.

His stomach clenched. The ease in his posture vanished.

He answered. "Delilah," he said, voice flat.

"I'm in Fayetteville," she said, her tone smooth and practiced. "We need to talk. The job is falling through, and I need your help."

The knot in his stomach tightened.

"What do you want?" he asked.

"Oh, I think you know," she said. "This mentoring empire you're building… I know exactly how you got the funding for it. And the strings attached."

The line went dead.

Chemelu stared at the screen, the image of Leha's smile now clouded by dread. He drew in a slow breath. He was a man of faith, not fear.

But tonight, fear had found him.

Chapter Twenty-Nine

A Risky Proposition

The morning after his dinner with Leha, Chemelu woke with a rare sense of peace — the kind that settles into a man who has finally allowed himself to imagine a future. But the peace didn't last. Delilah's call from the night before replayed in his mind like a warning he couldn't outrun.

By the time he pulled into the parking lot of a nondescript convenience store in Raeford, the knot in his stomach had tightened into something sharp.

The contrast hit him immediately.

Last night had been fullness — gold-painted walls, highlife music drifting through the room, the sweetness of plantains caramelizing in hot oil, Mama Abena's blessing, Leha's smile softening in candlelight.

This morning was the opposite.

The air was cool and metallic, carrying the faint smell of gasoline and damp asphalt. The pavement still held the night's moisture, reflecting the flickering neon **GAS & SNACKS** sign like a broken promise. A trash can overflowed near the entrance, buzzing with flies. A lone shopping cart rattled in the wind.

Everything felt stripped, exposed, unforgiving.

He sat in his car for a moment, gripping the steering wheel. The scent of The Taste of West Africa — ginger, spice, and the last trace of a room that had held him — had faded from his clothes, replaced by the stale tang of old upholstery and cold air. It felt like stepping out of a dream and into a consequence.

He had arrived early, using the drive to organize his thoughts. He'd chosen this meeting place away from Fayetteville under the pretense of checking out the new James A. Leach Recreation Center — a perfect future site for SCI youth activities. His alibi was solid. He even allowed himself a brief rise of hope, imagining a life with Leha in a quiet neighborhood like Turnberry, where a friend lived.

But the moment he saw Delilah leaning against her sleek sedan, arms crossed, posture dripping with entitlement, the future he imagined evaporated.

He stepped out of his car, gravel crunching under his shoes.

"Delilah," he said, voice clipped.

"Chemelu," she replied, her tone smooth and practiced. "You look… settled into yourself. Fayetteville must be treating you very well."

There was something in her smile — a sharpness, a knowing — that made his stomach twist.

"We're not here for pleasantries," he said. "You made demands. I'm here to listen."

She tilted her head, amused. "Always so serious. It's adorable, really. You act like you're above all this."

He didn't respond.

She pushed off the car, heels clicking against the pavement. "Fine. Let's get to it. The funding for my project fell through. I need cash. Fast."

"And you thought of me," he said bitterly. "After you cheated. After you left pregnant by someone else."

"That was then," she said, flicking her hand dismissively. "And you survived. Congratulations."

Her voice sharpened.

"But now? You've built something. Something big. That Global Community Initiative grant? That's real money. And I need a piece."

"It's a nonprofit," he snapped. "Not a scheme."

"Oh, please." She stepped closer, her perfume cutting through the cold air like a blade. "You think you're some saint now? You think people don't talk? I kept the records, Chemelu. The seed funding. The deal you made. The strings you pretended weren't there."

His blood ran cold.

She smiled — slow, cruel. "Imagine the grant committee finding out. Imagine your board. Imagine your precious Leha hearing the truth from me."

"What do you want?" he asked, voice low.

She named a number. A large one.

"A one-time consulting fee," she said. "You pay, and the records disappear. My silence is yours."

He stared at her, the dilemma pressing down on him like a force he couldn't ignore.

This was everything he stood against. Everything he had rebuilt his life to avoid. Everything he had promised himself he would never become.

But exposure could destroy SCI. Destroy Leha's reputation. Destroy the community work he believed in. Destroy the fragile trust he was building with the youth.

He looked around the empty parking lot — the cracked pavement, the neon sign sputtering like a warning, the cold morning air that smelled of gasoline and disappointment.

There was no "we" here. Only "I."

And the cost of the wrong choice could be catastrophic.

He closed his eyes for a moment, restoring his breath.

He was a man of faith, not fear. But today, fear had found him. And it wasn't letting go.

Meanwhile — Across Town

Tyashia stood in the bowling alley, the neon lights stuttering across her face.

Vince was pacing, muttering about his approach, his form, his "off day." His frustration radiated like heat.

She flinched when he snapped at her — the same force he used to dominate the lane was the force he used with her. Charming one moment, demanding the next. This wasn't connection; it was consumption.

Her phone buzzed.

Kendra: You missed a great night! Bishop T's message was fire. Still up to skate tomorrow? My treat!

A wave of longing washed over her. Kendra's world was bright music, genuine laughter, and the freedom of wheels on pavement. This world was neon glare, grease, and the heavy pull of Vince's demands.

Tyashia picked at a loose thread on her sleeve — her tell when she needed grounding.

She needed air.

She slipped away while Vince was focused on his approach.

The hallway toward the restrooms was dim and blessedly quiet, tucked beside the game room where arcade lights blinked in restless colors. A pinball machine chimed in the distance, its silver ball ricocheting once before the sound faded again.

Tyashia leaned against the wall and slipped in her earbuds, pressing play on Ahmad Latif's Ville Promises.

The beat rose up around her, passionate and textured, wrapping itself through the space like something familiar reaching for her. Ahmad's voice followed — low, direct, delivering that lived-in grit that felt like someone speaking from the middle of their own healing.

The sound didn't just ease her breathing; it sparked a small lift inside her chest — the kind of quiet, private joy that felt like an inside smile, an inside hug, an inside high-five she didn't have to explain to anyone.

A line from "Northside Lullaby" rose through the quiet— not the one that had struck her before, but another she'd never really heard until now:

Find the rhythm that belongs to you.

Her breath caught. It felt like a hand on her shoulder, guiding her back to herself.

Ten minutes later, she returned to the lane.

Vince was furious.

"Where the hell were you?" he hissed, grabbing her roughly by the elbow and yanking her toward him. Pain shot up her arm — sharp, immediate. His grip was a vise, the physical proof of everything Ron had warned her about.

"Bathroom," Tyashia muttered, pulling her arm free, anger sparking in her chest. "I needed a minute."

"You don't wander off when you're with me," Vince spat, leaning close, his eyes cold and possessive.

Something inside her snapped — not in fear, but in clarity.

"Relax, man," Meja said, strolling up with her usual detached calm. "She's back. Go bowl."

Vince shoved past her, muttering curses. He hurled another ball down the lane. It veered instantly into the gutter with a loud thud. He glared at Tyashia, blaming her.

Tyashia stood perfectly still. The noise of the alley thinned into the background, the crash of pins and arcade beeps blurring into nothing she needed to hear.

His control was brittle. His anger was a mask for the insecurity he transmitted like a shadow.

I am not an audience, she thought, staring at the red zero flashing on the screen. *I get to choose where I go, who I'm with, and what I wear.*

The moment was a quiet revolution — a shift she felt in her bones.

Something shifted, the ground beneath her didn't tremble from fear. It rose to meet her determination.

The Next Afternoon

The day brightened a little when Tyashia spotted Kendra waiting for her at the bus stop.

Kendra wasn't waiting for the bus. She leaned against a compact purple sedan — the kind of first car teens name and decorate. Hers had tiny silver stars scattered across the bumper and a small roller skate charm dangling from the rearview mirror, swaying with every breeze. The cheerful purple matched her oversized headphones, bright against the dull winter sky.

"I decided to skip the bus today," Kendra said, her smile warm and easy. "Figured I'd catch you instead. Hop in — I can drive you home."

Tyashia hesitated. The previous night's tension still clung to her skin. "Vince might not like that I rode with you."

"Vince isn't here," Kendra replied, unfazed. She swung open the passenger door. The car smelled faintly of vanilla and sunshine. "And you're allowed to like what you like."

Tyashia slid into the seat, closing the door on the cold afternoon. "He's… very specific about things."

Kendra pulled away from the curb. "Ron knows Vince pretty well, right? My dad knows Ron. Dad says Vince is all about control because he feels out of control at home. He used to hang with a rough crowd before he found his 'audience.' Don't let him decide your story, Tyashia."

Tyashia blinked. "Your dad knows Ron? Ron's my counselor."

"Yup. Fayetteville's small like that."

She turned the radio up slightly — bright pop music lifting the mood with every beat.

"Anyway," Kendra continued, "I got the deets on that 'Blue Anchor' bus project. Ms. Leha and her friend Chemelu are hosting a dinner soon to talk about it. They're looking for high school volunteers for a community grant thing."

Tyashia's mind flashed back to the bowling alley — the neon lights, the stale popcorn, the tight grip on her arm.

"What kind of project?" she asked quietly.

"It's about fixing up another old bus into a mobile resource center — library, art supplies, clothes closet, all that good stuff. It's about building Ubuntu. Using your strength to build up other people, not tear them down."

Ubuntu. The word dropped in her mind like a small ember.

"They want to talk to people who are interested," Kendra added. "Dinner's at Ms. Leha's house on Saturday."

Saturday. Vince would expect her to be available. He always did.

But this time, the expectation didn't feel like a command.

It felt like a choice.

Outside the window, a gust of wind lifted a dry leaf from the curb and sent it spiraling upward — caught in a current stronger than the one that tried to pin it down.

Tyashia watched it rise.

And something inside her rose with it.

Chapter Thirty

The Night the Village Formed

Saturday arrived with a cool breeze drifting through Fayetteville — the kind that hinted at winter without fully committing. The air felt clearer than it had all week, as if the city itself was trying to shake off the heaviness of the shutdown. Even Leha felt it as she stepped onto her porch, smoothing the front of her sweater.

Tonight mattered.

Tonight, the adults and youth she'd been guiding on parallel paths would finally sit at the same table.

Ubuntu in motion.

Inside, her home held a welcoming radiance. The dining room table was set with intentional care — mismatched plates that felt like family, cloth napkins folded neatly, and a centerpiece of eucalyptus and candles that filled the room with a grounding calm. The air smelled of roasted vegetables, spiced rice, and the rich aroma of Kenyan coffee brewing in the kitchen.

Chemelu moved with quiet purpose beside her, arranging serving spoons and nudging the lamp so its glow fell evenly across the table. His presence was calm, resolved — a quiet reassurance that she wasn't carrying this alone.

"This is good work, Leha," he said softly. "Bringing people together is sacred."

She exhaled, letting his words settle. "I just hope it lands the way it needs to."

"It will," he said simply. "Because it's rooted in truth."

The first knock came right on time.

Melodie stepped inside with her usual warm smile, carrying a tray of cornbread muffins and followed by two teens from her Rooted & Rising program. They greeted Leha with easy familiarity, their energy filling the room with life.

"Evening, Ms. Leha," one of them said shyly. "We brought extra creative kits for the bus — sketchbooks, colored pencils, little things the kids can use."

Leha's heart swelled. "Thank you. That means more than you know."

More knocks followed — mentors, community partners, a few parents, and finally Ron, who arrived with a stack of folders tucked under his arm.

"Ready?" he asked quietly.

"As I'll ever be."

Tyashia arrived last.

She stood on the porch for a long moment before knocking, her breath visible in the cool air. She tugged at the sleeve of her sweater — grounding herself the way Ron had taught her.

Choice, she thought. *This is a choice.*

When she finally stepped inside, the space opened around her — laughter, soft music, the smell of food, the bustle of community. It felt like stepping into a different world entirely.

Kendra spotted her first. "You made it!" she squealed, pulling her into a hug before Tyashia could protest. "Come on, I saved you a seat."

Tyashia followed her into the dining room, her eyes widening as she took in the scene. Melodie's teens were chatting with mentors. Ron was deep in conversation with Chemelu. Safiya was pouring spiced tea from The Gentle Ground Café. Everyone seemed connected — woven together like threads in a tapestry.

It was overwhelming. And strangely comforting.

Dinner began with a simple blessing from Chemelu — a quiet invocation of gratitude, community, and purpose.

As everyone slipped into their seats, Leha stood, her hands resting on the back of her chair.

"Thank you all for being here," she began, her voice calm but warm. "Tonight isn't just about food or planning. It's about building something bigger than ourselves. A space where our young people can find support, creativity, and belonging."

She glanced at Tyashia — not calling her out, but acknowledging her presence with a soft, encouraging smile.

"It's about Ubuntu," she continued. "I am because we are. None of us rises alone."

Melodie nodded, lifting her glass. "We rise by lifting others."

A murmur of agreement rippled around the table.

As the meal unfolded, conversations blossomed.

Ron spoke with Melodie's teens about their goals. Safiya shared stories about the café. Chemelu explained the vision for the new Blue Anchor bus — a mobile resource center that would bring books, art supplies, hygiene kits, and mentorship directly into neighborhoods that needed it most.

Tyashia listened quietly, absorbing everything.

At one point, Kendra nudged her. "Pretty cool, right?"

Tyashia nodded slowly. "Yeah… it is."

"Think you might want to help?" Kendra asked, her tone gentle, not pushy.

Tyashia hesitated.

Vince's voice slipped through her mind — sharp, controlling, dismissive.

Then another set of memories rose up, soft but insistent:

The feather lifting from the curb like a sign. The lyric that wrapped around her heart when she needed it most. The ache in her arm from Vince's grip — a bruise she refused to let define her. The calm of Ron's office, where she learned to breathe again. The candle she poured with intention, watching the wax settle into something whole. And now, the pulse of this room — people laughing, listening, choosing each other.

She took a breath.

"I think… I might," she said softly.

Kendra beamed. "Then you're sitting with us at the planning table."

Later, as the evening wound down…

Leha stepped outside to breathe in the cool night air. The porch light cast a soft wash across the steps. She heard footsteps behind her.

Tyashia.

"You okay?" Leha asked gently.

Tyashia nodded, pulling her sweater tighter around her. "Yeah. I just… I didn't know people could be like this."

"Like what?"

"Kind," she whispered. "Like… they actually want you here."

Leha's heart tightened. "You deserve that, Tyashia. You deserve community. You deserve choice."

Tyashia looked down at the step beneath her — worn smooth from years of visitors. "I think I want to help with the bus," she said quietly. "I think I want to… try."

Leha smiled, a sense of rightness floating through her. "Then we'll build it together."

Tyashia exhaled, a long, unhurried breath.

She didn't feel like she was falling anymore. She felt like she was moving.

Chapter Thirty-One

The Heart of the Circle

The week after the dinner at Leha's house, Fayetteville felt different — gentler in some places, heavier in others. Tyashia was moving toward community. Vince was tightening his grip. And Leha felt the shift in the air like a change in weather.

The work was growing. The youth were growing. And the mentors — the ones holding so much — needed tending too.

So she called a gathering.

The multipurpose room buzzed with quiet anticipation. Folding chairs formed a wide circle beneath warm pendant lights. A tray of pastries from a local bakery filled the air with cinnamon and butter — comfort disguised as food.

Ron entered first, carrying notebooks. A soft-spoken mentor followed quietly, offering a small wave. Teachers, Soldiers, social workers, retirees, and college students trickled in — people who showed up even when their own lives were fraying at the edges.

Leha stepped into the center.

"Today isn't about training," she said softly. "It's about tending."

The room exhaled.

She invited them to share one unseen burden. The stories that emerged were raw — burnout, grief, imposter syndrome, loneliness. The truth beneath the surface.

Ron demonstrated grounding techniques, guiding them through slow breaths and unclenched shoulders. The soft-spoken mentor shared the emotional strain of showing up for youth who reminded her of her younger self. Others shared quietly — the exhaustion of caregiving, the ache of divorce, the fear of not being enough.

Leha introduced new tools — digital journals, AI-assisted prompts, progress trackers — not to replace the heart of mentoring, but to sustain it.

"This isn't about making mentoring mechanical," she said. "It's about making it sustainable."

The mentors nodded, absorbing the wisdom like thirsty soil.

They closed with a candle, a quote, and a single word from each person — *hope, strength, clarity, courage, community.*

When the room emptied, Leha stood alone in the circle, letting the silence settle.

This — this tending — was the heartbeat of the work.

Two weeks later, the mentors gathered again — this time at Lake Rim Park. The morning sun filtered through tall shoreline trees, casting soft beams across the picnic shelter. The air smelled of dew and honeysuckle.

Ron led a grounding exercise, his voice carrying a worn gentleness. "I'm learning," he admitted, "that being strong all the time is its own kind of burden."

The soft-spoken mentor nodded. "I didn't know I was allowed to be vulnerable until this group."

When it was Leha's turn, she hesitated.

"I'm afraid," she said quietly. "Afraid that if I stop moving, everything will fall apart."

Ron leaned forward. "You don't have to hold all of this by yourself."

The group murmured in agreement — a soft chorus of support.

They sipped warm turmeric lattes from tiny cups, letting the heat settle into their bones. Then they walked the lake trail, sharing stories, laughter, and stillness. The water shimmered. The breeze carried the scent of pine. It felt like a reset — a collective exhale.

Leha left the retreat feeling held. And ready.

What came next was a night she could never have imagined.

The ballroom at the Crown Complex gleamed beneath the chandeliers. Gold accents shimmered against navy linens. Each table held candles, eucalyptus, and framed photos of mentors with their mentees.

It was the most elegant event they had ever hosted.

Leha stood near the stage, adjusting the microphone, heart fluttering. This night honored the quiet heroes — the mentors who held the community together.

Ron greeted guests with a presence that held firm. The soft-spoken mentor moved through the room with a gentle steadiness, offering hugs and quiet encouragement. Chemelu stood beside Leha, grounding her with his presence.

Tyashia entered with Kaymon — shoulders back, her bracelet catching a bit of motion as she sat.

When the program began, Leha spoke of legacy, lineage, and the quiet work of showing up. The youth choir sang *Rise Up*. Mrs. Greene received a lifetime award. Parents shared testimonies.

Then Tyashia stepped onto the stage.

"When I first came here," she said, voice trembling, "I didn't trust anyone. But my mentor saw something in me I couldn't see yet."

She looked at Leha.

"You taught me that healing isn't a straight line. And that I'm allowed to grow."

The room erupted in applause.

A donor pledged a major grant. The crowd rose to its feet. Leha stepped outside, overwhelmed by gratitude.

Chemelu joined her, slipping an arm around her waist.

"You built something beautiful," he murmured.

"We built it," she whispered.

He kissed her temple. "This is legacy."

Leha looked back at the ballroom lit softly — mentors laughing, youth celebrating, community rising — and felt something deep inside her settle.

This wasn't just a program. It was a movement. A foundation. A future.

And she was ready for whatever came next.

Chapter Thirty-Two

The Future We Build Together

A week after the retreat and the banquet, Fayetteville seemed to move with an unusual undercurrent — calm in some pockets, tense in others. The work was growing. The youth were growing. And the mentors needed tools that could grow with them.

That realization struck Leha one quiet morning at The Gentle Ground Café. She watched one of the mentors — a young teacher named Bri — sit at a corner table, staring at a blank notebook page. Bri sighed, tapped her pen, and whispered to herself, "I don't even know where to start."

Something clicked into place.

They don't just need support, Leha thought. *They need new strategies. New language. New ways to reach our kids.*

By the time the sun dipped low, she had rearranged the multipurpose room — a semicircle of chairs facing a projector screen, a low instrumental beat pulsing through the speakers, the scent of fresh coffee grounding the space. Overhead, the fixtures cast a clean, steady brightness that made every face easy to read, every intention clear.

Tonight wasn't about reflection. Tonight wasn't about healing. Tonight was about the future.

Ron entered first, raising an eyebrow at the setup. "You're bringing out the big guns tonight."

Leha smiled. "Something like that."

Mentors filtered in — teachers, Soldiers, social workers, retirees, college students — people who had been showing up long before the community realized how much they were carrying. They dropped into their seats with quiet curiosity.

When the room stilled, Leha clicked to the first slide:

AI + Mentoring: Tools for Equity, Connection, and Community Care

A ripple of interest moved through the room — a collective inhale.

"Before we begin," Leha said, "I want to be clear. AI is not here to replace us. It's here to support us. To make our work more sustainable. To help us reach youth in ways we couldn't before."

Marcus raised a hand. "Like robots?"

Laughter filled the room, warm and easy.

"No robots," Leha said. "Think of AI as a digital assistant. A tool. A partner."

She walked them through examples, each one landing with a quiet sense of possibility:

- AI-assisted journaling prompts for mentees who struggle to express emotions
- conversation starters for difficult check-ins
- cultural context summaries to help mentors understand youth experiences
- trauma-informed language suggestions
- goal-setting templates youth can personalize
- career exploration tools that open doors beyond Fayetteville

Ron leaned forward. "So this helps us prepare better?"

"Yes," Leha said. "It helps us show up with clarity. With intention. With language that heals instead of harms."

She clicked to the next slide.

Ethics + Equity

"This is the most important part," she said. "AI must be used responsibly. With cultural awareness. With trauma-informed practice. With Ubuntu."

She wrote the word on the board:

Ubuntu — I am because we are.

"This technology must serve community, not replace it. It must amplify our values, not erase them."

The mentors nodded, feeling her words land with a truth they all recognized.

Then Leha introduced a hands-on activity.

"Pair up," she said. "Use the AI tool to generate a conversation prompt for a mentee who's struggling with self-esteem."

The room buzzed with energy as mentors experimented, laughed, and shared discoveries. Screens flickered to life. Eyes widened. Hearts opened.

Ron looked up, surprised. "This actually helps."

"It does," Leha said softly. "And it's only the beginning."

As the workshop ended, one of the mentors approached her, eyes bright with new conviction. "You're shifting the whole landscape," she said. "This is the future."

Leha exhaled, feeling the truth settle into her bones.

Maybe it was.

As the mentors packed up their notebooks, Leha felt the spark of something bigger — a shift, an opening, a door easing itself ajar.

Chapter Thirty-Three

The First Act of Choosing

While the mentors were strengthening their roots — through circles, retreats, and new tools for the future — the young people they served were shifting too. And for Tyashia, the shift began quietly, the morning after Leha's dinner.

Sometimes the first step toward freedom is quiet— a shift so small only the heart can hear it.

The morning after the dinner at Leha's house, Tyashia woke with a feeling she couldn't quite name. It wasn't joy — not exactly. It wasn't confidence either. It was something quieter, like a drumbeat she hadn't heard in a long time.

She lay still for a moment, replaying the enchantment of Leha's dining room — the laughter, the stories, the way everyone seemed to belong to something bigger than themselves.

Ubuntu. I am because we are.

A quiet thought rose in her — maybe she could belong to something like that too.

Following her next session with Leha — and the conversation about Aunt Asiah — something subtle but powerful shifted inside her. It wasn't a dramatic revelation. It was quieter, like a truth she had always known but never named.

Asiah had wanted children her whole life. She would've been the kind of mother who packed notes in lunchboxes, who showed up to every school play, who clapped the loudest at every milestone. But life had written a different script for her — one with empty cribs and unanswered prayers. Maybe the cancer had been there long before she knew. Maybe her body had been fighting a silent battle while she was busy fighting for everyone else.

So she poured her love into her students instead.

A Title I school. Low pay. Outdated textbooks. Kids who carried hunger, grief, and chaos in their backpacks. Black, brown, white, Hispanic — a mosaic of children fighting poverty with a teacher who refused to let them feel small.

Asiah showed up for them anyway. Every day. Every year. With grit. With tenderness. With a belief that even the most overlooked child deserved to be seen.

Strength didn't have to be loud to be real. It could be quietly resolute. It could be rooted in compassion. It could be the act of loving children who weren't yours because your heart insisted they were.

That was the blueprint. That was the inheritance.

Keep rolling, Asiah used to say — not as a cliché, but as a way of surviving. A way of choosing herself. A way of choosing love even when life had been unkind.

Those words became Tyashia's quiet mantra, a reminder that preparation was its own kind of power.

Ron noticed the shift immediately.

"You're sitting taller today," he said gently as she settled into the chair across from him.

Tyashia shrugged, but a small smile tugged at her lips. "Just thinking about stuff."

"Good stuff?" he asked.

She nodded. "Yeah. Good stuff."

Ron helped her turn that internal shift into action.

"Fayetteville State University is a great school, Tyashia," he said one afternoon, handing her an application packet stamped with the FSU Broncos logo. "It's right here, part of the community foundation you're building."

The packet felt heavier than paper — like a beginning she could finally feel in her hands.

Tyashia accepted it, a gentle rise of genuine hope warming her chest. FSU wasn't just a college — it was a tangible path forward. A future she could shape herself, separate from Sylvia's rigid expectations or Vince's suffocating control.

She imagined herself walking across a campus filled with old trees and open sky. She imagined choosing her own classes. Her own clothes. Her own life.

For a moment, she let herself breathe in that freedom.

But her relationship with Vince and Meja was growing more toxic by the day. The small acts of resistance she practiced — wearing her favorite blue T-shirt under the blouse Vince insisted on, choosing a lunch seat that wasn't dictated by Meja's clique — created friction.

Tiny rebellions. Tiny reminders that she still belonged to herself.

One afternoon in the hallway, Vince cornered her after class. His shadow slid across her locker like a warning.

"I called you last night. Why didn't you answer?" His tone was low, demanding.

"I was doing homework," Tyashia replied, keeping her voice even. She refused to look away. Asiah's resolve — quiet, firm, unshakable — held her upright.

Vince scoffed. "Homework. You missed our movie night. I told you we were watching *Creed*."

His voice was sharp, but beneath it she heard something else — fear. The same fear Ron had named. The fear of being overlooked. The fear of losing control.

She didn't soften. She didn't apologize.

Instead, she tightened her grip on the FSU application in her hand. The edges pressed into her palm like a reminder.

Asiah hadn't survived by bending to anyone's demands. She had survived by choosing her own path, by refusing to let anyone else define her worth.

Tyashia stepped back, creating space between them. "I had things to do," she said simply.

Vince's jaw clenched. "Don't start acting brand new."

But she already was.

As she walked away, the application packet rustled in her hand — not just a form, but a declaration.

A declaration that she was building a life rooted in her own choices. A declaration that she was ready — not for Vince's script, but for her own.

And she felt the ground beneath her tilt toward freedom.

Chapter Thirty-Four

Talk Show Dreams

As Tyashia began choosing herself in small, quiet ways, the world around her began opening too — in places she never expected.

She woke with a different kind of awareness — like a door inside her had unlatched during the night, letting in a breeze she hadn't realized she'd been blocking out. Something felt different that Saturday. Still thick with Carolina heat, but eased somehow, as if the world had made room for her.

For months, loneliness had pressed against her ribs — constant, heavy, familiar. Every street corner echoed the life she'd left behind. But after watching people laugh, build, and dream together in Leha's kitchen, the stress she accepted had loosened. Not gone. Just… no longer the only thing she felt.

As she approached the community center, she spotted Kendra.

She stood near the entrance juggling a thick stack of magazines — *Teen Vogue*, *Essence*, *Girls' Life*, and a couple of old *Oprah* issues she kept for the interviews — plus a large iced coffee balanced against her hip. A pair of roller skates hung from her backpack straps, the wheels knocking every time she moved. She looked like a one-girl newsroom on wheels.

"Oh Lord, I am so sorry! My hands are full and my mind is on *The View* probably," Kendra blurted, her words tumbling out like they were racing each other.

Tyashia blinked. "It's okay."

"I basically live here," Kendra said, shifting her magazines. "They should start charging me rent. I'm in the little studio room every day."

"Studio?" Tyashia asked.

Kendra nodded toward the side hallway. "It used to be a storage closet, but they put a ring light and a mic in there for the teens. I practice my intros, interview questions, all that. One day, I'm gonna have a real set — but for now, that closet is my Oprah room."

Tyashia smiled. "You love talk shows that much?"

"Love them," Kendra said, her voice softening with sincerity. "It's about connection. Everybody has a story. One day, I want a show where girls like us get to tell the truth — the real truth — and breathe a little easier because of it."

The words hit deeper than Kendra knew. Tyashia thought of the half-finished FSU application on her desk. She thought of the youth circle. She thought of the girl on the news saying, *We protect each other.*

She glanced toward the hallway. Tyashia had seen the studio room once — the ring light, the taped-up backdrop, the stack of donated magazines Kendra organized like sacred texts.

Maybe even she had a story worth telling — someday.

"I brought my skates," she said quietly. "You said you had a sweet spot?"

Kendra's face lit up. "Come on. I'll show you. It's totally private."

They walked toward the park path.

"Sometimes I just need to move," Kendra said, "and not think about everything going on."

"Everything?" Tyashia asked.

Kendra sighed, her shoulders dropping. "The news. The ICE stuff. Did you see the protests at FSU yesterday?"

Tyashia shook her head.

"They shut down part of Murchison Road," Kendra said, eyes bright with urgency. "Students were chanting, 'We protect each other,' and 'Families belong together.' They were loud, Tye. Loud and brave."

A small surge of something — fear, recognition, anger — moved through Tyashia's chest.

"One girl said on camera, 'We're not letting ICE snatch people out of our community.' I swear, I replayed that clip like ten times."

Tyashia swallowed. "People really said that?"

"Loud," Kendra said. "And proud. That's why I love talk shows. That's why I want my own one day. So girls like us can talk about stuff like this — ICE, police in schools, mental health — without being shut down."

The words landed with power. Not heavy — clarifying.

Maybe she wasn't just choosing a school. Maybe she was choosing a future where she could stand up too.

The community center felt quieter than usual that afternoon — the kind of quiet that made every sound feel sharper. Soft overhead fixtures cast a smooth, even shimmer across the room, bright enough to work but gentle enough not to sting her eyes.

Tyashia sat across from Ron, her notebook open but her thoughts drifting far beyond the page.

"You're drifting again," Ron said gently, closing his planner. "Must be some current pulling you."

"It's just… a lot," she sighed. "Picking one thing feels like ignoring everything else that's a mess."

She thought of Kendra's relentless energy — the talk-show chatter, the honesty about the news, the way she promised skating without hesitation. It was confusing, disruptive, and strangely comforting.

Ron leaned forward. "The 'one thing' isn't about ignoring the mess. It's about finding a point of return. One solid thing to hold onto when the waters rise."

He paused, something unspoken passing in his eyes. "I used to be in a situation where everything felt like a current. My focus was always on managing the chaos — the demands of others."

Tyashia looked up, surprised. Ron, too?

"What changed?"

"I found my still point," he said. "It meant learning to say no. To prioritize my own worth. To trust that not everyone leaves."

He tapped her notebook. "That's what this assignment is. What are you going to hold onto for yourself, Tyashia?"

She looked down at the blank page. Something inside her clicked into place.

She thought of Kendra — her bright headphones, her talk-show dreams, her honesty. She thought of the FSU students chanting, *We protect each other*. She thought of the soft, tentative opening that maybe, one day, she could tell her own story too — even if she didn't yet know how.

Maybe trust wasn't about certainty. Maybe it was about choosing what to hold onto.

She picked up her pen. "I think my 'one thing' is going to be boundaries," she said, writing the word in bold strokes. "Learning how to set them and keep them."

Ron nodded. "That's a good one. Boundaries are the best guides there are."

For once, the word didn't feel like a wall. It felt like a doorway.

The building was quiet that evening, just Leha and Ron finishing paperwork. The center had that end-of-day stillness — bright posters from past youth events lining the hallway, their corners lifting slightly from the day's traffic, and the distant hum of cars along NC-87. A few leftover tutoring worksheets sat in a neat stack on the counter, edges curling from use.

Leha's phone buzzed. Safiya.

Relief washed through her as she answered.

"Hey, how is she?" Leha asked.

Safiya's voice was weary but sure. "She's tough, L. Lakena's stable now. But seeing her like that… it brings everything back. Home. The Fruitbelt."

They talked about Peach Street, the Neighborhood House, the drill team, Jessie who fixed bikes, Ms. Beverly who made every child feel like the most important person in the room.

"Those people built the foundation for a whole generation," Safiya said. "It wasn't grants or paperwork. It was a promise to pay it forward."

Leha closed her eyes for a moment, letting the truth settle into her bones. That was what she and Ron were doing here. That was what they were trying to be for Tyashia.

When the call ended, the room felt softer somehow — like the past had pulled up a chair beside them.

Ron gave the stack of flyers a firm pat. "Sounds like those people made a difference."

"They did," Leha said softly. "And we're doing the same."

Ron chuckled. "You're the Ms. Beverly. I'm just the old guy fixing the bikes."

"You're more than that," Leha said warmly. "You're the quiet presence that keeps the center balanced."

"Exactly. Ubuntu."

Just then, the outer door chimed — a small, bright sound cutting through the stillness.

Ron and Leha looked up.

Tyashia stepped inside, her face determined, though her eyes looked heavy — the kind of tired that came from thinking too much, feeling too much, and trying to choose differently than she had before.

"Tyashia? What are you doing here this late?" Ron asked.

She approached the desk, stopping in front of Leha.

"I need to go to church with you on Sunday," she said, her voice small but finding its footing. "I need to find my faith again."

Leha felt something shift — not in the room, but in the girl standing before her. A quiet courage. A choosing.

And as Tyashia stood there, clutching the strap of her bag, Leha noticed a folded sheet of paper tucked into the side pocket — a page filled with scribbles, half sentences, and crossed-out thoughts. Not quite a journal. Not quite a story. But something trying to become one.

A seed. A beginning.

This wasn't just progress. This was a turning point. A girl choosing her direction.

Chapter Thirty-Five

The Sanctuary and the Storm

As Tyashia began choosing her own foundations, the next step came quietly — a decision she never would have made a month ago.

Some places don't just welcome you — they remind you who you were always meant to be.

Sunday morning arrived with a soft chill in the air, the kind that made Fayetteville feel briefly like fall again. The sky was pale, the breeze cool, and the city felt suspended between seasons.

Leha's car turned into the long driveway of Simon Temple AME Zion Church — a place that stood like a promise on the hill.

The church rose ahead of them, stately and serene. A wide brick façade. Tall white columns catching the early sun. A manicured lawn stretching out on either side. The steeple reached upward, clean and bright — a quiet declaration of hope.

Families streamed toward the entrance, dressed in winter coats and warm colors. The air buzzed with greetings, laughter, and the soft thrum of gospel music drifting from inside.

Tyashia sat in the passenger seat, staring at the building with a mixture of awe and nerves.

"It's big," she whispered.

"It's home," Leha said gently. "At least, it has been for me."

Inside, the sanctuary opened around them — rows of soft royal-purple chairs arranged with care, each one facing the pulpit with quiet intention. Soft gold filtered through the high windows, catching on the choir loft where singers in coordinated purple were warming up, their harmonies rising like a tide.

Tyashia paused at the entrance, taking it all in.

The space felt alive. Not loud — alive. Like the walls themselves remembered every prayer ever whispered here.

Leha touched her shoulder. "You ready?"

Tyashia nodded, though her heart thudded in her chest.

They found seats halfway up, close enough to feel the energy but far enough back that Tyashia didn't feel exposed. The choir launched into an opening hymn, voices blending in rich, layered harmony that filled the sanctuary from floor to rafters.

Tyashia felt the sound in her bones.

It wasn't like the music she used to drown out her thoughts. This music didn't drown anything. It lifted.

Then the pulpit shifted — a subtle movement, a ripple of expectation.

Bishop Brian R. Thompson, Sr. stepped forward, presence moving through the sanctuary like a low vibration — the kind that made people sit up straighter without realizing it.

But he wasn't alone.

Standing just behind him, radiant in a deep plum clergy robe, was Rev. Felica R. Thompson — his partner in ministry, his equal in calling. She stood with one hand resting on the pulpit rail, the other free, ready to wave, ready to affirm, ready to pour her own spirit into the room.

"Good morning, Simon Temple," Bishop Thompson began, his voice warm and resonant.

"Good morning," the congregation echoed.

Rev. Felica lifted her hand, palm open toward him. "Teach, Bishop," she called, her voice ringing with both pride and conviction.

A few people chuckled softly — not at her, but with her. This was familiar. This was home.

"We gather today as a community — not perfect, not polished, but present," Bishop Thompson said. "And sometimes, presence is the greatest act of faith."

"Say that," Rev. Felica murmured, nodding, her hand slicing gently through the air in agreement.

Tyashia swallowed hard. Presence. She had shown up. That had to count for something.

Then Bishop Thompson shifted — subtly, intentionally — into the kind of sermon that lived in the marrow of Black history.

"Family," he said, "we are living in a time where storms are not just weather. They are policies. They are shutdowns. They are systems that shake the ground beneath our feet."

A murmur rippled through the sanctuary.

Rev. Felica leaned forward, eyes bright. "Help us, Lord."

He continued, his voice carrying a quiet power.

"Some of you are furloughed. Some of you are working without pay. Some of you are wondering how to stretch a dollar when the government you serve has forgotten your worth."

Heads nodded. Shoulders sagged. A few people whispered, "My Lord."

Rev. Felica lifted her hand again, this time in a slow, sweeping arc. "You're talking right, Bishop."

"And some of you," he said, "are watching ICE roll through our communities like a cold wind — snatching fathers, mothers, neighbors. Trying to make fear our daily bread."

The sanctuary stilled.

Rev. Felica pressed a hand to her heart. "Cover Your people, God."

"But hear me," he said, leaning forward, voice rising with conviction. "This is not the first time our people have faced storms. The Black church has always been a sanctuary — a place where we gathered to share information, to protect each other, to plan, to resist, to rise."

He paused, letting the long memory of history settle.

Rev. Felica stepped closer, her voice ringing out: "We've been built for the storm!"

"We are not new to this," Bishop Thompson echoed. "We are built for this."

Tyashia felt something inside her shift — a recognition she couldn't name.

"God does not abandon His children in the storm," he continued. "He equips them. He strengthens them. He sends people — reminders — to show them they can stand."

Rev. Felica nodded deeply. "Yes, Lord. Send the reminders."

Leha glanced at Tyashia, but didn't speak.

Tyashia's throat tightened. Reminders. Ron. Leha. Kendra. Even Sylvia, in her own rigid way. And maybe… herself.

"Some of you are fighting battles no one sees," he said. "Some of you are carrying struggles you never asked for. But you are still here. And that means your story is not over."

A tear slipped down Tyashia's cheek before she could stop it.

She wiped it quickly, embarrassed — but then she noticed others wiping tears too. Grown men. Elderly women. Teenagers. Mothers. Veterans. People who looked like her. People who didn't.

Everyone carrying something. Everyone trying to stand.

When the choir rose for the altar call, the sanctuary swelled with sound — drums, organ, voices layered in harmony that felt like a warm embrace.

Rev. Felica lifted both hands now, ushering the Spirit forward, her voice rising above the music: "Come on, church. Come on and receive what you need."

Tyashia's chest ached. Not with fear. With release.

She leaned toward Leha. "Can I… go up there?"

Leha's eyes softened. "Of course."

Tyashia stood, legs trembling, and walked slowly down the aisle. The carpet felt soft beneath her sneakers. Each step made the aisle feel more alive around her.

At the front, she bowed her head.

She didn't know what prayer to say. She didn't know what words to use.

So she whispered the only truth she had:

"I don't want to be afraid anymore."

A warm hand rested gently on her back — one of the prayer ministers, murmuring a blessing she couldn't fully hear but felt deeply.

When she returned to her seat, Leha squeezed her hand.

"You did something brave today," she whispered.

Tyashia nodded, breath shaky. "I think… I think I want to help with the bus project. And maybe… maybe I want to join the youth group here."

Leha smiled, eyes shining. "Then we'll walk that path together."

Outside, the winter sun had risen higher, reaching across the church lawn in slow, bright strokes. The breeze lifted, carrying the faint sound of the choir's final chords into the open air.

Tyashia stepped into the morning letting it meet her.

Something in her lifted, subtle but sure — as if she was rising too.

Chapter Thirty-Six

When the Community Stands Up

The next afternoon, the community center met her differently. Not safer — not yet — but steadier beneath her feet. Like the sanctuary at Simon Temple had left a quiet imprint on her, a reminder that she didn't have to face storms alone.

She walked through the main activity room with her backpack slung over one shoulder, the faint buzz of the vents and the chalky scent of well-used gym mats lingering in the air. A few kids played ping pong in the corner. Someone laughed near the game table. An ordinary day.

Until it wasn't.

The room's high fixtures cast a blunt, icy brightness that made every shadow look like a warning.

Vince stepped into her path.

His jaw was tight. His eyes wild with something she recognized now — fear wearing the mask of anger.

"We need to talk," he said, grabbing her arm before she could react.

His fingers clamped down hard, yanking her toward the exit.

"Let go!" Tyashia snapped, jerking her arm free. The suddenness of his grip jolted her — a line crossed so clearly it erased any lingering confusion about who he really was.

Her heart pounded, but she didn't shrink. Not this time. Not after everything she'd learned. Not after watching FSU students chant *We protect each other.* Not after standing at the altar whispering, *I don't want to be afraid anymore.*

"Is there a problem here, son?"

Ron's voice rolled through the room, low and firm — a warning wrapped in calm authority.

He stepped out of the office doorway, posture solid, eyes locked on Vince.

Leha appeared behind him, her expression sharpening instantly as she took in the scene — Vince's flushed face, Tyashia's braced stance, the tension vibrating through the air.

"Tyashia," Leha said gently, "come stand with us."

The room shifted. Not loudly. Not dramatically. But unmistakably.

Kids stopped playing. Staff voices tapered off. A few teens moved closer, not touching, but forming a loose semicircle — a quiet show of solidarity.

Vince's eyes darted around the room. The confidence he wore like armor cracked at the edges.

"This is between us," he muttered.

"No," Ron said, stepping forward. "Not when you put your hands on her."

Vince's nostrils flared. "She's my girl."

Tyashia felt something inside her harden — not anger, but clarity.

"I'm not," she said.

The words landed like a stone dropped into still water.

Vince blinked. "What?"

"I'm not your anything," she said, voice even. "Not anymore."

A murmur rippled through the room — not gossip, but recognition. A girl claiming her own name.

Vince took a step toward her.

Ron moved instantly, placing himself between them. "That's enough."

Leha crossed her arms, her tone cool and unyielding. "You need to leave, Vince."

"You can't tell me—"

"I can," she said. "And I am."

The authority in her voice wasn't loud. It didn't need to be. It rose from years of standing between young people and the storms that tried to claim them.

Vince looked around again — at the staff, the teens, the mentors, the community that had quietly closed ranks around Tyashia.

He wasn't just facing Ron and Leha. He was facing a whole room that refused to let him isolate her.

His bravado faltered.

"This isn't over," he muttered, backing toward the door.

Ron didn't move. "It is for today."

Vince pushed through the exit, the door slamming behind him.

Silence followed. Then a breath. Then another.

Tyashia's knees wobbled, but she stayed upright.

Ron turned to her, voice gentle now. "You okay?"

She nodded, though her throat felt tight. "Yeah. I… yeah."

Leha stepped closer. "You weren't alone."

Tyashia swallowed hard. "I know."

And she did, in a way she never had before.

The community center hummed back to life — slowly, cautiously — but something had changed. Not just for Tyashia, but for everyone who had witnessed what happened.

This wasn't just a confrontation. It was a line drawn. A girl choosing herself. A community choosing her too.

And somewhere deep inside, beneath the fear and adrenaline, Tyashia felt something rise — not loud, but unmistakable.

Strength. Claimed, not borrowed. Her own.

Chapter Thirty-Seven

The Break That Becomes the Beginning

The call came just after sunset, slicing through the gentleness of the community center's administrative hub. A small television mounted in the corner played the local news on low volume, the anchor's voice drifting through the room as she reported on possible school closures across the county. Outside, the sky was a deepening indigo, the last streaks of daylight fading behind the dark edge of the woods.

Her phone vibrated.

The moment she heard Tyashia's voice — thin, trembling, frayed at the edges — she stood up so fast her chair rolled back.

"Leha," Tyashia choked, breath hitching. "I did it. I broke up with them."

The words were soaked in heartbreak and exhaustion. But beneath the pain, Leha heard something else — a tremor of courage, the kind that that arrives when you choose yourself without apology.

"Oh, T…" Leha breathed, her voice warm with admiration. "I'm so proud of you. Are you safe? Where are you?"

"I'm at home," Tyashia sniffed. In the background, Ahmad Latif's *Ville Promises* played softly — a quiet anthem of resilience. "Vince was furious. His mask totally dropped. Meja, too. It was awful, Leha."

Across the room, Ron looked up from his desk, concern sharpening his features. Leha switched the phone to speaker.

"Tyashia, this is Ron," he said, voice threaded with calm. "You made a very brave decision today. The hardest part is over."

"He said it wasn't over," she whispered. "He promised more conflict. And Meja… she was so bitter."

A surge of protectiveness rose in Leha's chest. *Not on our watch.*

"We're here for you," she said firmly. "You're not alone in this."

Ron nodded, his tone carrying quiet conviction. "Leha and I were just talking about making our support more tangible. We're building something stronger here — a real network of adults who show up for young people. The kind of support we had growing up. The kind of support you deserve."

"That sounds… amazing," Tyashia whispered. "But Vince…"

"Vince needs boundaries now," Leha said, her voice firm. "And you've already set the first one."

Ron added, "I'll call Sylvia tonight. She and Leonard will want to know what's going on. You deserve a safe perimeter, and Vince needs to understand the consequences of crossing lines."

A small, shaky breath — relief, fear, gratitude tangled together.

"Okay," she whispered. "Thank you."

When the call ended, Leha exhaled slowly, the moment sinking into her bones with a silent force.

"Okay," she said, turning to Ron. "Let's make this happen. Let's start building what will help her stand."

They stayed late, drafting a plan for deeper community support — mentors, parents, elders, neighbors. Earlier, the hub had felt almost hollow after the last youth left for the day, but now the space carried a different kind of movement — the soft clicking of keyboards, the shuffle of folders, the low murmur of ideas taking shape.

Community wasn't abstract. It was action. It was structure. It was showing up.

Tonight, they weren't just reacting. They were building something. Something that would outlast fear.

Life after Vince wasn't quiet; it was simply a different kind of loud.

At home, the shift was noticeable. Aunt Sylvia and Uncle Leonard didn't hover, but their presence wrapped around the house like a soft circle. Sylvia kept the porch light on later than usual. Leonard started walking her to the bus stop on mornings he didn't have early shifts. They didn't ask for details — they didn't need to. Their quiet vigilance said everything:

We see you. We're here. You're not facing this alone.

Even Tasha, who usually moved through the house with teenage indifference, had been watching her more closely. One evening, as they both reached for the orange juice in the fridge, Tasha spoke without looking up.

"I heard some stuff at school," she said, voice low. "About Vince. About how he acted when you walked away."

Tyashia froze. "What did you hear?"

Tasha shrugged. "Just… people talking. Saying he was mad. Saying he looked stupid trying to get your attention and you didn't even blink." A tiny smirk tugged at her mouth. "They said you handled him."

Tyashia blinked. "They said that?"

"Yeah." Tasha finally met her eyes. "And… I'm glad you're done with him. For real."

It wasn't an apology. It wasn't a speech. But it was the closest thing to a peace offering Tasha had ever given.

And it mattered.

Tyashia moved through the high school hallways with her new boundaries held close, feeling the sharp sting of isolation at first. Meja ignored her completely — a silent form of contempt that Tyashia chose to interpret as peace. Vince tried a few times to reassert his presence: a glare in the cafeteria, a scoff near her locker, a muttered comment meant to unsettle her.

But the line she'd drawn held.

"Boundaries," she whispered to herself like a mantra, the word written in bold across the top of her notebook. It strengthened her more than she expected.

She accepted Kendra's invitation to join the college prep workshop Ron was hosting after school. Instead of riding in Vince's controlling sedan, she walked home, the crisp November air a cleansing buffer between who she had been and who she was beginning to claim.

The trees along the sidewalk shed their last leaves, scattering them across her path like quiet reminders of change — of letting go.

Then, one afternoon, just as the final bell rang and students spilled into the hallways, Vince approached her near the main entrance. His expression was a mix of anger and calculation — the look of someone losing control and scrambling to reclaim it.

"Heard you're suddenly all about FSU," he sneered. "Decided you want to be a local loser?"

Tyashia didn't look up from her phone. She felt his presence ripple through the space, the demand for attention, the old chaos calling her name.

"There's a good program," she said evenly. "And I'm not a local."

"You hang out with Ms. Leha and her church friends now? The do-gooders?" he pushed, voice rising. "Mr. Ron must be putting ideas in your head."

Tyashia put her phone away and finally met his eyes. "I'm putting ideas in my own head, Vince. And my boundary is that I don't talk to you anymore."

He froze, thrown off by her firmness. "Your boundary?" he scoffed — but the usual power behind the word was gone. It sounded hollow now, like a threat that no longer had teeth.

Tyashia simply turned and walked away, leaving him standing in the crowded hallway. Her legs trembled as she made her way toward the bus stop — adrenaline buzzing — but the profound sense of victory was worth every shaky step.

On the bus, she pulled out her phone and called Leha.

"What I chose for myself held," she said quietly.

"I am so proud of you, T," Leha replied, her voice lit with quiet certainty. "The hardest part is over. Now we build."

And—unexpectedly—Tyashia believed her.

The bus rumbled forward, carrying her through familiar streets that suddenly felt different. Tyashia rested her forehead against the cool glass, feeling a small current of momentum move through her — her own choice echoing back to her.

She wasn't running. She wasn't hiding. She was moving — on her own terms.

And that was enough.

Chapter Thirty-Eight

A Promise Kept

The idea for the trip came quietly — the way important things often do.

Two nights after Tyashia told Leha she wanted to find her faith again, she sat at the kitchen table long after everyone else had gone to bed. Her acceptance letter from FSU lay open beside her, the words *We are pleased to inform you…* glowing softly in the kitchen light.

Aunt Asiah should have been here for this moment. Her laughter. Her chaos. Her belief in Tyashia's brilliance long before anyone else saw it.

Sylvia found her there, shoulders hunched, eyes distant.

"You're thinking about her," Sylvia said quietly.

Tyashia nodded. "I feel like… I'm moving forward. But she's still back there. In Philly. In that grave with no headstone."

Something softened in Sylvia's face — something rare, something real.

"Then let's go," she said simply. "Before graduation. Before everything changes. Let's go see her."

And just like that, the decision was made. Not out of obligation. Not out of guilt. But out of love — the kind that grows in the cracks of a complicated family.

The Philadelphia air hit Tyashia with a familiar bite — sharp, metallic, unapologetically northern. She stepped off the train with a steadiness she hadn't possessed a year ago. Behind her, Sylvia followed, posture straight but softened by the long ride and the quiet conversations they'd shared along the way.

There was a new quality to Sylvia now. Not fragile — but less rigid. The furlough had shaken something loose in her: the truth that order could collapse, systems could fail, and even the most disciplined life could be thrown off balance.

They took a taxi to the quiet cemetery on the edge of the city. The closer they got, the tighter the knot in Tyashia's stomach pulled. When they reached Asiah's resting place, her stride faltered.

A temporary plastic plaque sat in the earth — a placeholder where permanence should have been.

It twisted something deep inside her.

"I kept my promise, Aunt Asiah," she whispered, sinking to the cool ground. "I made it. I'm graduating soon."

She talked about everything — Ron's guidance, Leha's mentorship, Kendra's friendship, the bus project, the boundaries she'd learned to hold, the acceptance letter from FSU. Beneath her coat, her Faith Over Fear shirt rested against her chest like a heartbeat. Tucked under her arm were her white leather skates — the pom poms faded, but still hers.

The tears came — not from raw grief, but from release.

This was closure. This was honoring. This was the moment she had carried like a stone in her chest for months.

Sylvia stood silently beside her, staring at the bare patch of earth. In her aunt's sharp eyes, Tyashia saw something she had never seen before — regret, guilt, love, and acceptance, all flickering across her face like shifting light.

"You deserved better than a temporary marker, Asiah," Sylvia murmured. She dabbed her eye. "You always did things your own way… lived in the mess of things." A small smile touched her lips. "I… I missed that sometimes."

She reached into her coat pocket and pulled out a simple sketch — a design for a black granite headstone.

"I ordered this for you this morning," she said softly. "A permanent place."

Tyashia stared, stunned. The same efficiency she once resented was now being used for love.

And beneath that gesture lived something else — the humility of a woman who had finally learned that permanence was never guaranteed.

The train ride back to Fayetteville was quiet in a way that felt earned. Sylvia dozed beside her, the sketch tucked safely in her purse, while Tyashia watched the landscape blur past the window.

She didn't feel hollow this time. She felt aligned.

By the time they stepped off the platform and the warm Carolina air wrapped around them, she knew she had brought a different version of herself home — one who had faced the truth, honored it, and could now move forward without flinching.

The next afternoon, she and Kendra sat on the thick green grass near their "sweet spot" — the community center park where the refurbished bus often parked. The once bare winter trees were now lush with late spring foliage. A soft breeze carried the scent of new growth — a scent that now meant safety.

"I still can't believe we're graduating early," Kendra said, adjusting her rhinestone-covered cap.

"I can't believe I'm staying here," Tyashia replied, smiling. "This transient, military town is… my home now."

They talked about FSU — Tyashia majoring in community development, Kendra chasing journalism and talk show dreams. The past year no longer felt like a blur of survival.

It felt like a map — one she had drawn herself.

"We did it, girl," Kendra whispered.

Tyashia nodded, leaning back on her hands. "Yeah," she said. "We did."

The victory wasn't loud. It was quiet. Earned. Entirely their own.

And somewhere in the distance, the bus engine purred — a reminder of the community that had held her together when everything else felt uncertain.

Chapter Thirty-Nine

The Chapter She Writes Herself

Graduation day rose inside Capel Arena like a wave — overhead fixtures reflecting off wide concrete floors, families fanning themselves with programs, and the low, electric swell of pride filling every corner of the space. The air conditioning fought the Carolina heat but couldn't cool the emotion in the room. Rows of blue seats stretched toward the stage, each one holding someone who had prayed, pushed, or persevered to get here.

And somewhere in the middle of it all sat Tyashia, wrapped in her gown, feeling the meaning and wonder of a year that had reshaped her from the inside out.

The "one thing" assignment from Leha had grown far beyond a single goal. It had become Kendra. The community. The decision to carry her past not as baggage, but as a map. She had poured her energy into others — tutoring on the community bus, skating with kids at the center, showing up for people the way others had shown up for her.

Under her graduation gown, a new T-shirt — soft blue cotton with the white letters **Still Growing** — clung to her like a second skin, a private promise to keep choosing courage.

"Tyashia Harrington!"

The world narrowed to the sound of her name. She rose like someone who knew she belonged.

The cheers blurred into a distant hum as she crossed the stage. She shook the principal's warm hand and accepted her diploma. When she stepped forward, her eyes found Leha and Chemelu seated together near the aisle — both of them clapping with a pride that reached her before their smiles did.

That moment felt more significant than the parchment in her grip.

The celebration at the community center buzzed with barbecue smoke, laughter, and the relief of teenagers who had finally crossed the finish line. Kendra was a whirlwind, cornering guests for impromptu "interviews" for her future talk show. Teachers, mentors, and community elders stopped Tyashia with congratulations — Leha, Chemelu, Melodie, Wesley.

The community that once felt foreign now wrapped around her like a warm embrace.

Near the entrance, Wesley stood with a paper plate of pasta salad and a quiet smile.

"Proud of you, young lady," he said. "You walked a hard road and didn't let it break you."

His words reached her with a calm importance — not heavy, but grounding.

Melodie approached next, handing her a cup of punch. "I've been watching you," she said. "Not in a weird way. In a 'this girl is going places' way."

Tyashia laughed softly. "I'm just trying to help where I can."

"No," Melodie said. "You're doing more than helping. You're leading. The kids on the bus look for you. They listen when you talk. That's not something you can teach — that's something you carry."

She nodded toward the bus parked outside, its colors catching the last traces of the day.

"We're expanding," Melodie said. "More routes. More resources. More youth leadership. And I want you in those conversations. Not as a volunteer — as part of the next generation shaping what this becomes."

"Me?" Tyashia whispered.

"Yes, you," Melodie said. "You're not just surviving anymore. You're building. And we need builders."

Later, she noticed Wesley and Melodie working side by side — Wesley lifting heavy trays with ease, Melodie directing volunteers with quiet efficiency. They moved like two parts of the same rhythm.

"Always the anchor," she teased.

"And you're the compass," he replied.

The weeks after graduation unfolded slowly, like a long breath finally released. Fayetteville didn't change — she did. The city met her with a new kind of clarity, the kind that comes when you've survived something and can finally look around without flinching.

She spent early summer helping Melodie with the community bus expansion, tutoring kids who reminded her of younger versions of herself — sharp, restless, waiting for someone to see them. Some afternoons she skated through the neighborhood with her pom poms bouncing, the warm Carolina air brushing her skin like a quiet reminder that she was no longer moving through life on defense.

Her acceptance packet from Fayetteville State University arrived in mid-July — thick, official, pulsing with new direction. She held it for a long moment before opening it, letting the meaning settle into her palms.

This wasn't running. This wasn't escape. This was the next chapter she was choosing with intention.

Move-in day came with its own kind of heat, the kind that shimmered off the brick buildings and made the campus feel alive. Her dorm room was small, but it was hers. She taped her **Still Growing** shirt to the inside of her closet door — a reminder of the girl she had been and the woman she was stepping toward.

That night, lying on her new twin XL bed, she whispered a quiet promise to herself:

No shrinking. No hiding. No returning to old versions of me.

She didn't know what her first week of classes would hold — only that she was ready for it. Ready for the learning. Ready for the stretching. Ready for the becoming.

College wasn't an escape. It was an arrival.

She felt prepared to meet whatever waited for her.

.

Chapter Forty

Becoming the Sociologist

By Thursday, campus felt familiar enough for her to breathe in it. She crossed the quad with her backpack slung over one shoulder, the morning sun warming the brick buildings around her. This was her first real step into the life she had chosen — not rushed, not forced, but earned.

That morning, the air in the Sociology lecture hall carried a charged stillness — the kind of quiet electricity that meant Professor A.L. had something planned. The room, tucked inside the old brick humanities building at Fayetteville State University, hummed with the low murmur of early morning students. Hoodies, half-finished coffees, notebooks flipped open with lazy anticipation.

But the moment they saw the portable speaker on the podium, curiosity sharpened the room.

Tyashia slid into her usual seat beside Kendra. The metal chair creaked beneath her, familiar now — a small constant in her new academic world.

"Uh oh," Kendra whispered. "She brought props."

Professor A.L. stepped forward, her locs pulled into a loose bun, her glasses perched low on her nose. She didn't greet them. She didn't take attendance. She simply pressed play.

A low, pulsing beat filled the room — unmistakably Fayetteville. Raw. Rhythmic. Honest.

Ahmad Latif. *"Poor Man Randy."*

The lyrics painted a portrait of generational struggle — poverty, systemic barriers, quiet resilience. The kind of story that lived in neighborhoods like Murchison Road, B Street, Bonnie Doone. The kind of story Tyashia once lived without having the language to name it.

When the chorus faded, Professor A.L. paused the track.

"This," she said, tapping the speaker, "is sociology."

She paced slowly, her voice warm but incisive.

"'Poor Man Randy' is not just a song. It's a case study. It's social stratification. It's structural inequality. It's the lived experience of poverty in a city many of you call home."

Hands shot up. Students debated. The room came alive.

But something else caught Tyashia's attention — movement outside the window.

A line of students in royal blue and pearl white jackets strolled across the yard, synchronized, confident, electric. The Lambda Rho Ladies.

Behind them, a group of men in matching colors followed, stepping in rhythm as they crossed the quad — the Phi Rho Gentlemen, their brother organization.

Kendra's breath hitched. "Oh my gosh — that's them. My future sisters."

Tyashia watched, mesmerized. The unity. The pride. The history in every step.

Professor A.L. noticed the distraction and smiled knowingly.

"Ah. Our Legacy Line Organizations," she said. "Another form of social structure. Born from exclusion. Built on scholarship, service, sisterhood, and brotherhood."

She clicked to a slide showing the founding years of each organization.

"These groups were created because Black students were denied entry into white fraternities and sororities. So they built their own — stronger, deeper, rooted in purpose."

Kendra whispered, "This is why I want Lambda Rho. They're about service. About community. About being refined."

Something shifted in Tyashia — a recognition of lineage, of legacy, of belonging.

Professor A.L. continued, "When you see them strolling, stepping, serving — you're witnessing history in motion. You're witnessing resistance turned into ritual. You're witnessing community turned into culture."

The room quieted, the weight of her words settling like truth.

Tyashia wasn't drifting anymore. She was supported. Not by fear. Not by survival. But by understanding. By authorship. By the realization that she wasn't just living her story — she was learning how to study it, name it, and eventually, change it.

After class, she stepped into the hallway feeling… different. Expanded. Like someone had handed her a new lens and the world had shifted into focus.

Every conversation she overheard. Every flyer on the wall. Every student rushing past.

It all felt connected — part of a larger system she was finally beginning to understand.

As she crossed the quad, her phone buzzed.

Melodie: *Hey Tye — Wesley and I are setting up for the veterans' resource event at the community center. If you're free, come through. Even just to observe. It's all sociology in motion.*

Tyashia stared at the message, her heart catching.

Sociology in motion.

Professor A.L.'s words echoed in her mind.

This is sociology.

Maybe the classroom wasn't the only place she was meant to learn.

She texted back:

On my way.

Wesley spotted her the moment she walked in and waved her over.

"You volunteering today?" he asked.

"I… didn't know this was happening," she admitted.

Melodie smiled. "You're welcome to help. Or just observe. Sometimes witnessing is its own kind of service."

Sam and Sandra approached, their faces lighting up when they saw her.

"Tyashia!" Sandra said, pulling her into a gentle hug. "Look at you — a whole college student now."

Sam nodded with quiet pride. "You're walking a good path. Keep going."

A warm breeze drifted through the open door, lifting the corner of a pamphlet on the table. Wesley tapped it with his foot to keep it from sliding away.

"Life has a way of showing us what to release," he murmured. "And what to hold on to."

Sam chuckled softly. "That's truth right there."

Sandra added, "And we grow because of it."

The message brushed against her with a steady, unhurried clarity.

This — this quiet room full of stories, this partnership between Wesley and Melodie, this unwavering presence of Sam and Sandra — was another kind of classroom. A place where she could see how individual struggles connected to larger systems, how community filled the gaps those systems left behind, how people became bridges for one another.

She picked up a stack of pamphlets and moved toward the entrance, ready to greet the next veteran who walked through the door.

Ready to serve. Ready to learn. Ready to rise.

.

Chapter Forty-One

The Question That Wouldn't Let Go

The evening settled gently around Leha's townhouse — the kind of stillness that arrived only after long days spent holding other people's stories. The kitchen carried the lingering warmth of dinner: garlic, roasted vegetables, the faint sweetness of cornbread cooling on the counter. Outside, cicadas hummed their steady chorus, a reminder that summer hadn't loosened its grip.

Leha rinsed the last dish and set it in the rack, her mind drifting back to Tyashia's voice earlier that afternoon — bright, hopeful, but threaded with something she couldn't quite name.

Her phone buzzed on the counter.

Chemelu: How's your spirit?

She smiled despite herself and picked it up.

Leha: Full. But something Ty said today won't let me go.

A moment later, the phone rang. She answered on the first ring and put him on speaker as she wiped the counter.

"She sounded lighter today," Chemelu said, his voice warm through the line. "College looks good on her."

"It does," Leha agreed. "But there was a moment… when she mentioned her mother. It was quick. Almost nothing. But it didn't sit right."

"What did she say?" he asked.

Leha hesitated, searching for the shape of the feeling. "She said she's been thinking about why her mother left. And then she said, 'Maybe some people disappear because they're tired of being disappointed.'"

On the other end of the line, she could almost hear his brow furrow.

"That doesn't sound like her mother's story," he said.

"That's what bothered me," Leha murmured, leaning against the counter. "It felt like she was repeating something she'd been told, not something she believed."

She moved to the small table by the window — the place where she often debriefed the day with herself. The lamplight cast a warm circle over her notebook and mug, softening the edges of the room.

"You know," Chemelu began, his tone shifting into that thoughtful cadence she'd come to recognize, "in my research, I've come across cases where people disappear not out of abandonment, but out of survival. Especially women. Especially when powerful men are involved."

Leha looked toward the window, the word landing with a quiet thud in her chest.

"Survival?" she repeated.

"Yes," he said. "When the threat is real — political, domestic, systemic — disappearing becomes a strategy. A way to protect the child. A way to stay alive."

She thought of the gaps in Tyashia's story. The inconsistencies. The way Asiah had always deflected questions about Philadelphia. The way Tyashia carried her mother's absence like a wound she'd learned to hide.

"What if she didn't leave her?" Leha whispered. "What if she ran for her?"

There was a pause on the line, the weight of the possibility settling between them.

"It's not far-fetched," Chemelu said quietly. "Especially if the father was involved in something dangerous."

Leha blinked. "Henry."

Recognition flickered in his voice. "I've seen that name before. In the archives. Philadelphia activism. A developer with a reputation for intimidation. There were threats. Escalations. And then… silence."

A chill moved through her, subtle but certain.

"This is bigger than we thought," she murmured.

"It might be," he agreed. "If Henry was targeted, and the mother was caught in the crossfire… disappearing might have been the only way to protect the baby."

Leha's breath tightened. The pieces were aligning — painfully, clearly.

She reached for her laptop, pulling it toward her with a resolve that felt like stepping into cold water.

"I need to look deeper," she said. "Dates. Names. Records. Anything that connects."

"You won't do it alone," Chemelu replied. "Call me when you hit a wall. Or before."

She smiled faintly. "You always say that."

"Because it's always true," he said.

They hung up, and the house fell quiet again.

Leha opened a new document and typed the first line:

Tyashia Investigation — Initial Findings

The cursor blinked, waiting.

Outside, the cicadas quieted for a moment, as if the night itself were listening.

Leha exhaled, her voice barely above a whisper.

"This changes everything."

Chapter Forty-Two

The Story Beneath the Story

Chemelu sat at his FSU office desk, preparing notes for an upcoming lecture on the African Diaspora, though his mind kept drifting back to something Leha had said earlier — her speculation about Tyashia's mother, survival, and the invisible threads that tie stories together. His office smelled faintly of old paper and dust, the scent of stories waiting to be uncovered. Outside his window, campus buzzed with late-afternoon energy, but inside, the air felt still — charged with an unspoken current.

He exhaled, trying to refocus, when a soft knock tapped at his door.

"Come in," he called.

Dr. Ankrah stepped inside, grinning broadly, holding a small gold-wrapped box like it was a national treasure.

"I brought you something to elevate your palate," he announced, placing it on Chemelu's desk with ceremonial flair. "Midunu Chocolates. Real chocolate. Not that American sugar-coated confusion."

Chemelu laughed. "You've been telling students that since before I arrived."

"Because it is true," Dr. Ankrah said, chest lifting with Ghanaian pride. "Ghanaian cocoa is the heartbeat of the world."

Chemelu raised an eyebrow. "Ah, here we go."

"What is that supposed to mean?" Dr. Ankrah challenged, arms crossing.

"It means," Chemelu said, leaning back with a grin, "that you forget Kenya exists. We may not be known for chocolate, but we know flavor. We know spice. We know chai that can resurrect the tired and humble the proud."

"Chai is not chocolate, my friend."

"No," Chemelu said, opening the box, "but it is superior."

They both laughed — the warm, familiar laughter of two African scholars who had carried their homelands across oceans and into their classrooms.

Chemelu broke off a piece of the Midunu chocolate and let it melt on his tongue. The flavor bloomed — rich, layered, unmistakably Ghanaian.

"Fine," he conceded. "This is excellent."

"Of course it is," Dr. Ankrah said, already heading for the door. "Great scholarship requires great chocolate."

"And great chocolate requires humility," Chemelu called after him.

"Humility?" Dr. Ankrah scoffed. "That is for Kenyans."

The door closed, leaving Chemelu smiling to himself. The chocolate lingered on his tongue — a reminder of home, of Africa's vastness, of the shared pride that connected them even across different nations.

And somehow, it sharpened his focus.

He turned back to his computer, refreshed, and began searching the university directory again.

That's when he saw the name: Henry — a history professor known for his work in African American history and community engagement. Henry had a reputation for innovative teaching and strong local partnerships.

Chemelu drafted a professional email proposing a meeting to discuss curriculum synchronization and a potential guest lecture series.

A Few Days Later…

They met at The Gentle Ground Café, the cozy spot that had become a quiet hub for thinkers, writers, and community leaders. The warm scent of roasted coffee beans filled the air, and their conversation flowed easily — from the challenges of teaching sensitive history to the importance of cultural literacy in a divided world.

"It's about making history tangible for the students," Henry said, stirring his coffee. "Showing them individuals, not just broad categories and statistics. The local angle always hits hardest."

"Exactly," Chemelu agreed, mentioning his work with the community center and the refurbished bus project. "We're always looking for strong educators to partner with."

As they talked, Henry shared pieces of his background — a quiet but firm history that included his early life in Philadelphia before moving to North Carolina. He spoke briefly about his activism days, pushing back against a powerful developer. The details were subtle, but they aligned almost perfectly with the articles Chemelu had skimmed in the archives weeks earlier.

A chill moved through Chemelu despite the warmth of the coffee.

The Philadelphia connection. The activism. The timeline. The tone of Henry's voice when he mentioned "a complicated past."

It was too specific to ignore.

When Henry stepped away to get a refill, Chemelu quickly jotted down his full name and the timeframe he'd mentioned. His pulse quickened as the pieces began to align.

This is the connection, he realized, the truth settling over him like a revelation. This is how it all links together.

What began as academic collaboration had become something far more personal — the key to unlocking the mystery of Tyashia's mother.

The groundwork was laid, and the investigation that would soon consume both him and Leha had quietly begun.

Leha's discreet investigation unfolded late at night, the blue glow from her laptop shining softly as she worked at The Gentle

Ground Café. The café was silent at this hour, its usual bustle replaced by the stillness of an empty room. The air smelled faintly of stale coffee and old paper as she scrolled through digitized newspaper archives and public records.

The quiet around her stood in stark contrast to the scandal unraveling on her screen — a story nearly eighteen years old, but still pulsing with danger.

The articles were grainy scans, but the story was unmistakable — a prominent Philadelphia city councilman, a very public affair, a furious wife, whispered threats, and then a disappearance that had once dominated the local news cycle.

But beneath the sensationalism, Leha noticed something else — inconsistencies, gaps, and a pattern of omissions that felt intentional.

Councilman's Wife Linked to Questionable Nonprofits Federal Grant Irregularities Under Quiet Review Mistress Vanishes Amid Scandal

The deeper she read, the clearer it became: the affair had been the distraction. The real story was the corruption pipeline — city contracts funneled through shell nonprofits, federal money disappearing, signatures that didn't match. And the councilman's wife was at the center of it.

Leha found a police report documenting the mother's disappearance, along with a chilling note left behind — a raw, unfiltered threat that hinted at violent intent.

She didn't abandon her, Leha realized. She was terrified — for her life and for her baby's.

A wave of profound sadness washed over her. Tyashia had spent her entire life holding the ache of rejection, wearing it like a heavy coat. But the truth was far more complex — her mother had made a desperate, protective choice.

Then a smaller detail caught her eye — a name she recognized.

Henry.

The records implied he was the actual father. The councilman's wife, blinded by jealousy and desperate to protect her corruption network, had believed the child was her husband's. But the truth pointed elsewhere — toward a hidden relationship, a different man, and a secret buried beneath layers of scandal and fear.

The stakes shifted instantly — from abandonment to protection, from shame to truth.

"This changes everything," Leha whispered into the empty café.

She closed her laptop, the screen going dark with a soft click. Outside, the cool night air stung her face as she walked to her car. She dialed Chemelu, her voice tight with urgency.

"You were right," she said as soon as he answered. "It was survival. But it's more complicated than that."

She explained the councilman, the threats, the corruption, the disappearance — and the real father, Henry.

"So Tyashia isn't even the councilman's child?" Chemelu asked, disbelief sharp in his voice.

"No," Leha said, leaning against her car door. "She was an innocent victim of a paranoid woman's rage — and a political machine that needed her mother silenced."

"This is explosive information," Chemelu said. "But we'll figure it out. Together."

Leha exhaled. "Before we bring this to her, we need Ron. This truth is a live wire."

Ron arrived at The Gentle Ground Café before sunrise, the sky still bruised with the last traces of night. He found Leha already inside, sitting at their usual corner table, her hands wrapped around a mug she hadn't touched.

"Leha," Ron said softly. "You look like you've been fighting shadows."

"I have," she whispered. "And the shadows are real this time."

She turned the laptop toward him. The headlines. The police report. The threatening note. The corruption trail. The name Henry.

Ron read in silence, his jaw tightening, his eyes darkening with anger and sorrow.

"She's been carrying the wrong story her whole life," he said quietly.

Leha nodded. "She thinks she was abandoned. She thinks she wasn't wanted. But her mother… she ran because she was terrified. She disappeared to save her."

Ron leaned back, rubbing a hand over his face. "This is going to break her heart before it heals it."

"I know," Leha whispered. "That's why I need you."

"You have me," Ron said simply.

They met Tyashia at the community center later that afternoon. She arrived with her backpack slung over one shoulder, her FSU lanyard hanging proudly around her neck. She looked tired — the kind of tired that comes with new independence and new responsibilities — but she also looked settled into herself.

"Hey," she said, smiling. "What's going on? You both look serious."

Ron stepped forward. "Tye, we need to talk to you about something important. Something about your mother."

Her smile faltered. "My mother?"

Leha motioned for her to sit. "We found some information. About what happened in Philadelphia. About why she left."

Tyashia sat slowly, gripping the edge of the chair. "Okay," she whispered. "Tell me."

Leha took a breath — the kind you take before stepping into cold water.

"Your mother didn't abandon you," she said softly. "She ran because someone threatened her life. And yours."

The words hit like a physical blow.

"What?" Tyashia gasped.

Ron leaned in, voice low and calm. "There was a powerful man. A scandal. His wife believed you were his child. She made threats. Real ones. And she was involved in something bigger — something dangerous."

Tears gathered instantly. "But… I thought… she left because she didn't want me."

"No," Leha said, her own voice breaking. "She left because she loved you enough to disappear."

"And the man you thought was your father…" Leha continued gently, "he wasn't. Your mother was close to someone else. A man named Henry."

Tyashia's head snapped up. "Henry? My father is… Henry?"

Ron nodded. "We're still confirming everything. But yes."

Tyashia stood abruptly, pacing, her hands shaking. "All this time… all this time I thought I wasn't wanted. That she just left me. That I wasn't enough."

Leha stepped toward her. "Tye, look at me."

Tears streaked her face as she stopped.

"You were worth everything," Leha said. "Your mother risked everything to keep you alive."

Tyashia's knees buckled, and Ron caught her before she hit the floor. She sobbed into his chest — raw, guttural, years of pain cracking open all at once.

Ron held her, unwavering. "Let it out," he murmured. "You don't have to carry this alone anymore."

Leha knelt beside them, her hand on Tyashia's back. "This truth is heavy," she whispered. "But it's yours now. And we're here. Every step."

Minutes passed. Maybe hours. Time softened around them.

When Tyashia finally lifted her head, her eyes were swollen but clear — clearer than they had ever been.

"So what happens now?" she asked, voice hoarse.

Ron exchanged a look with Leha. "Now," he said, "we help you find the rest of your story."

Leha nodded. "And we do it together."

Tyashia wiped her face, a trembling breath escaping her lips.

"Okay," she whispered. "Okay."

The truth had broken her open.

But it had also set her free.

Chapter Forty- Three

A Prayer and a Promise -Henry

The Philadelphia air had never felt so heavy, so choked with the scent of fear and betrayal. Henry stood in the empty apartment, the silence a deafening roar that echoed the finality of their disappearance. Sarah and their little girl, Tyashia, were gone. The police had been less than helpful, their interest fading the moment the powerful councilman's name entered the conversation. The case was closed quickly, filed away as a "voluntary disappearance."

Voluntary?

Henry slammed his fist against the kitchen counter, the cheap laminate rattling. He knew the threats, the vengeful wife's rage. But there had been something else too — something Sarah never fully explained. A tension in her voice. A fear that didn't match the story the public believed. Sarah hadn't left; she had run for survival.

He spent the next weeks in a blur of desperate action. He combed public records, hit dead ends, and found every door closed by bureaucracy and the councilman's influence. The deeper he pushed, the more resistance he met — not just from the wife's fury, but from a system determined to keep the truth buried. He felt helpless, stripped of his strength, unable to protect the woman and child he loved. He wasn't the respected man people saw in public; he was just a heartbroken father who had lost his family before it truly began.

One night, exhausted and defeated, he sat in a dimly lit bar, the stale smell of beer and smoke stinging his eyes. He picked up his drink, his reflection in the dark glass a stranger's face — tired, angry, hollow.

Is this who I am now?

He remembered his father's words, a quiet conviction that had shaped him since boyhood: *"The best thing a man can be is reliable, son. Dependable."*

Henry set the glass down, a wave of clarity washing over him. The immediate search might be blocked at every turn, but his life didn't have to be. He could become the man who deserved to be their father, just in case he found them again. He could build a life they would be proud of — a life of purpose and integrity, not anger and despair.

He left the bar that night and never looked back.

He enrolled in graduate school for history, channeling his pain into a quiet resolve. He moved to Fayetteville, North Carolina — far from the memories that still scraped at him — into a town shaped by uniforms, departures, and homecomings. Distance didn't erase anything, but it opened a small, necessary space. Enough for him to breathe. Enough for him to gather what had splintered. Enough for him to grow into someone who could carry the past without letting it break him.

He kept one photo — a baby picture of Tyashia, a small, steady reminder of the promise he made to himself.

I will be ready, he promised the picture every night.

Years passed. He earned his PhD, became a professor at Fayetteville State University, and built a life of purpose. He was a good man, dependable, just as his father had taught him. He worked hard, found joy in teaching, and became a consistent source of support for his students and the community. He poured into young people the stability he wished he could have given his own daughter.

But the ache never left. It lived in the quiet moments — the empty passenger seat on long drives, the unasked questions, the birthdays marked only by a whispered prayer.

The day Ron and Leha called him about a student who might be his daughter, the floodgates of hope burst open. He drove to The Gentle Ground Café, his heart pounding a fierce rhythm, the scent of coffee and warm spices a welcome distraction from his anticipation.

He was ready. He had kept his promise.

Chapter Forty-Four

What Was Lost, Now Found

Tyashia was a bundle of raw nerves in the minutes before the meeting. She had learned only yesterday that Henry — her father — was real, alive, and teaching history at Fayetteville State University. Just a few miles away. Just… here.

The revelation had cleared the anger she'd carried for years, but now a fragile, trembling hope had taken its place. She ran her hand over the hem of her blue T-shirt — the one Aunt Asiah had given her. The faded words *Hope Endures* brushed against her fingertips like a reminder she wasn't sure she deserved.

Her heart hammered against her ribs.

Leha had chosen The Gentle Ground Café for the meeting — a place where mismatched mugs lined the counter, local art covered the walls, and the steady movement of baristas kept the space feeling alive. Students typed at corner tables. A pair of elders played dominoes near the window. The espresso machine hissed softly as someone pulled a shot. It wasn't quiet. It wasn't loud. It was the kind of place where big moments could land without breaking you.

She and Ron were already seated in a corner booth — not looming, not hovering, just present in that way people are when they refuse to let you face something life-changing alone.

"He'll be here any minute," Leha murmured, her hand warm on Tyashia's arm.

"I know," Tyashia whispered, eyes fixed on the door. *What do you say to a ghost made real?*

And then Henry walked in.

He looked older than the fragments she'd imagined — a few gray strands at his temples, a deeper quiet in his posture — but the core was unmistakable. The kind eyes. The gentle smile. And something else too: gratitude, the kind that comes from surviving storms without letting them harden you.

He spotted her instantly. His expression cracked open — relief, awe, grief, gratitude — all at once.

Tyashia didn't hesitate. She stood, crossed the space between them, and folded into his arms. He held her like someone who had been waiting years for this moment. She breathed in the scent of him — soap, starch, and something warm that felt like home.

"Oh, Tyashia," he murmured into her hair, his voice thick. "I can't believe this is real."

She pulled back just enough to see his face.

"You knew about me?" she whispered.

Henry nodded, eyes shining. "I did. From the beginning."

He swallowed hard.

"I tried to find you. I reached out to Asiah more than once. I begged her to tell me where you were. But your mother…" He hesitated, choosing his words with care. "She was terrified. She asked Asiah to keep you hidden. To keep you safe. And Asiah honored her promise."

Tyashia's breath caught. Aunt Asiah had carried that secret — for her. For her mother. For all of them.

Henry continued, voice trembling. "I didn't stop looking. Not ever. I prayed every day that you were alive, that you were loved, that one day I'd get the chance to be your father in whatever way you'd let me."

Tears blurred her vision. "I'm here now," she whispered. "I'm here."

He cupped her face gently. "And I'm not going anywhere."

Chapter Forty-Five

Where the Water Holds Us

The week after the truth shattered and remade her — after learning who her father was, after letting herself collapse into Ron's arms, after feeling the ground shift beneath her feet — Leha moved through her days as if carrying a quiet tide inside her. A pull she couldn't name. A weight she couldn't set down.

She held space for Tyashia's healing, for the new mentee referrals, for the audit meetings piling on her calendar, but her own breath stayed shallow, caught somewhere between responsibility and exhaustion.

Chemelu noticed the way her shoulders curved inward. He noticed how she lingered at her desk long after the building emptied. He noticed the way her smile thinned at the edges, as if it were working too hard.

On Thursday evening, as she packed up her laptop at the community center, he appeared in the doorway — steady, warm, a quiet certainty in his eyes.

"Come with me," he said.

She blinked. "Where?"

He didn't answer. He simply held out his hand.

Something in his expression — gentle, sure — made her follow without hesitation.

He drove her to the airport.

"Chemelu..." she whispered, half laughing, half stunned. "What are we doing?"

He placed a small envelope in her hand. Inside was a boarding pass.

Fayetteville → Montego Bay. Departure: Tonight.

Her breath caught. "You're taking me to Jamaica?"

"I'm taking you somewhere the water can hold you for a while," he said softly. "Somewhere you can breathe again."

The words loosened something deep inside her.

The moment they stepped off the plane, the air wrapped around her — warm, humid, fragrant with salt and hibiscus. It felt like stepping into a gentler version of the world, one where she didn't have to be the anchor for everyone else.

"Welcome to Jamaica, my Leha," Chemelu murmured, taking her hand.

Their taxi wound along the coast toward Ocho Rios, the landscape unfolding in vibrant color — emerald mountains rising sharply from the earth, bursts of bougainvillea spilling over fences, glimpses of turquoise water shimmering like glass. Steel drums drifted from roadside shacks, the rhythm loosening the tightness in her chest.

By the time they reached the small private villa, the sun was sinking low, painting the sky in strokes of tangerine and violet. From the balcony, the sea stretched out in endless blue, waves whispering against the shore as if inviting her closer.

Leha leaned on the railing, breath catching. "It's stunning."

Chemelu stepped behind her, his hands warm on her waist. "You deserve beauty," he said quietly. "You deserve rest."

She closed her eyes, letting the moment settle into her bones.

The next morning, he surprised her again — tickets to the Bob Marley Nine Mile Tour.

They drove deep into the mountains, the air cooling as the road climbed. The guide spoke of Marley's childhood, his philosophy, his music as resistance and prayer. Chemelu listened with a reverence she rarely saw in him, asking questions, connecting threads between Marley's worldview and his own Ubuntu.

Leha watched him, her heart swelling. He hadn't just brought her on a trip. He had brought her to a place that fed both of their spirits.

She'd tried to go vegan that month, but the jerk chicken didn't stand a chance — she could practically hear her father teasing her, "Didn't even make it a week, huh?" The thought made her laugh into her napkin.

That evening, after jerk chicken and sweet plantains, they returned to the balcony. The moon rose full and silver over the water, casting a shimmering path across the waves. The sound of the surf was steady, rhythmic — a heartbeat she didn't have to control.

Chemelu guided her to the lounge chair, sitting beside her, their fingers lacing together.

"This," she whispered, "is the most thoughtful gift anyone has ever given me."

He turned to her, eyes soft. "You carry so much, Leha. The stories. The children. The community. Even the pain that isn't yours. I wanted to give you a place where you could set it down."

He leaned in, kissing her slowly — a kiss warm as the island air, patient as the tide, full of promise.

When they finally pulled apart, she rested her head on his shoulder, the moonlight brushing her skin, the sea breathing below them.

Her breath deepened. Her shoulders eased. Her heart finally quieted.

Chemelu brushed a thumb along her hand, his voice low. "There are chapters ahead of us," he murmured. "Beautiful ones."

She didn't know what he meant — not yet — but something in his tone made her chest flutter.

Below them, the waves rolled in and out, steady and sure, as if the water itself were holding them in its gentle, endless embrace.

By the time they flew home, Leha felt unruffled — ready to step back into the stories waiting for her in Fayetteville.

Chapter Forty-Six

History Made Personal

The FSU History Department hallway smelled of old paper, dust, and the faint sweetness of floor polish. It was late afternoon, and the hall was mostly empty, students scattered to study groups or the Bronco Bistro. Tyashia walked beside Henry, a lightness in her step she hadn't felt a year ago. This quiet time on campus had quickly become their ritual — after her sociology classes and before his evening office hours.

"Professor A.L. was talking about social foundations in class today," Tyashia said, pausing beside a display case filled with historical artifacts, a worn bronze compass resting on faded velvet. "How community structures act as lifelines for marginalized groups."

Henry smiled, a warm expression that still eased something in her chest every time she saw it. "Professor A.L. is brilliant. And she's right. History isn't just dates and battles, Tye. It's about survival. It's about how ordinary people find their way through extraordinary circumstances." He paused, his gaze softening. "It's our story."

"It makes sense," Tyashia said, feeling the connections click into place — her mother running for survival, Henry becoming a dependable man just in case he found them, Asiah providing a haven, Ron and Leha building a net for kids like her. "It's about finding strength when the world tries to break you."

"Exactly," Henry affirmed, gesturing down the hall toward his office. "The history of our people, especially Black history, is a testament to resilience. It's about creating community where none existed — just like the men in my own family back in Philadelphia," Henry said. "My grandfather used to organize block clean-ups and neighborhood watches long before the city cared about our street. He always said, 'If the world won't build a place for you, you build one for yourself.'"

They reached his office, a comfortable space overflowing with books, maps, and historical prints. Henry motioned for her to sit in a worn leather armchair while he settled behind his desk.

"You know," Henry continued, his voice lowering, "part of my research now focuses on how military families use community as a stabilizing force. Especially here, near Fort Bragg." He pulled open a drawer and retrieved a folder. "The separation, the stress of deployment — they push people to build their own immediate support networks. It's community-building born out of necessity."

Tyashia absorbed his words, seeing the pattern everywhere. It was the same strength she saw in Melina, in Ron, in Aunt Sylvia. It was the same strength her mother had drawn on when she fled a political machine that could have swallowed them whole.

"It's everywhere once you know to look for it," she said.

"It is," Henry agreed. "It's why the work Leha and Ron do at the Rooted & Rising program is so vital. They provide those structural supports, those points of stability, for the quiet people who slip through the cracks." He looked at her, his eyes serious and proud. "You have that strength in you, Tyashia. You didn't just survive — you built supports around yourself here."

Tyashia looked around the office — the maps, the books, the sepia-toned photographs — and felt something shift inside her.

Not heaviness. Not fear. Something clearer. Something like a breath she'd been holding for years finally releasing.

"It's strange," she said quietly. "I used to think history was something that happened to other people. But now… it feels like it's holding me. Like I'm part of a story that didn't break, even when everything tried to."

Henry's eyes softened. "You are," he said. "And you're carrying it forward."

A surge of pride rose in her chest. She wasn't fleeing her past now — she was stepping into the lineage that had kept her alive.

"I am the author of my own story," she said softly, quoting Leha's affirmation — and meaning it more than ever.

Henry nodded, a proud smile touching his lips. "That's my girl. And it's a powerful story, Tye. Now, let's go get some chicken and waffles at Uptown's. I think you've earned a treat."

Tyashia laughed, the sound bright and unforced.

She was exactly where she was supposed to be — held by history, surrounded by love, and facing a future she was finally ready to write.

Chapter Forty-Seven

You Survived Me

The night before her flight, the house felt unusually still — not rigid, not cold, just… suspended. Sylvia hovered in the doorway of the kitchen, watching Tyashia fold the last of her clothes into a small carry-on. The zipper clicked shut, soft but final.

"You have everything?" Sylvia asked, her voice too even.

"Yeah," Tyashia said. "I'm ready."

Sylvia nodded, but something in her posture drew tight. Her hands clasped together, knuckles whitening as if she were holding onto a truth she wasn't sure she could release.

"London is far," she murmured.

"I know."

A silence stretched between them — not hostile, not tense, but weighted. Sylvia's gaze drifted toward the window, unfocused, as if she were looking at something years away.

"When you see your mother…" she began, then stopped. Her throat worked around a word she couldn't seem to push out. "Just remember she… she wasn't always like this."

Tyashia frowned. "Like what?"

Sylvia blinked hard, the mask snapping back into place. "Never mind. It's not my story to tell."

But the way she said it — tight, trembling at the edges — told Tyashia there was more. Something buried. Something Sylvia had spent decades refusing to touch.

Sylvia turned away, reaching for her keys. "Let's go. You'll miss your flight."

As she walked past, Tyashia caught the faintest whisper under her breath — a name spoken like a bruise.

"Sarah…"

And then Sylvia straightened, armor restored, and said nothing more.

With Henry's presence grounding her life in ways she hadn't expected, it was Sylvia who helped Tyashia find her mother.

It began one quiet evening at the kitchen table. Sylvia sat across from her, hands folded tightly, as if bracing herself against a truth she could no longer hold alone. After a long breath, she opened her Bible — the one she kept on the counter, pages softened by years of use — and pulled out a worn envelope tucked between Psalms and Proverbs.

"This came after Asiah passed," Sylvia said, her voice low. "I should have told you sooner. I just… wasn't ready."

The envelope was addressed in Sarah's handwriting. Inside was a single page — a brief apology, a forwarding email address, and one line that made Tyashia's breath catch:

If I am gone, tell my daughter I never stopped loving her.

Sylvia's eyes glistened. "I didn't tell you because I was afraid," she admitted. "Afraid of losing you. Afraid of reopening things I buried. Afraid of facing what I didn't do for my sister when we were young." Her voice wavered. "I didn't want to break what we finally had."

It wasn't anger that rose in Tyashia — it was understanding. Sylvia had loved her the only way she knew how: tightly, imperfectly, protectively.

With the email address in hand, Tyashia sent the first message — a tentative, trembling note heavy with years of silence and unasked questions. She watched it sit in her outbox for what felt like forever before her mother's reply appeared.

I'm so sorry, Tyashia. Every day, I lived with the ghost of the little girl I left behind.

They moved to phone calls. The sound of her mother's voice was a jolt— familiar and distant at the same time. The thin crackle of the long-distance line couldn't hide the raw emotion. The threats were long gone, the councilman's wife disgraced years earlier, but Sarah's fear had hardened into habit. She had lived in isolation for so long that safety felt like a foreign language.

"We found Henry," Tyashia told her mother one evening, explaining how Leha and Chemelu had used their academic networks to confirm his identity. "He's a history professor here in Fayetteville now. We met him."

"Henry? There?" Sarah's voice was a mix of surprise and relief, a faint tremor threading through each word. "Does he hate me? Is he okay?"

"He's okay, Mom," Tyashia assured her. "He understands. He just wants you to be safe. And he wants to see you too."

Days passed in a rhythm of cautious hope — short emails, longer phone calls, moments where silence did more healing than words. Slowly, the distance between them began to thin.

With Sylvia's blessing — and her quiet, trembling pride — Tyashia planned the trip. She used a portion of her scholarship money, a symbol of her independence, to fund this final act of healing. She booked her flight, packed her bags with a mix of excitement and fear, and soon she was on a plane heading across the Atlantic.

London was a whirlwind of new sights, sounds, and smells. The weather was damp and cool, the air tinged with diesel fumes and old stone. Double-decker buses rumbled past as she made her way to the quiet café where they had agreed to meet. Inside, it smelled of strong tea and pastries.

Her mother was already there.

Sarah looked older, with fine lines around her eyes, but her gaze was unmistakable. Her rich cocoa-brown complexion and slim, graceful build were unchanged, though the years of stress had left their mark. Her dark hair was pulled back in a simple bun. She carried herself with a quiet elegance that seemed hard-won.

This is real. She is real, Tyashia thought as she approached the table.

"My God, you're beautiful," Sarah whispered, standing to pull her into a fierce hug. The warmth of her mother's embrace felt like a missing piece clicking into place.

They talked for hours. Sarah spoke of the constant fear, the desperate choice to run, and the pain of leaving her child behind.

"I lost myself, Tyashia," Sarah confessed, tears streaming down her face. "I traded my identity for survival, and then I forgot how to live again. Your father was a good man, dependable, but I was so young, so lost, chasing a joy I couldn't find, and I nearly got us both killed. I let the fear control me, and I never found my way back."

Tyashia thought of Henry — the calm he moved with, his quiet certainty, the way he had rebuilt himself in her honor. The contrast between her parents' journeys was stark, but the thread between them was the same: survival against systems that were never built to protect them.

The next day, Sarah suggested they visit a neighborhood book event she'd been attending for years.

"It's called the Kensington Book Swap," she said, a small smile touching her lips. "It's… community. I think you'll like it."

They walked through streets lined with brick flats and small shops until they reached a modest square. Tables were set up beneath a gray sky, stacked with books of every size and color. Handwritten signs read *Take One, Leave One* and *Stories Travel Further Together*. The air smelled of rain, paper, and street-corner coffee.

People milled about — elders with canvas totes, teenagers in hoodies, parents with strollers. Snatches of different languages floated through the air. A volunteer in a bright scarf greeted them with an easy smile.

"Welcome to the Kensington Book Swap. Find something that speaks to you."

Tyashia wandered the tables, fingers trailing over spines. She saw novels from Nigeria, Jamaica, Brazil, the U.S. — stories of migration, resistance, love, and loss. It felt like a living archive, a global version of the Gentle Ground Café shelves back home.

Sarah watched her quietly. "When I first came here," she said, "I didn't talk to anyone. I just… stood at the edge and listened. It reminded me that the world was bigger than my fear. That other people had survived things too."

Tyashia picked up a worn paperback by a Black British author, the cover creased from many hands. On a nearby table, a small sign invited visitors to leave notes inside the books they donated.

"Do you have anything you want to leave?" Sarah asked gently.

Tyashia pulled her notebook from her bag, tore out a page, and wrote a single line:

For the ones who survived in silence and are finally ready to speak.

She folded the note and tucked it inside the book before placing it back on the table.

In that moment, she felt the connection stretch across continents — Fayetteville, Philadelphia, London — threaded together by stories, by people who refused to disappear.

"You survived for me," Tyashia said later, as they sat on a bench near the square, watching people trade books and laughter. She wiped a tear from her mother's cheek. "And because you did, I survived too. Your choice was an act of faith, not just fear."

Sarah gripped her hand. "I don't deserve your forgiveness."

"Maybe not," Tyashia said softly. "But you have it anyway. And now we get to decide what comes next."

She had both parents in her life now — a father reborn by love, and a mother whose survival carved a path back to her.

Her future in Fayetteville — and beyond — felt wide open.

As she boarded the early morning flight back to North Carolina, London still clung to her — the cool air of Kensington, the murmur of the book swap crowd, the memory of her mother's hand in hers. She took no souvenirs except a single folded note from her mother and the memory of stories traded in a quiet square.

By the time the plane lifted into the sky, she knew she wasn't just returning home.

She was returning changed.

Chapter Forty-Eight

The Return Home

The flight back to North Carolina felt different. Not lighter — not exactly. But clearer.

Tyashia sat by the window, forehead resting against the cool glass as the plane cut through a sky streaked with soft morning gold. Below her, the Atlantic shimmered like hammered metal, each ripple revealing itself like a truth surfacing after years underwater.

Her thoughts drifted to London — to the Kensington Book Swap, the tables of worn paperbacks, the handwritten signs inviting strangers to trade stories. She could still feel the cool air on her cheeks, still see her mother watching her slip a folded note into a donated book.

For the ones who survived in silence and are finally ready to speak.

The moment wrapped around her like a quiet promise, a reminder that stories could travel farther than fear ever could.

Her mother's voice still echoed in her ears — trembling, apologetic, full of a love that had survived distance, danger, and silence.

You survived for me, Sarah had said. And Sarah's tears had answered everything.

Now, as the plane descended toward Fayetteville Regional Airport, a new truth rose in her: she wasn't returning as the same girl who had left.

She was returning with a father. With answers. With a story that finally made sense.

Ron and Leha were waiting for her at baggage claim, standing side by side like the pillars they had always been. Ron held a paper cup of hot tea, steam rising in a soft curl. Leha held a small bouquet of eucalyptus and lavender — calming, intentional, steadying.

The moment Tyashia saw them, her breath caught.

She didn't run. She walked — measured, sure — and let herself be pulled into their arms.

"You did something brave," Leha murmured into her hair.

Ron nodded, his hand warm on her shoulder. "And you came back whole."

Tyashia swallowed hard. "I met her. And him. And… it was everything."

They didn't rush her. They didn't ask for details. They simply held space — the kind of space that lets truth settle without splintering.

Later that afternoon, they sat together at The Gentle Ground Café — the same place where the investigation had begun, where truth had first started to unspool. The air smelled of cinnamon, roasted beans, and something warm and familiar, like a room that had been waiting for her return.

Tyashia stirred her chai latte slowly, watching the steam rise in soft spirals.

"I thought knowing the truth would break me," she said quietly. "But it didn't. It… rebuilt me."

Ron nodded. "Truth has weight. But it also has shape. And now you can carry it differently."

Leha leaned forward. "How do you feel about Henry?"

A small smile tugged at her lips. "Safe. Like… like he's been waiting for me."

"And your mother?" Ron asked gently.

Tyashia's eyes softened. "She's still healing. But she's alive. And she wants to know me. That's enough for now."

Leha exhaled, relief easing across her features. "You're allowed to take this slow, T. There's no timeline for healing."

"I know," Tyashia said. "But I'm ready."

As they walked out of the café, the late-afternoon sun cast long shadows across the pavement. A scrap of notebook paper — someone's forgotten list or reminder — lifted in the breeze and drifted across her path before settling near her shoe.

She picked it up, turning it over in her hand.

Not a symbol. Not a sign. Just a small, ordinary thing carried by the wind.

But it reminded her of something simple and true: she had been carried too — by people, by love, by truth — and now she was learning how to stand on her own.

That evening, back in her dorm room at FSU, Tyashia opened her laptop and began typing. Not an assignment. Not a journal entry. Something else.

A story. Her story.

She wrote about Philadelphia. About Fayetteville. About fear and survival. About boundaries and the people who honored them. About the mother who ran to save her. About the father who waited to find her. About the community that held her through every unraveling.

The words came like a letting-go, like someone finally stepping into her own voice. When she finished, the room held the aftermath — chairs slightly shifted, a pen rolling a few inches across the table, laughter drifting in from the hallway as life moved on around her.

She leaned back, breath even, heart full.

She wasn't writing to escape anymore. She was writing to understand. To honor. To claim.

She saved the document under a new title:

"Where We Hold Each Other."

The next morning, as she walked through the student lounge, a flyer on the community board caught her eye — simple, blue, and impossible to ignore.

From Spark to Story A Creative Writing & Storytelling Workshop Fayetteville Technical Community College — Summer Session Instructor: Dr. Mariah Ellison

Her body reacted first before her mind caught up.

A writing class. A storytelling class. A chance to finally give shape to everything she had carried.

Later that afternoon, she showed the flyer to Leha.

"This looks like you," Leha said, her voice warm. "You've been writing pieces of your story for months. Maybe it's time to learn how to tell it."

Tyashia traced the edges of the flyer with her thumb. "Do you think I'm ready?"

"I think you're shifting," Leha said. "And this class… it could be the next place where your footing finds you."

Two weeks later, Tyashia walked into the FTCC classroom — bright lights, clean desks, the faint smell of dry-erase markers and new beginnings. Students of all ages filled the room: veterans, single parents, retirees, young adults like her.

The instructor smiled as she entered. "Welcome to *From Spark to Story*. You're here because your story matters."

Something opened inside her — a quiet certainty.

This wasn't just a class. It was a doorway.

By the end of the first session, she had written a single sentence in her notebook:

"I survived, and now I'm learning how to speak."

FTCC had become something else entirely — a place where her healing found its footing, where her past and future finally faced each other, where the spark inside her rose into story.

.

Chapter Forty-Nine

When a Voice Finds Its Light

A few days after returning from London, Tyashia felt something shift as she crossed the walkway toward the Rudolph Jones Student Center — not a lightness, but a new kind of awareness. The morning sun over Fayetteville had the same familiar warmth, but she noticed things she had never paused to see before: the way students clustered in small circles, how certain groups moved with ease while others hovered at the edges, the invisible lines that shaped who felt at home and who felt like they were still learning the choreography.

It was the kind of noticing Professor A.L. had been pushing her toward all semester.

She slowed near the Divine Nine plots, the brick markers catching the early sun in a way that made their colors feel newly awake. Royal blue, crimson, purple, pink, gold — each shade rising from the ground like a living archive. She thought of London's Tube stations, where people created temporary communities on crowded platforms, and of the homelessness project Professor A.L. assigned — how culture shaped not just who had shelter, but who had dignity.

In London, she had watched people sleep near the Thames wrapped in silver thermal blankets, while tourists stepped around them with practiced indifference. She remembered thinking, *This isn't about individual choices. This is about systems.* And she smiled —

because she could hear Professor A.L.'s voice in her head, warm and insistent: *Look for the structure beneath the story.*

She headed toward the student lounge, where Leha and Ron were finishing a brief meeting with a few students as part of a short-term partnership SCI had formed with the university. When they saw her, their faces brightened — not with surprise, but with the quiet recognition of people who had already held her through the first wave of truth.

"You're moving differently," Leha said, pulling her into a hug. "Like something in you found its footing."

Ron studied her with a thoughtful calm. "London didn't just give you answers. It widened your lens."

Tyashia exhaled, a soft smile forming. "It did. I kept seeing things… the way people formed community in places that weren't meant to hold them. The way silence travels through families. The way survival looks different depending on where you stand."

She shook her head, almost amused. "I swear, I kept thinking about that homelessness project. About how culture shapes what we call 'normal.' I didn't expect sociology to follow me across an ocean."

Leha's eyes warmed. "That's what growth feels like. When the world starts speaking back."

"And your mom?" Ron asked gently, already knowing but giving her space to name it again.

Tyashia's voice softened. "We talked again last night. She's trying. And Henry… he's consistent. Present. It feels real."

Ron nodded, satisfied. "Good. You're not just coming back from a trip. You're coming back with clarity."

Over the next few days, the impact of London followed her like a soft echo.

In class, she found herself raising her hand more. In the dining hall, she sat with new friends instead of shrinking into corners. In her dorm, she slept without the old nightmares clawing at her chest.

Even Professor A.L. noticed.

"You're sharper," she said after class, handing back her essay with a rare smile. "More grounded. Your sociological imagination is deeper."

Tyashia smiled. "I think… I finally understand where I come from."

Professor A.L. nodded, eyes warm. "And that makes all the difference."

That night, as she studied for finals, her phone buzzed.

Mom — London Just checking in. Proud of you. Call me when you can.

Tyashia pressed the phone to her chest, breath catching. The message wasn't dramatic — it was simple, consistent. A mother reaching back across an ocean, building something new with her daughter.

The ripple effect wasn't loud. It was quiet. Transformative. Rooting.

While Tyashia was finding her footing again, the people who had anchored her were navigating their own storms.

…

Ron's apartment smelled of cedar and chamomile tea — a soft contrast to the sterile brightness of the ER where Melina had spent her day. She sank into his sofa, exhaustion settling deep in her bones.

Ron emerged from the kitchen with a tray. "Drink this, Mel. You look worn out."

She wrapped her hands around the warm mug. "Thanks, Ron."

He sat across from her, leaning forward. "Long shift?"

"Aren't they all?" she sighed. "But that's not why I came."

Ron waited — calm, patient, present in the way he always was when someone needed space.

Melina stared into her tea. "I keep choosing men who need saving," she said quietly. "I pour myself out until there's nothing left. I don't know how to break the pattern."

Ron turned a cookie between his fingers, thoughtful. "You're not broken," he said gently. "You have a healer's heart. But even healers need someone who can meet them where they are — not drain them."

He looked at her then — really looked. "You deserve someone who sees you. Someone who shares the load."

The silence between them shifted — not rushed, not dramatic, just honest. A connection that had been growing quietly for months finally had room to breathe.

Then Ron's phone buzzed. He read the message, his expression tightening.

"It's Leha," he said. "A new mentee referral. A girl named Brianna. She's been having panic episodes at school, and her grandmother doesn't know how to help."

He met Melina's eyes. "Leha asked if you could come too. Not as a mentor — as someone who understands what fear looks like in a young person's body. She thinks your presence might help the girl open up."

Melina felt something settle inside her — not frantic purpose, but a quiet calling.

"Yeah," she said softly. "I can do that."

They weren't just becoming a support for the community. They were becoming a support for each other.

Chapter Fifty

The Tamron Hall Show
When a Voice Steps Into Its Future

The days that followed moved with a quiet momentum. The Blue Anchor bus was fuller than ever, the mentoring sessions steadier, the youth more open. Something had shifted — not loudly, but unmistakably. The community was standing taller, speaking clearer, believing deeper.

And as the work deepened, so did the attention around it.

Two days later, as Leha sorted through her inbox between mentoring sessions, a subject line stopped her mid-scroll.

TAMRON HALL SHOW — Inquiry: The Power of Mentoring

Her breath caught, the words blurring for a moment.

A producer had seen a short video Melodie posted of the Blue Anchor bus — kids reading, volunteers tutoring, Ron kneeling beside a child sounding out words, and Kendra interviewing a grandmother about why she brought her grandson every week. The video had quietly gone regional, shared by teachers, parents, and local organizers.

The producer wrote:

We're planning a segment on Black mentorship networks. We'd love to feature a young woman who has been shaped by mentoring — someone articulate, passionate, and community rooted. Melodie suggested Kendra.

Leha didn't hesitate.

She forwarded the email to Melodie with one line:

This is her moment.

Kendra burst into the community center an hour later, breathless, her rhinestone-studded water bottle clutched to her chest.

"Leha!" she squealed. "Melodie told me — is this real? Like… Tamron Hall real?"

Leha grinned. "It's real. They want you in the audience. And if the moment feels right, Tamron may call on you to speak."

Kendra covered her mouth with both hands, eyes wide. "Oh my gosh. Oh my gosh. I'm gonna pass out."

Melodie laughed, sliding a folder across the table. "Don't pass out. Read this. It's the briefing packet. And we're getting you a new outfit."

"A new outfit?" Kendra blinked.

Leha nodded. "You're representing the community. You're representing the kids. And you're representing yourself. We want you to feel confident."

Kendra's eyes filled. "Y'all… I don't even know what to say."

"Say yes," Melodie said simply.

And she did.

The Tamron Hall Show

The studio lights were brighter than Kendra expected — warm, golden, almost theatrical. The air buzzed with energy as audience members filed in, guided by cheerful staff in black headsets.

Kendra clutched her laminated audience pass, her hands trembling.

BACKSTAGE ACCESS — SEGMENT 2: The Power of Mentoring

She wore a soft blue blazer Melodie had picked out, paired with white sneakers "for comfort and confidence," as Leha insisted. Her coils were stretched into a half-up style, pearl clips catching the light, her makeup soft and glowing.

"You ready?" a producer asked, adjusting her mic.

Kendra swallowed. "I think so."

"You're going to be great," Leha whispered from behind her. "Just speak from your heart."

The show began with applause. Tamron Hall stepped onto the stage in a sleek emerald dress, her presence commanding yet warm.

"Today," she said, "we're talking about the power of mentoring — how Black communities build structures that hold their youth up."

Photos of the Blue Anchor bus flashed across the screen — kids reading, volunteers tutoring, Ron kneeling beside a child sounding out words.

Kendra felt her pulse quicken.

Tamron continued, "We have someone special in our audience today — a young woman from North Carolina whose life has been shaped by mentorship."

The producer touched Kendra's shoulder.

"You're up."

Kendra stood, legs trembling but held by a courage she hadn't realized was already rising in her.

Tamron smiled at her. "Hi, sweetheart. What's your name?"

"Kendra," she said, voice shaking. "I'm from Fayetteville."

"And you've been part of a mentoring program there?"

"Yes, ma'am. I… I've seen what it looks like when adults show up. When they stay. When they care."

The audience murmured softly.

Kendra continued, her voice gaining strength.

"I used to think I had to do everything alone. But then I met mentors who saw me — really saw me. They taught me how to use my voice. How to tell stories. How to believe in myself."

Tamron's eyes softened. "That's powerful."

Kendra nodded, tears gathering. "Mentoring didn't just change my life. It gave me a future."

The audience erupted in applause.

Tamron stepped closer. "Thank you, Kendra. Your voice matters. And your community is lucky to have you."

After the Show

A staff member guided Kendra to a small lounge where Tamron Hall herself entered, still radiant under softer lights.

"Kendra," she said warmly, "you were incredible."

Kendra's breath caught. "Thank you. I… I want to tell stories like this. For real. On TV. For our people."

Tamron smiled knowingly. "Then keep doing exactly what you're doing. Start local. Stay rooted. And never underestimate the power of your voice."

She handed Kendra a signed card.

Keep telling the truth. — Tamron

Kendra pressed it to her chest, overwhelmed.

When she returned to Fayetteville, the community center erupted in cheers. Tyashia hugged her so tightly she squeaked.

"You were amazing!" Tyashia cried. "Girl, you were on Tamron Hall! You're basically famous."

Kendra laughed, wiping tears. "I just told the truth."

Leha placed a hand on her shoulder. "And that's how change begins."

Melodie added, "This is only the beginning for you."

Kendra looked around — at the people who had believed in her before she believed in herself.

"This is what keeps me," she whispered.

And she meant it.

Chapter Fifty-One

The Strength of Many Hands

Fayetteville State University had become a kind of rebirth for Tyashia — a place where the angry, isolated girl she once was had dissolved into someone clearer, more resolved, and alive with new direction.

One warm afternoon, Leha surprised her with a text:

Meet me at the Gentle Ground Café at 4. Bring your notebook. Trust me.

Tyashia arrived early, nerves buzzing under her skin. The café smelled of cinnamon and Kenyan coffee, sunlight slanting across the wooden tables. She spotted Leha near the back — and beside her sat Ahmad Latif.

For a moment, Tyashia forgot how to breathe.

His music had gotten her through nights when she felt invisible, unheard, and drowning in silence. *'Ville Promises* had been the soundtrack to her healing — the first voice that told her she wasn't alone.

Leha stood, smiling. "Tyashia, this is Ahmad. He's in town for a youth arts panel. I told him about you."

Ahmad rose and extended his hand, his presence calm and unassuming. "I've heard a lot about your journey," he said. "It's an honor to meet you."

Tyashia's voice caught. "I… your music… it helped me survive things I didn't have words for."

He nodded, eyes soft with understanding. "That's why I make it. To remind folks that their story matters — even when the world tries to silence it."

She sat across from him, hands trembling as she spoke. "I used to listen to *'Ville Promises* on repeat. It felt like you were talking to girls like me."

"I was," he said simply. "Girls who carry more than they should. Girls who rise anyway."

Leha watched them with quiet pride.

Ahmad leaned forward. "Leha told me you're writing now. That you're finding your voice."

"I'm trying," she whispered. "Sometimes it feels too big. Or too messy. Or like I don't have the right to tell it."

He shook his head gently. "Your story is the kind that saves people. Not because it's perfect — but because it's true."

Her eyes stung.

"Can I ask you something?" she said. "How did you know your voice mattered?"

Ahmad smiled, a little sad, a little knowing. "I didn't. Not at first. But I kept speaking anyway. And eventually, the world caught up."

He tapped her notebook. "Keep writing. Even when it scares you. Especially when it scares you."

She nodded, breath unsteady but full.

Before he left, he said, "Your story is what *'Ville Promises* was written for — finding your voice even when the world tries to drown it out. Keep going, Tyashia. You're already becoming who you needed."

When he walked out, Tyashia sat in stunned silence, her heart beating with a new kind of certainty.

She had found her voice — and now she knew it mattered.

She began mentoring with the community center's youth program, leading candle-making sessions for younger mentees. It was during these sessions that she began spending more time with Kaymon — the quiet warrior from Leha's mentoring circle.

Their connection surprised everyone — including themselves.

A week later, the FSU student union buzzed with energy. The poetry slam pulsed with chatter, popcorn, and the low thrum of music drifting from the stage.

But tonight, something else electrified the room.

A row of students in royal blue and pearl white jackets entered — the Lambda Rho Ladies, known across campus for their elegance, service, and razor-sharp sisterhood. Their presence commanded attention.

Behind them, their brother organization — the Phi Rho Gentlemen — followed, stepping in rhythm as they took their seats. Their cadence was crisp, intentional — a rhythm shaped by generations.

Kendra squeezed Tyashia's hand. "That's my future. Right there."

The host bounded onto the stage, sequined beret sparkling under the lights.

"Tonight," he announced, "we honor legacy, voice, and the Legacy Line Organizations who paved the way!"

The room erupted.

The Phi Rho Gentlemen performed a short step — powerful, precise, echoing the heartbeat of tradition. The Lambda Rho Ladies followed with a stroll that was smooth, poised, and radiating the kind of refinement that made the whole room lean in.

"Lambda Rho women don't just lead," Kendra whispered. "They lead with purpose. Their National Chairwoman built her whole platform on youth empowerment. That's the kind of legacy I want to walk in."

Goosebumps rose along Tyashia's arms.

"This," Kaymon whispered, "is HBCU culture. This is family."

The poets took the stage — stories of survival, identity, and the long work of becoming oneself. Every poem felt like a mirror.

"Everyone has a story," Tyashia murmured. "Just like Kendra said."

"And you're finding yours," Kaymon replied.

She rested her head briefly on his shoulder, letting the rhythm of the room settle into her bones.

She wasn't just absorbing everyone else's truths. She was starting to trust she had one of her own.

A few days later, she stood in front of her mirror, adjusting her sweater for the tenth time. A "first date" after Vince felt strange — less about excitement and more about relearning how to simply be herself with someone new.

Kaymon arrived in dark jeans and a clean, fitted shirt — simple, calm, grounding.

They drove to a small Italian restaurant a few towns over. Over plates of pasta and the scent of oregano and garlic, their conversation deepened.

He talked about his passion for music production, his dream of building something on his own terms.

"J. Cole proved you can succeed out of here," he said. "I want to be the first me."

"And you?" he asked gently. "Your big dream. Do you ever get nervous about leaving all this behind?"

"Sometimes," she admitted. "But I think I'm more nervous about staying. I want to be somewhere where ambition isn't a threat."

"You deserve that," he said, touching her hand lightly. "You're a force of nature, T. Don't let anyone contain that."

He spoke about growing up in the foster system — the uncertainty, the instability, the deep gratitude he felt for the Millers, who finally gave him and his siblings a home.

She noticed the small things — how he never left food on his plate, how he helped the server clear dishes. Quiet habits that spoke volumes.

When he walked her to her door, he didn't try to kiss her. He simply smiled.

"It's a great start," he said softly — and somehow, it felt like a promise.

And it was.

Weeks passed. The mentoring program was growing faster than any of them expected — and so was something quieter, more intentional, between Leha and Chemelu.

One quiet Friday evening, The Gentle Ground Café was warm with the scent of roasted coffee and cinnamon. Safiya had closed early for a private event. Leha was organizing books when Chemelu approached, the grounding scent of sandalwood preceding him.

"I finished the grant proposal for the Blue Anchor expansion," he said. "Two buses. More mentors. A full mobile classroom."

"You always show up," she said, her smile softening.

He guided her to their corner booth — the place where their partnership had first shifted into something deeper.

"You remember that night?" he asked. "You told me how guarded you were. And I told you that fear is the illusion of separation."

She nodded, breath catching.

"The foundations we've built — for Tyashia, for the children, for the community — they're all manifestations of Ubuntu," he said. "I am because we are."

He reached into his pocket and pulled out a small wooden box.

Her heart pounded.

"My gratitude is my prayer," he said, opening the box to reveal a simple, elegant ring. "You helped me see that my purpose is intertwined with yours. You are the 'us' that makes 'I am' possible."

He didn't kneel — the booth was too small — but his gaze was reverent.

"I want us to be a strength for each other. For our community. For our future. Leha Harrington… will you marry me?"

Tears blurred the café lights into soft halos.

"Yes," she whispered. "Yes, I will."

Chapter Fifty-Two

Where Love Finds Its Ground

The engagement ring caught the light of the small bookstore and bistro as Leha sat across from Chemelu in their familiar corner booth at The Gentle Ground Café. It shimmered softly — not flashy, not loud, but intentional. A quiet testament to the promise they had just made. The world around them felt hushed, as if the café itself were holding its breath.

Safiya appeared from behind the counter, wiping her hands on a linen towel. She had closed early for a private event, but she'd stayed close, sensing something was unfolding.

"Is that what I think it is?" she asked, eyes widening.

Leha lifted her hand, the ring catching the warm hues of the café's wooden shelves and honey-colored walls.

Safiya let out a joyful gasp and rushed over, pulling Leha into a fierce, love-soaked hug. "Oh my goodness — that's a man who sees your whole soul." She let her hand hover, unsure where to place the feeling. "Alhamdulilah."

Chemelu laughed softly. "I'm grateful she said yes."

Safiya beamed at him. "And I'm grateful you show up for her the way you do."

She slipped back behind the counter, giving them space but staying close enough to witness the moment — her smile warm, knowing, and full of blessing.

"We should call them," Chemelu said, a smile tugging at his mouth.

"The army of support," Leha replied, pulling out her phone.

She called her mother first. Martha answered on the first ring.

"Mama, I have some news," Leha said, her voice bright with joy.

"Oh, honey, what is it? You sound wonderful."

Leha told her everything — the proposal at The Gentle Ground Café, the talk of Ubuntu, the reminder that fear is the illusion of separation.

A moment opened. Then Martha's voice, warm and sure: "He sounds exactly like the man you described. A good grounding point. I'm so happy for you both."

Next, she called her father, Sam. His reaction was loud, joyful, and completely on brand.

"My son-in-law," he boomed. "Now that's something worth celebrating! And Sandra's already planning the menu — yes, there'll be trees and twigs for you vegans."

Leha laughed, warmth blooming in her chest. Her family was sprawling, imperfect, and deeply supportive — a constellation of waypoints she had once feared she'd never have.

Later that evening, she called her sister Melina on speakerphone. The two laughed, teased, and immediately launched into planning engagement parties and bachelorette trips while Leha drove home, her heart impossibly full.

Tonight was for quiet certainty. For shared truths. For the soft, powerful knowing that what she'd been seeking had been beside her all along.

It was the perfect end to the beginning of their shared story.

The house held the soft traces of a lived-in morning. On the counter, the Keurig's last brew cycle left a thin ribbon of steam drifting above a half-full mug. Beside it sat the wooden cutting board with the letter L carved deep into the grain — a gift from

Chemelu — and the heart-shaped planter where a spider plant spilled over the edges in bright green arcs.

Leha sat at the kitchen table, a well-worn copy of *Reclaiming Stolen Moments* by Felica Raines Thompson open before her. The words blurred as her mind spun through the whirlwind of the past weeks — Tyashia's healing, her engagement to Chemelu, and the quiet tug of something she hadn't yet named.

Her phone buzzed beside her.

Subject: Ubuntu Model Inquiry — East Africa

Her breath paused.

That email had been sitting at the top of her inbox for two days. She hadn't opened it yet. Not because she wasn't curious — but because something in her knew it would shift the ground beneath her feet.

She closed the notification and reached for her coffee instead. One thing at a time. One breath at a time.

But the thought lingered, hovering at the edges of her mind like a sunrise she wasn't ready to look at directly.

She smiled softly, remembering her conversation with her mother the night before. The "civil wall" between them had crumbled long ago, replaced by mutual respect forged through their separate journeys of rediscovering themselves.

But now, her focus returned to the challenge before her — the email she had avoided opening.

A dream opportunity. A global invitation. A whisper she could no longer ignore.

She finally tapped the message.

A consulting invitation. Nairobi. The chance to replicate the SCI model across East Africa.

Her heart thudded — not with fear, but with recognition.

This wasn't sudden. This was the whisper she'd been feeling for weeks. The call she'd been avoiding. The circle she hadn't yet admitted was closing.

She picked up her phone and called her mother.

"Mama… I need advice. About Nairobi."

Martha's voice softened. "That's a big decision, honey."

"The book I'm reading talks about prioritizing what matters most," Leha said. "I built this life on integrity and community. Choosing Nairobi feels like it might disrupt that foundation."

Her mother exhaled, the sound carrying years of wisdom. "Leha, I made a choice once to leave a life of duty because I felt trapped. I lost myself. I chose wrong because I didn't communicate my needs. You have a choice now that I didn't have then."

She paused, letting the truth settle.

"And Nairobi isn't a disruption," Martha added gently. "It's an expansion. It's the global version of the work you've already built."

A wave of clarity washed over Leha.

"You're a strong woman," Martha said. "Follow your purpose. Reclaim your time."

After she hung up, Leha wiped tears from her eyes — tears of clarity, not fear.

The future — the one with Chemelu, the one with Nairobi — felt limitlessly open.

Nairobi wasn't just a job. It was the birthplace of Ubuntu. It was the global echo of everything she had built in Fayetteville. It was a circle closing and opening at the same time.

She wasn't being pulled away. She was being called forward.

The smell of rich Kenyan coffee — Spring Valley Coffee, the same blend Chemelu always brought back from Nairobi — filled Leha's kitchen. It grounded her instantly.

It felt like a sign. A reminder. A thread tying her present to her future.

Chemelu, ever the man of simple elegance, had left the honeymoon planning entirely in her hands with a warm smile and a single instruction:

"Surprise me, my love. I trust your vision completely."

Leha opened her laptop, excitement fluttering in her chest. Bali had always been at the top of her travel list. It was time to call Iris Martin — owner of Surreal Journeys Travel, curator of experiences, architect of her unforgettable Kenyan trip.

"Leha, congratulations!" Iris exclaimed when she answered. "Chemelu is a lucky man."

"Thank you," Leha said. "We're finally planning the honeymoon. I'm thinking… Bali."

"Oh, the magic waiting for you!" Iris laughed. "You're going to fall in love with it. Bali is the ultimate haven for relaxation and rejuvenation."

Leha leaned in as Iris painted a vivid picture — vibrant greens, rice terraces, jungles dripping with moisture, volcanoes standing guard, private villas with infinity pools, temple bells, incense, a pace of life that forces you to slow down.

Forces you to slow down. That was the key.

Her life with Chemelu was about intentionality, presence, and community. Bali seemed to embody those same principles.

"It sounds perfect," Leha murmured. "Tyashia needs places to hold onto… but maybe I do too."

"Exactly," Iris said. "I'll draw up a custom itinerary."

Later that evening, Leha shared the plan with Chemelu over dinner. His face lit up when she said the name.

"Bali," he repeated, reverence softening his voice. "The Island of the Gods. It will be the perfect start to our life together."

On the table between them sat a small tin of Kericho Gold tea, a gift from Mama Akinyi the week before. Its golden label caught the light, a quiet reminder of the world they were building — one that stretched from Fayetteville to Nairobi to Bali.

Leha reached across the table, her hand resting on his. The engagement ring sparkled the way his smile softened when he looked at her.

The date was set. The destination chosen. The guard officially dropped.

The future — the one with Chemelu — felt limitlessly open.

Two weeks later, the address led Leha and Chemelu to a quiet, tree-lined suburban street. His parents had immigrated years ago and built a life here — a blend of Kenyan heritage and American reality.

Leha felt a jittery nervousness rise in her chest. Meeting the in-laws was always a milestone, but tonight the cultural gap felt particularly wide.

The door opened to Mama Akinyi — warm, vibrant, and fragrant with cardamom and spices. She pulled Leha into a fierce hug.

"Welcome, Leha," she said. "Come in, come in."

The house was beautifully decorated — American furniture blended with African art, carved sculptures, colorful fabrics, framed photos of Kenyan landscapes. On a side table sat a woven basket filled with Kahawa 1893 coffee beans and Ketepa Pride tea, staples of any Kenyan household. The air was filled with the aroma of nyama choma and ugali.

Chemelu's father, Baba Kamau, sat in the living room — serious, measured, a man of few words. His handshake was firm, his gaze assessing.

Dinner was joyous. Mama Akinyi filled the room with stories of Kenya — community life, harvest festivals, the challenges of adapting to American culture.

"Here, everything is so individual," she said. "In Kenya, community is everything. My garden is for everyone."

She placed a steaming pot of chai made with Ketepa's Tangawizi blend on the table, its ginger-cardamom scent drifting through the room. Leha loved her instantly.

But Baba Kamau remained quiet, observing. His gaze followed Leha's movements — not unkind, but unreadable.

Later, as Leha helped Mama Akinyi clear the table, she finally voiced her concern.

"He is not a man for many words," Mama Akinyi said gently. "But he respects you. He sees a strong woman."

Relief washed through Leha.

After dinner, she found Baba Kamau on the back porch, staring out at the suburban yard. A small tin of Dormans Coffee sat beside him — a taste of home he never let himself run out of.

"It is a big world," he said. "Kenya is far."

"I know," Leha replied softly. "But the world needs places that hold people together. Community."

He looked at her then, a flicker of understanding warming his eyes. He nodded once — a gesture that spoke volumes.

"Chemelu is a good man," he said. "He is lucky."

"I'm the lucky one," Leha said honestly.

He nodded again, turning back to the yard.

It was simple. It was enough. She was ready for Kenya.

Chapter Fifty-Three

When Joy Begins Its Work

The morning after the engagement unfolded around her with a gentler kind of calm, as if the world had tilted a few degrees toward joy. Leha woke with sunlight spilling across her comforter, the ring catching the light in quiet glimmers. It wasn't the size of the stone that made her breath deepen. It was the meaning. The intention. The steadiness of it.

She reached for the So Lit Candle she and Chemelu had poured together at the So Lit Candle Shop — the one scented with the blend Alexis Leenese had suggested. Warm amber, soft plum, black rose, and a whisper of vanilla. She lit it carefully, watching the flame rise and settle into its own rhythm.

The fragrance unfurled through her kitchen, draping the room with a tenderness that felt like memory and new beginnings. It steadied her instantly — a reminder of the day they made it, laughing over spilled wax and choosing scents that felt like home.

She sat at the table with her notebook open. The first page was blank, but her heart was full.

A wedding. Her wedding.

Not the rushed, obligatory kind she had once feared. Not the performative kind she had seen others endure. But a ceremony rooted in Ubuntu, community, and intention.

Her phone buzzed.

Chemelu: Good morning, my love. Ready to start dreaming.
Leha: Meet me at The Gentle Ground Café in an hour. Bring your ideas.

The Gentle Ground Café was already carrying its own pulse when she arrived. Sunlight pooled across the mismatched tables, catching on the edges of ceramic mugs and the brushed steel espresso machine behind the counter. A barista wiped down the chalkboard menu, leaving faint streaks of lavender-colored dust in her wake. At their usual table, Safiya had placed a slim vase of eucalyptus — a small, intentional blessing for whatever this new chapter would ask of them.

The air held warm spices, roasted beans, and the sweetness of cardamom pastries cooling on parchment, wrapping around her with a familiarity that steadied her feet.

Chemelu walked in moments later, his presence calm and centering. He kissed her forehead before sitting across from her.

"So," he said, eyes bright, "where do we begin?"

Leha opened her notebook. "With intention. With what matters."

They talked about everything — not logistics, not budgets, not colors — but meaning.

"What do we want people to feel?" she asked.

"Connected," he said. "Like they're witnessing something rooted, not rushed."

"Like they're part of the story," she added.

"Because they are," he said softly.

They agreed on a small ceremony, something intimate and deeply personal. A blending of cultures. A celebration of lineage. A gathering of the people who had held them through storms.

As they talked, Leha jotted down the ideas rising naturally between them — a natural, sacred location; music that honored both Carolina and Kenya; food that blended warmth and spice; vows written by hand and spoken from the heart; a circle of community that included children, mentors, and elders.

The Nairobi decision hovered at the edges of her mind — not as a threat, but as a question waiting for clarity. She didn't bring it up yet. Today was about joy.

Later that afternoon, they visited a small event space on the outskirts of Fayetteville — a converted barn with tall windows, exposed beams, and a field of long grass swaying behind it. The space carried the earthy sweetness of fresh growth and sun-kissed soil.

"This feels like us," Chemelu said, running his hand along the wooden railing.

"It does," Leha agreed. "Simple. Honest. Beautiful."

They stood in the center of the room, imagining the ceremony — the circle of chairs, the soft music, the faces of the people who had shaped them.

Leha felt a swell of emotion rise in her chest.

"This is really happening," she whispered.

Chemelu took her hands. "We're building something that will outlast fear. That's what enduring bonds do."

She leaned into him, letting the truth of that settle.

That evening, back at home, Leha curled up on the couch with her notebook. She flipped to a fresh page and wrote:

Wedding Planning — Phase One • Vision • Values • Community • Ceremony • Anchors

She paused, tapping her pen against the paper.

Should she call her mother? Should she loop in Melina? Should she tell Tyashia?

She smiled.

There would be time for all of that. Time for the women who shaped her to step into this new chapter with her. Time for the community to gather around her.

But tonight, the beginning belonged to her and Chemelu.

She closed the notebook, placed her hand over her heart, and whispered the truth she had finally learned to trust:

"My life is opening, and I am opening with it."

Chapter Fifty-Four

The Shape of What Holds Us

In the weeks following Leha and Chemelu's engagement, Fayetteville moved into a new rhythm. The mentoring program was expanding, the Blue Anchor bus was reaching more neighborhoods, and the people who had once been scattered by trauma and circumstance were now moving in quiet harmony. It was a season of deepening — where each person in their circle began confronting their own foundations, their own faith, their own healing.

The city moved with a new softness. More connected. As if the work they had been doing — the mentoring, the meals, the late-night conversations, the shared grief — had begun to stitch something sacred back together.

The Gentle Ground Café smelled of ground espresso and old paperbacks — Safiya's favorite combination. Evening light drifted through the windows in warm honey-brown tones, illuminating dust motes that floated lazily in the air. The café was calm at this hour, the kind of calm that invited reflection.

Safiya was marking her place in a biography of Maya Angelou when a shadow fell across her book.

David stood there — tall, easy-voiced, kind-eyed. The logistics manager from the base. He'd visited the café several times since they met at a community meeting, always ordering coffee, always sitting nearby. But tonight, he approached her directly.

"Closing time soon, Safiya?" he asked.

"Just about," she said, smiling. "Getting your evening fix?"

"Something like that." He hesitated, then continued with gentle sincerity. "I was hoping to ask you something. Not too forward — just something I've been sitting with."

Safiya set her book aside. "Ask away."

"I admire how established you seem," he said. "I've never met a Black Muslim woman before you. I'm curious about your path… your guiding point."

Safiya appreciated the honesty — and the absence of judgment. She closed her book fully, giving him her full attention.

Behind her, the shelves held the quiet lineage of her thinking: bound copies of *The Crisis*, a few issues of *The Final Call* tucked beside Baldwin, and a worn paperback of Du Bois's *The Quest of the Silver Fleece* — the book she always said taught her that stories could be both resistance and refuge.

"My faith is my guiding point," she said simply.

He nodded, absorbing her words. "And your best friend, Leha — she's deeply Christian. You two are close. How do you bridge that gap?"

Safiya smiled softly, her gaze drifting to the books behind her — Toni Morrison, James Baldwin, bell hooks — the thinkers who had shaped her understanding of humanity.

"It's not about bridging a gap," she said. "It's about recognizing we're drawing water from the same well."

She spoke with quiet conviction. "In Islam, we have a term — *Ihsan* — the beauty and excellence of our actions and intentions. My faith asks me to live with compassion, justice, and service. The five daily prayers aren't a burden; they're a rhythm that keeps my life aligned with what is good."

She paused, letting the truth settle between them. "When Leha and I look at each other's lives, we see the same principles in action. Her faith drives her to serve her community. Mine drives me to serve mine. The foundation is kindness, respect, and a shared mission to do good. That's enough."

Safiya stepped into the back room to retrieve her prayer rug, leaving the café bathed in amber quiet.

Leha wandered toward the counter, her eyes drawn — as they always were — to the highest shelf. The book sat there like a patient witness:

The Weight of Quiet Women by Amara Ellison. Soft green cover. Gold script. A line drawing of two hands — one open, one closed.

Tonight, she reached for it.

She opened to a page near the middle.

"There are women who hold the world together without ever being seen doing it. Their strength is not loud. It is the kind that keeps the roof from caving in while everyone else sleeps."

Her breath caught.

She turned another page.

"A quiet woman is not a woman without pain. She is a woman who learned to fold her ache into corners no one checks."

Her mother's face rose in her mind — the tired eyes, the careful silence, the devotion she had once mistaken for distance.

She flipped to one more passage — one she didn't know she needed.

"Daughters often inherit their mothers' unfinished prayers. Not to carry them, but to complete them — to speak aloud what their mothers whispered into the dark."

Leha closed the book gently, pressing her palm to the cover as if settling something inside herself.

Safiya returned, pausing when she saw the book in Leha's hands.

"That one waits for people," she said softly. "It finds you when you're ready."

Leha swallowed. "I think it just did."

Safiya smiled — a knowing, tender smile. "Some truths arrive quietly. But they arrive right on time."

She turned off the lights, and the café relaxed into its evening hush.

Across town, the world Kaymon lived in was far less forgiving — a place where lifelines were often severed before they could hold.

He was in his garage studio, tweaking a bass line, lost in the music. The dim light cast soft shadows across the posters on the wall — J. Cole, Kendrick, Lauryn Hill — the artists who had taught him that truth could be a lifeline.

When Mrs. Miller answered the house phone, he barely noticed. But moments later, she appeared in the doorway — pale, trembling.

"Kaymon," she whispered. "It's the social worker. It's about your father."

He knew instantly.

An overdose.

The next hours blurred into paperwork and grief. His father — the man who had chosen addiction over his children — was gone. No dramatic ending. No redemption arc. Just a quiet, devastating finality.

Tyashia came over that evening. She didn't try to fix it. She simply sat beside him, her hand warm in the chaos. Jada and Malik were quiet, their usual banter replaced by a shared grief for the father they never truly had.

"I hate him," Kaymon whispered. "He chose that life over us."

"It's okay to be angry," Tyashia said softly. "But Ron told me strength is a choice. You can choose anger… or you can choose to honor the man you are now."

Her words didn't erase the pain, but they gave it shape.

Later that week, Kaymon stood alone at his father's simple grave. No funeral. No mourners. Just him and the wind moving through the grass.

He took a long breath.

"I choose forgiveness," he whispered. "I choose my own path. I choose my family."

He pulled out a small speaker and played his newest track — a melody threaded with grief, hope, and resilience.

He smiled — a genuine, unburdened smile.

He had chosen compassion over bitterness. He had chosen his own soundtrack. His own life.

And for Tyashia, there was one place in Fayetteville that always reminded her of the people who had held her when she couldn't hold herself.

The Simon Temple A.M.E. Zion fellowship hall was quiet on a Thursday evening. Tyashia was organizing donations for the mentoring program's food pantry when Henry set down a heavy box beside her.

"You've been moving different lately," he said gently. "Lighter. Stronger."

Tyashia gave a small smile. "I'm trying."

Henry nodded, then exhaled. "I missed a lot of your life, didn't I?"

"Yeah," she said quietly. "You missed a lot. Not recitals — I didn't have those. But Aunt Asiah made sure my world didn't feel small."

She paused, letting the memories rise.

"She taught me to skate. Took me on SEPTA and NJ Transit all the way to New York so I could see off-Broadway shows. We'd come right back the same night because she couldn't afford a hotel. And whenever she could, she'd take me to Harriett's Bookshop in Philly. We'd ride the bus, walk those blocks, and she'd let me pick one book — even when money was tight."

Her voice softened. "Jeannine talked to me like I mattered. Like stories mattered. Like I was supposed to take up space in the world."

Henry's face tightened — regret, awe, something tender. "Your aunt… she had a way of turning a little into a whole world."

"She did," Tyashia said. "She gave me the best of who she was. Even when she was exhausted. Even when the bills were stacked."

Henry swallowed hard. "I wish I'd known. I wish I'd had the chance to thank her. To tell her what she did for you."

Tyashia looked at him — surprised, softened.

He continued, voice low. "Maybe… maybe one day I could go with you to Philly. To her gravesite. To pay my respects. If that's something you'd want."

Something in her chest loosened — not forgiveness, not yet, but the first shimmer of recognition.

"She'd like that," Tyashia said. "She always wanted people to show up for each other."

Henry nodded, eyes shining. "And maybe after we visit her… we could stop by Harriett's together. Pick out a book. Something that marks a new chapter for us."

The suggestion landed gently — hopeful, careful, real.

Tyashia's breath deepened. "Yeah," she said softly. "I'd like that."

Henry nodded again, voice thick. "I'm sorry I didn't know where you were. I'm sorry I didn't push harder to find you. I'm sorry I missed all those years."

The words didn't erase anything. But they landed honestly — finally.

"Aunt Asiah held me together," Tyashia said. "But I still wondered about you. I wondered if I mattered."

"You did," Henry said. "You always did. I just didn't know how to reach you."

She let out a slow breath. "Strength is a choice. I'm choosing to believe that now. For both of us."

Henry's voice softened. "So what do you choose next?"

"Presence," she said. "I choose presence."

He picked up a small speaker — similar to the one Kaymon used — and turned it on. A warm R&B track filled the hall.

"How about we reclaim a little of that lost time right now?" he asked, extending a hand.

Tyashia didn't hesitate.

They danced among the boxes of canned goods — quiet, imperfect, profoundly healing. A father and daughter rebuilding their footing, one simple step at a time.

Aunt Asiah's love had carried her this far. Now, she was letting Henry step into the space she once believed was permanently closed.

The melody wasn't lost. It had simply been waiting.

.

Chapter Fifty-Five

Where Forever Finds Its Root

The air at the Cape Fear Botanical Garden carried the sharp scent of pine, the soft perfume of blooming jasmine, and the unmistakable sound of shared joy. The late-afternoon sun filtered through the canopy of towering oaks, casting warm, dappled light across the lawn. It felt as if the earth itself had paused to witness this moment.

Rows of chairs lined the lawn, filled with the "army of support," a living testament to the community Leha and Chemelu had built. Mentors, elders, students, neighbors — people whose lives had been shaped by their work, their love, their presence.

Leha stood nearby, radiant in a simple, elegant white gown. Her mother, Martha, adjusted a final detail on the veil, her honeysuckle-and- lavendar perfume carrying the adoration of her own reclaimed joy. Sam watched from his seat beside Sandra, his posture relaxed, his expression peaceful — a man who had lived through storms and now witnessed his daughter's sunrise.

Chemelu stood with his father, Baba Kamau, whose serious expression softened when he caught Leha's eye. The groom was impeccable, the subtle scent of sandalwood and shea butter drifting gently on the breeze. His hands were steady, but his eyes reflected a gratitude that ran deep.

Tyashia and Kaymon sat together in the second row — a picture of quiet, healthy love. Safiya sat nearby, serene and contemplative, her presence a reminder that faith could build bridges where walls once stood. Melina, glowing in her bridesmaid dress, wore a single smudge of purple eyeliner like a joyful signature.

Ron stood just behind them, hands clasped loosely, his expression full of the kind of pride that didn't need words. He had watched Leha grow into her calling, watched Chemelu become a brother in the work, and now he stood as witness — not as counselor or mentor, but as family. The kind of family chosen through service, trust, and years of showing up.

The officiant stepped forward, voice warm and sure. "We gather here today to celebrate not just the union of Leha and Chemelu, but the power of the roots that brought them here. Strength is a choice — and today, this community chooses love."

Safiya smiled softly. In recent weeks, her reflections had deepened her belief: faith wasn't a boundary. It was a foundation.

Chemelu turned to Leha, his gaze reverent. "Leha, you taught me that integrity isn't just about truth, but about action. Ubuntu — 'I am because we are' — is our shared grounding place. My gratitude is my daily prayer, and marrying you is my greatest act of faith. I promise to be your home, always, in this life and in the life we build together in Kenya."

Leha's voice trembled. "You taught me that fear is the illusion of separation. You saw past my walls to the person I was afraid to be. With you, I am ready for the world — ready for Kenya — ready for anything. I am because you are, and I can't wait to see what beautiful chaos we grow through next."

Their kiss was soft and profound, sealed by cheers from the entire community. As they walked back down the aisle, applause rose like a wave, blending with the wind moving through the tall pines. It felt like a blessing — ancient, collective, and deeply earned.

The applause followed them all the way to the garden gate, a warm tide of love rising behind them. By the time the sun dipped below the pines, the world had already begun to shift — gently, intentionally — carrying them toward the next beginning.

The overwater villa in Bali was a quiet sanctuary. Moonlight spilled across the room, draping the sheer netting around their four-poster bed in soft silver. The ocean lapped gently beneath them. Frangipani blossoms perfumed the humid air.

Leha stood on the balcony, watching the water ripple under the moonlight. Chemelu stepped behind her, wrapping his arms around her waist.

"My wife," he murmured.

"My husband," she replied.

He turned her gently. "You have no idea, Leha. Seeing you walk down that aisle… you were the divine made physical. Your strength. Your intention. Your brilliant mind."

Something inside her softened — the last remnants of her emotional guard dissolving in the warmth of his voice.

She rested her forehead against his. "I've never felt more certain of anything."

They stayed like that for a long moment, the ocean moving beneath them like a steady breath.

Later, they lay beneath the canopy, the room quiet except for the soft hum of the night. Leha traced the line of Chemelu's hand, thinking of everything that had brought them here — the healing, the community, the lineage, the courage to choose joy.

And beneath it all, the Nairobi invitation pulsed like a quiet promise — not a disruption, but a widening of the world they were building together.

She exhaled slowly, letting the truth settle.

Forever wasn't a destination. It was a series of choices. And they were choosing each other — again and again, across oceans, across seasons, across whatever came next.

Outside, the moon drifted higher, casting a soft glow across the water.

Inside, their future stretched open — wide, bright, and waiting.

.

Chapter Fifty-Six

Foundations in Motion

The SCI office was in full motion — not frantic, not chaotic, but focused. Volunteers moved through the space with an ease that came from knowing exactly where they fit. Clipboards snapped open. Pens tapped against tables. Someone rearranged a stack of supply bins while another sorted sign-in sheets with practiced hands. From the hallway came a burst of laughter, bright and unfiltered, folding itself into the work happening inside the room.

Leha took it in with a long, gentle breath. Tyashia and Kaymon planned a study group in the corner, their heads bent together in easy partnership. The space felt lived-in and expanding — a testament to the seeds they had planted and the roots that had taken hold.

Chemelu slipped his hand into hers. "Feels good, doesn't it?" he murmured. "Seeing all these foundations we've set."

"It does," she said, leaning into him. She felt light. Whole. Ready.

Her phone buzzed.

Subject: Global Community Initiative — Ubuntu Model Application

Her breath paused.

A consulting invitation. Nairobi. The chance to replicate the SCI model across East Africa. The dream she had whispered into the universe years ago — now standing at her door.

"It's finally here," Chemelu said softly.

But the joy dimmed when she asked about the early funding.

"We were transparent with the local board," he said. "But the global review will want every detail. Every receipt. Every origin point."

"And the gaps?"

"We'll face them," he said. "Together."

The air shifted. The world wasn't holding its breath for her answer. It was holding its breath for theirs.

"Then we finish this," she said. "With integrity."

He nodded. "With integrity."

The old community center was a mess — chipped paint, bare floors, dust thick enough to write in. But to Leha, it looked like potential. A blank canvas waiting for purpose.

Tyashia spun in a slow circle. "We can fit a hundred kids in here."

"A hundred and one," Kaymon added, nudging her shoulder.

The "army of support" arrived in waves — Sandra with paint rollers, Martha with snacks, Jada and Malik eager to help, elders offering stories and extra hands, teens buzzing with pride at building something that belonged to them too.

By sunset, the hall had transformed. Not perfect — but unmistakably alive. A foundation taking shape.

Leha stood in the doorway, watching the room hum with possibility. This wasn't just a building. It was a promise.

She didn't know yet what she would do with all the words she carried now — the ones she whispered to herself in the dark, the ones she wished someone had said to her sooner. But she knew this: she wanted to give them away. To girls like her. To girls she hadn't met yet. To anyone who needed a reminder that they were made of more.

The thought took hold inside her like a small, steady light — something she could build from, something that felt like beginning.

As the last volunteers packed up, someone turned on the small TV mounted in the corner. Roland Martin's voice cut through the chatter with his signature mix of fire and clarity.

"Breaking news tonight," he said. "Former congressional aide Delilah Carter is under federal investigation for misappropriation of nonprofit funds and falsifying grant documentation."

Leha stilled.

Chemelu's jaw tightened — not with fear, but with recognition.

Roland continued, "Sources confirm Carter attempted to funnel money through several community organizations without their knowledge. One of those organizations — the Sandhills Community Initiative — avoided entanglement only because its leadership refused early funding that lacked transparency."

A photo of Delilah appeared on the screen — composed, confident, and now unmistakably cornered.

Roland shook his head. "Integrity isn't just a moral stance. It's a safeguard. And in this case, it protected a youth program doing real work in Fayetteville."

Leha exhaled slowly.

Chemelu wrapped an arm around her shoulders. "We dodged a storm we didn't even know was coming."

"No," she said softly. "We chose integrity. And it protected us."

"And the kids," he added.

The volunteers murmured, some shaking their heads, others whispering prayers of gratitude.

The moment wasn't triumphant. It was clarifying. A reminder that their work lived inside systems — and their choices shaped the safety of everyone connected to them.

Across the room, Kaymon knelt beside a younger boy struggling with a paint roller, guiding his hand with a patience that surprised even him. There was a serenity in his movements now — not loud, not performative, just present. Healing had carved out room inside him for something new, something he hadn't known he could offer: responsibility. A quiet kind of leadership.

Tyashia watched him for a moment, her expression softening. Growth wasn't always loud. Sometimes it was a boy choosing to show up differently than the men before him.

Tyashia approached Sylvia's house with a quiet confidence she had earned through fire. The house still smelled of lemon polish and rigid order — the scent of a woman who once believed structure could save the world.

But the furlough months earlier had cracked Sylvia's armor. Forced stillness had humbled her, softened her, opened a door neither of them had known how to approach.

Tyashia wore one of her new affirmation shirts — *Made of More* — the words resting across her chest like a truth she had finally grown into.

"I wanted to say thank you," she began. "For taking me in. I'm doing well at FSU. I'm mentoring kids now."

"That was the plan," Sylvia said. "Structure and accountability."

"It was," Tyashia agreed. "But structure is a foundation — not a cage. I don't need perfection anymore. I am enough."

Sylvia's mask shifted. "I was terrified," she whispered. "Taking Asiah's place… knowing I couldn't be the aunt she was. And after the furlough… I realized how much I'd been holding together with fear."

"You were the mentor I needed when my wheels were stuck," Tyashia said softly.

A small, genuine smile touched Sylvia's lips.

Peace settled between them — quiet, earned, real.

Later that night, long after the volunteers had gone home and the building had settled into its familiar creaks, Leha sat alone at the folding table near the front window. The only light came from the desk lamp she'd dragged across the room — a small circle of brightness in the wide, quiet space.

Tyashia's affirmation shirt — *Made of More* — lay draped over the back of a chair, forgotten in the rush of cleanup. The words felt like they were waiting for her.

Leha reached for it, smoothing the fabric between her fingers.

Made of More.

The phrase carried truth — not just for Tyashia, but for every girl who had walked into her office carrying more than any teenager should. For every boy who had been told to be strong before he was ready. For every mentor who had held someone else's story until their own hands shook.

She exhaled, the weight of the day settling into something composed.

Foundations weren't built in a moment. They were built in motion. And tonight, everything was moving in the right direction.

Chapter Fifty-Seven

A New Branch on the Tree

Morning unfolded over The Gentle Ground Café with a sense of anticipation — the kind that gathers before the first rush of the day. Safiya moved through the space with her usual calm. Behind the counter, the grinder released a soft scatter of beans into its hopper, and someone restocked the display of lemon-ginger scones beside a stack of well-thumbed poetry chapbooks. Light fell across the floorboards, catching on the edges of mismatched mugs and the brass bell above the door that chimed whenever someone stepped inside.

Ron arrived first.

He paused in the doorway, not with dread, but with a tenderness he hoped to carry well. His presence felt perpetual, thoughtful, as if he had spent the night choosing his words with care.

Safiya looked up. "You're holding something big."

He nodded once. "I am."

She didn't ask more. She simply offered a gentle, knowing glance — a blessing without words.

A few minutes later, Leha stepped inside.

She went still, breath suspended when she saw Ron's expression — not troubled, but full. Full of something he hadn't yet spoken. Safiya watched them both with quiet understanding.

"Okay," Leha said softly. "What's going on?"

Ron exhaled, not in fear, but in release. "I wanted to talk before the day gets away from us. Before Nairobi. Before everything shifts."

Leha's pulse quickened. "Tell me."

He stepped closer, voice warm. "Melina and I… we've grown close. It surprised us both. And we've been trying to find the right moment to tell you."

Leha blinked, startled but not wounded. "You and Melina?"

Ron nodded. "Yes. And there's more."

The bell over the door chimed again.

Melina stepped inside, her hands clasped in front of her, her eyes bright with both fear and hope. She looked softer than usual — not fragile, but open in a way Leha hadn't seen since they were children.

"Leha," she whispered. "I'm pregnant."

The world tilted — not in shock, but in awe.

Leha pressed a hand to her mouth. "Mel… oh my God."

Melina's eyes filled. "I didn't want to hide it. I just… wanted to tell you in a way that honored you. And honored this."

Ron's voice softened. "This isn't a mistake. It's a blessing. A new beginning. And I want to do this right — with integrity, with love, with family."

He hesitated, then added quietly, "There's something else we need to tell you."

Melina reached for his hand.

"We got married," she said softly. "Just the two of us. A small ceremony. We weren't hiding it from you — we just… needed a moment that was ours before the world had opinions."

Ron nodded. "We're still deciding when to have the full wedding — before the baby or after. But we wanted you to know now. We wanted you to hear it from us."

Leha's breath trembled. "You're… married?"

Melina nodded, tears slipping free. "We are."

Leha stepped forward, her eyes shining. "You're giving Mama and Daddy a grandbaby… and you're giving our family a new branch."

Melina laughed through her tears. "Yeah. We are."

Leha pulled her into a hug — not tight, but full. Full of surprise, full of love, full of the kind of joy that rearranges a family.

"You're not alone," she whispered. "You will never be alone."

Ron stepped closer, his voice warm. "This child will be loved. Held. Surrounded."

Safiya placed a hand over theirs, her voice a soft invocation. "Ubuntu," she murmured. "I am because we are."

The moment didn't break them. It expanded them.

A new branch on the family tree. A new heartbeat in the lineage. A new future rising in the quiet morning light.

The reckoning wasn't about mistakes. It was about truth. About love. About the courage to grow.

And the world — the whole world — exhaled.

And when the community gathered that night, it felt less like an event and more like a homecoming.

Chapter Fifty-Eight

The Night of a Thousand Anchors

The evening settled over the community center like a soft shawl — warm, familiar, threaded with the hum of people gathering themselves. Inside, the building felt alive in a way that made the walls seem to breathe. Not with urgency. Not with pressure. But with gratitude.

Leha stood near the entrance, watching the room fill in waves.

Kaymon carried in a speaker, nodding to the beat already pulsing through the space. Safiya arranged trays of sambusas beside a stack of mismatched plates. Sam and Sandra set out desserts with the quiet rhythm of people who had done this a thousand times. Martha placed flowers near the stage — simple, elegant, intentional.

Ron and Melina moved through the room with a new, gentle joy, their hands brushing in small, unspoken ways. Tyashia helped a group of middle schoolers hang a banner across the back wall:

WE ARE BECAUSE WE ARE.

As she stepped back to look at it, something in her shifted. She noticed how the kids organized themselves — who took charge, who hesitated, who waited for permission that no one needed to give. She saw how community formed itself in real time, how belonging wasn't just emotional but structural. Professor A.L.'s voice rose in her memory: *Look for the patterns. They'll tell you what people believe about themselves.*

And here, in this room, the pattern was simple: **Everyone mattered. Everyone had a place.**

The room buzzed with life — the kind that didn't need permission to exist.

And then the door swung open again.

Simon burst in first, clutching a sketchbook. "Miss Leha! I finished the mural idea!" he announced, flipping it open to reveal a bright, swirling design of hands, roots, and roller skates. "I put wheels on the roots so they can keep moving."

Leha laughed, her heart warming. "Of course you did."

Cassidy followed behind him, rolling her eyes with affection. "Don't let him fool you — he made me hold the flashlight for two hours while he drew."

Tasha nudged her. "And you loved every minute."

Cassidy shrugged. "Maybe."

Uncle Leonard stepped in next, carrying a stack of folding chairs. He nodded at Leha — a quiet, respectful gesture that held more apology and pride than words ever could.

And then came Kendra.

She swept into the room like she'd been waiting her whole life for this entrance — bright blazer, curls bouncing, mic clipped to her collar. She held a stack of glossy tickets fanned out like playing cards.

"Alright, Fayetteville!" she called, voice ringing with talk show sparkle. "I've got something special for y'all tonight!"

Heads turned. Kids perked up. Even Leonard's mouth twitched into a smile.

Kendra lifted a ticket high.

"**Roll, Bounce, Speak!** — a youth skate night at Round A Bout Skating Rink. And guess who's going live from the middle of the floor?"

The room erupted.

Tyashia froze — in the best way — because the words hit her like a memory wrapped in music. Asiah's laughter. The pom poms on her skates. The way she'd say, *Keep rolling, Tye. Even when it's hard.*

Kendra crossed the room and pressed the first ticket into her hand.

"Your aunt started this," she said softly. "You get to carry it forward."

Tyashia blinked hard, breath catching — not in pain, but in gratitude.

Kaymon nudged her shoulder. "You skating backwards this time?"

Simon piped up, "I can teach you! I've been practicing."

Cassidy groaned dramatically. "Lord, don't let me break my ankle in front of the whole city."

Tasha smirked. "I'll help with the interviews. Somebody's gotta keep Kendra from talking too much."

Kendra gasped. "Excuse you — I am a professional."

Laughter rippled through the room — warm, unforced, alive.

When the music softened, Sam stepped onto the small stage.

"We're not here to talk about programs," he said. "We're here to honor the people who built this place — together."

He gestured to the crowd, then to Leha. "And to the woman who taught us that community isn't built by one person — it's built by all of us."

Applause rose like a wave.

Youth stepped forward — Malik with a robotics story, a little girl who simply said, "This place makes me feel safe." Simon held up his mural sketch, cheeks warm with pride. Cassidy shared how the center helped her "stop shrinking." Tasha admitted she'd learned how to apologize — and mean it.

Their words were brief, but they landed with a force that stilled the room.

And from the second row, Aunt Sylvia dabbed her eyes with a handkerchief, nodding along as each child spoke. For a moment

— just a breath — her gaze drifted somewhere far beyond the room.

Not to a single memory, but to a feeling she had spent a lifetime smoothing over: the tremble of raised voices behind thin walls, the way she used to gather Sarah and Asiah close when the house felt like it might split in two. A childhood stitched with instability, with secrets she still carried like folded paper in her pocket.

She inhaled, slow and steady, and the present returned — the warmth of the room, the safety these children didn't have to question.

"This is the harvest," she whispered, just loud enough for Leha to hear. "Every seed you planted is standing up tonight."

Safiya stepped forward. "Ubuntu isn't a word," she said. "It's a way of breathing. And tonight, I see a room breathing together."

Tyashia spoke last, her voice carrying a quiet strength. "Whatever comes next — we can hold it. We can hold each other. Because healing isn't just personal… it's communal. It's structural. And we're building something here that holds all of us."

Leha felt tears spill down her cheeks. Because she believed her.

The lights dimmed. A slideshow moved across the wall — snapshots of the center being built, painted, opened. Youth smiling. Volunteers laughing. A community learning the shape of itself.

The final slide read:

WE ARE READY.

The room erupted in cheers.

And then — as the cheers softened — a little girl tugged at Leha's sleeve, her eyes wide with the kind of pride only children carry without hesitation. She held up a crayon drawing she'd made during the slideshow: a bright butterfly with wide, uneven wings, colored in blues and purples and a single streak of yellow down the middle.

"I made this for you," she whispered. "It looked like tonight."

Leha pressed a hand to her heart as the child placed the drawing on the welcome table — a small, imperfect, beautiful offering. The butterfly seemed to glow in the projector's light, its wings open as if mid-flight, as if blessing the room with the promise of becoming.

Later, the core team gathered beneath the wide Carolina sky — Ron with his quiet strength, Safiya with her prayerful calm, Sam with his steady wisdom, Melina with her blooming joy, Tyashia with her new certainty, Kaymon with his emerging leadership, Simon clutching his sketchbook, Cassidy leaning into her growth, Tasha standing taller than she ever had, Leonard with his softened edges, and Kendra still glowing from her big announcement.

They didn't hover. They didn't crowd. They simply were — a circle of people who had held her through every season.

Safiya stepped forward first. "May your steps be guided," she said. "May your work be blessed."

Ron added, "May you walk in truth."

Sam said, "May you remember where you come from."

Melina whispered, "May joy find you."

Tyashia smiled, eyes bright. "May you know you're never alone."

Leonard nodded. "May you always have a place to land."

Kendra grinned. "And may you roll, bounce, and speak wherever you go."

Chemelu took her hands. "May the world meet you with the same grace you've given it."

The blessing settled over her like a mantle — light, warm, ancestral.

"Amen," she whispered.

Inside, the building glowed — not with urgency, but with the slow gathering of people finding their places. The night held its breath, full of promise.

And Leha stood in the doorway, letting the light stretch toward her like an invitation.

A lineage made whole. A community ready. A future opening.

She placed a hand over her heart, feeling its calm rhythm.

Then she stepped forward — toward the horizon waiting for her name.

.

Chapter Fifty-Nine

Where We Lay Down What We Carried

The night air outside the community center was cool, touched with the faint scent of pine and the soft hum of a city settling into itself. The celebration had ended, but the warmth of it still clung to the walls — laughter echoing faintly, the last notes of music drifting like smoke.

Leha stepped outside to breathe, her heart still full from the blessing circle. She wasn't alone for long.

Martha stood near the edge of the parking lot, arms wrapped loosely around herself, not in cold but in contemplation. Sam stood a few feet away, hands in his pockets, shoulders relaxed in a way Leha hadn't seen in years.

They weren't speaking. They were simply… standing. Two people who had shared a life, a home, a history — and a quiet ache neither had ever fully named.

Leha hesitated, unsure whether to approach, but Martha turned and offered a small, gentle smile.

"You can come," she said softly. "This moment belongs to you and Melina too."

Sam nodded, his eyes gentle. "We're just talking. Or… trying to."

Melina joined them, slipping beside Leha, her hand brushing her sister's. The four of them formed a loose circle beneath the streetlamp's glow.

For a long moment, no one spoke.

Then Martha exhaled — a long, trembling release that seemed to come from a place she'd kept locked for decades.

"You know," she began, voice steady but soft, "there was a picture frame in our old house. The one in the hallway. It was always crooked. No matter how many times I straightened it."

Sam's head lowered, a rueful smile touching his mouth. "I remember."

"I used to fix it every morning," Martha continued. "Every single morning. I thought if I kept that frame straight, maybe everything else would stay straight too."

Her voice wavered, but she didn't look away.

"But the truth is… I was holding up more than a picture. I was holding up a man who didn't know how to come home from war. I was holding up a family that didn't know how to talk about the things that scared us. I was holding up a marriage that was breaking under the weight of silence."

Sam swallowed hard. "Martha…"

She shook her head gently. "No blame. Not tonight."

Sam's eyes shone. "I didn't know how to come home. I didn't know how to put down the things I saw. I didn't know how to be soft again. And you… you carried all of it. You carried me."

"I carried us," she corrected. "Until I couldn't anymore."

Silence settled — not sharp, not bitter, but honest.

Melina wiped her cheek. "Mama… Daddy… we never knew."

"You weren't supposed to," Martha said. "You were children. You deserved a childhood, not our battles."

Sam stepped closer, his voice low. "Ending the marriage wasn't failure. It was mercy. For both of us."

Martha nodded. "We didn't stop loving each other. We just stopped being able to live inside the same walls."

They stood in that truth, the air softening around them.

"We did our best," Martha said.

"And now," she added, her voice warming, "a new life is coming into this family… a reminder that even after the hardest seasons, something beautiful still chooses us."

Sam's breath deepened — not in pain, but in awe.

Melina pressed a hand to her belly, her eyes shining. "This baby… it feels like a beginning."

Sam nodded. "A new branch on the tree."

A soft flutter brushed the quiet. A small bluebird landed on the wooden fence a few feet away, its feathers catching the streetlamp's glow in a wash of cobalt. It tilted its head, watching them with a stillness that felt almost like understanding.

Martha's eyes softened. "Well," she murmured, "would you look at that."

Sam let out a quiet laugh. "A blessing."

"A reminder," Martha said. "That life keeps moving. Even when we don't feel ready."

The bluebird lingered for a breath — calm, unhurried — then lifted off, wings brushing the air with a soft whisper before disappearing into the night.

Martha squeezed Sam's hand once before letting go.

"We did our best," she said again, softer this time.

"We did," Sam agreed.

"And now," Martha added, turning to her daughters, "we get to build something new. Not as a broken family. As a changed one."

Leha felt her throat tighten. Melina leaned into her shoulder.

Sam placed a hand over his heart. "I love you girls. That never changed."

"We love you too," Leha whispered.

The four of them stood beneath the Carolina sky — not as the family they once were, but as the family they had become. Separate. Whole. Healing.

Leha saw her parents not as the pillars she leaned on, but as people — flawed, tender, brave in their own quiet ways.

People who had carried more than anyone knew. People who had finally put it down.

She breathed in the night air, feeling something settle inside her.

A lineage made honest. A past made gentle. A future made possible.

And somewhere deep within her, a horizon whispered her name.

When the Horizon Opens Its Hands

A small yellow ladybug drifted down onto the pavement outside the SCI office, its tiny wings catching the late winter light as it paused — easy-going, certain — before lifting off again. It moved the way courage often does: quietly, without announcement, following a path only it could sense.

Leha watched it through the conference room window, feeling something settle inside her chest. Not the ache she once carried. Not the fear she once obeyed. Something steadier. Something earned.

The night before had shifted something in her — the way her parents stood beneath the streetlamp, honest and human; the way Melina's hand rested over her belly; the way Sam and Martha released each other with grace instead of bitterness. A family once held together by silence had finally spoken its truth. And somehow, that truth had made room for all of them.

Healing wasn't loud. It was a soft rearranging. A quiet making space.

And for the first time in her life, she felt the difference between being held up and standing on her own. Both mattered. Both had shaped her. But this moment — this breath — belonged entirely to her.

Inside the office, volunteers moved with the familiar rhythm of a place that knew its purpose. Printers hummed. Youth laughed in the hallway. The scent of lemon cleaner lingered in the air. But beneath it all, a new calm pulsed — the kind that comes when a community knows it can stand.

She closed her laptop gently, as if the opportunity resting inside it were a living thing.

Chemelu entered with a mug of Kenyan coffee, its rich, earthy aroma warming the air between them.

"You're quiet," he murmured.

"I'm listening," she said.

"To what?"

She looked toward the window, where the ladybug had been. "To what's calling me."

He didn't rush her. He never did. He simply sat beside her, his presence a shoreline she could lean against.

Later that afternoon, she walked the Cape Fear River Trail alone. The water moved slowly beside her, reflecting the sky in soft ripples. She thought of the painting in their home — the Maasai mother walking forward, warriors behind her, a child held close. A lineage of courage. A lineage of protection. A lineage of movement.

She thought of her mother's quiet strength. Her father's steady hands. Ron's integrity. Safiya's faith. Tyashia's becoming. Melina's new life blooming. The "We Are Ready" banner. The "Made of More" shirt. The community center rising from dust and chipped paint. The blessing circle beneath the Carolina sky.

Every thread pointed in the same direction.

Forward.

A breeze lifted off the river, cool and certain. It brushed her cheek like a blessing.

She stopped walking. Closed her eyes. And let the truth settle into her bones.

She finally understood the shape of her own becoming — how individual stories braided into collective ones, how healing rippled outward like a widening circle.

"I'm ready," she whispered.

Not because everything was perfect. Not because every fear was gone. But because she finally understood that readiness wasn't a feeling — it was a choice.

She pulled out her phone with steady hands. Opened the email. Typed two words:

Let's begin.

And hit send.

As she lowered her phone, a soft movement caught her eye.

A small yellow ladybug had landed on the railing beside her, its wings folded neatly, as if it had been waiting for her to look up. It didn't move at first. It simply rested there — steady, bright, unafraid — the way she finally felt inside her own skin.

Then, with a slow unfurling, it lifted into the air and drifted forward, following the path ahead of her as if pointing the way.

Leha's breath steadied.

"I'm coming," she whispered.

And she stepped toward the horizon, the ladybug rising with her, both of them moving into the light.

May the road rise to meet her, may the truth walk beside her, and may every step forward honor the ones who carried her here.

EPILOGUE
When the Work Comes Full Circle

Morning rose gently over the community center, the light soft and patient, as if the world itself were taking a breath with her. Leha stepped inside, the stillness wrapping around her like a familiar embrace — not empty, but expectant, as though the building understood she was preparing to cross a threshold.

On the welcome desk sat a small basket — the same one the volunteers had filled weeks earlier. Inside were two gifts placed with intention:

- a bag of Kenyan coffee, signed by the mentors
- a box of West African–inspired artisan chocolates, tied with a gold ribbon

A handwritten note rested between them:

For the journey. For the soil. For the world you're about to touch. We're with you. Always.

Leha pressed the note to her chest. It wasn't a gift. It was a blessing — a benediction from the community that had shaped her into the woman she was becoming.

A yellow ladybug rested on the rim of the basket, still and bright, as if keeping watch. It lingered for a breath, then lifted into the morning air and disappeared into the light.

Leha didn't speak. She didn't need to.

Outside, the morning air held a quiet clarity. Chemelu waited by the car, loading their bags — one for Nairobi, one for the work they would carry with them.

He held up a thermos. "Kenyan coffee for the road."

She smiled. "You know me too well."

They sipped together, the aroma rising like a promise — every early morning they had survived, every late night they had planned, every moment they had chosen courage over fear.

"Ready?" he asked.

She nodded. "Almost."

Before leaving, they returned to the community center one last time. A small group had gathered — Ron, Melina, Safiya, Sam, Tyashia, Kaymon, Malik, Mrs. Thompson, and a handful of parents and youth.

No speeches. No ceremony. Just presence.

Safiya stepped forward, hand over her heart. "Ubuntu goes where you go."

Ron nodded. "And we'll keep things steady here."

Behind him, the veterans from Fort Liberty stood in quiet solidarity — men and women who understood service, sacrifice, and the kind of leadership that leaves its mark. Their simple salute carried more meaning than words.

Tyashia held up a small drawing — a map with a star at the center. "This is where you taught us to rise."

Kaymon and Malik stood beside her in their FSU hoodies, the gold and blue catching the morning light. "Bronco Pride travels," Kaymon said. "You taught us that too."

Melina handed Leha a small pouch. Inside were two chocolates — a taste of home and heritage. "For your first night in Nairobi."

Mrs. Thompson dabbed her eyes. "You've built something that will outlive all of us."

Leha's eyes warmed. This wasn't goodbye. This was expansion.

As they drove toward the airport, the city slowly waking around them, Leha rested her head against the window.

She thought of the girl she once was — small, guarded, unsure she deserved community or purpose. She thought of the woman she had grown into — open, steady, whole. She thought of the youth who had found their voices, the parents who had found relief, the mentors who had found direction, the elders who had found renewal.

She thought of the lineage that shaped her — Divine Nine sisters, HBCU legacy, military community, cultural symbols that reminded her she belonged to something larger.

And she thought of the world waiting on the other side of the ocean.

Chemelu reached over, taking her hand. "Whatever happens next," he said, "we walk it together."

She squeezed his hand. "Together."

At the airport gate, Leha opened her bag one last time. On top sat:

- the Kenyan coffee, reminding her of the mornings that shaped her
- the artisan chocolates, reminding her of the lineage she was stepping into

- the note from her community, reminding her she was never walking alone

She closed the bag gently.

A truth rose within her — clear, steady, undeniable:

Community wasn't just a feeling. It was a structure. A system. A living network of choices that shaped lives as surely as any policy or institution.

The boarding announcement echoed through the terminal.

Leha stood. Chemelu stood with her.

And together, they stepped toward the horizon — not leaving home behind, but carrying it with them.

ACKNOWLEDGEMENTS

This book was not written in isolation. It was shaped, held, and carried by a community of people who believe in the power of story, the necessity of truth, and the beauty of Ubuntu — *I am because we are.*

To my parents, **Sam and Macieon Hairston**, and my aunt **Alberta Martin** — though you are no longer here in body, your love and legacy continue to guide every step I take. You are the soil from which every chapter of my life grows.

To my husband, **Al** — thank you for being my encourager, my steady place, and my quiet strength through every late night and revision.

To my children, **Ahmad and Alexis** — your brilliance, creativity, and wisdom echo through these pages. And to my grandchildren, **Elijah, Ahli, Chloe, and Carter** — you are my joy, my inspiration, and the future I write toward. A special thank you to **Bella**, whose care and devotion to the children continues to bless our family in meaningful ways.

To my mother-in-law, **Trudy**, and my father-in-law, **Clarence** — thank you for your enduring support, your kindness, and the way you have embraced my journey with grace.

To my siblings, nieces, nephews, and all of my family near and far — thank you for loving me across distance, seasons, and becoming. Your laughter, your prayers, your presence, and your belief in me have been a quiet wind at my back. I carry your names, your stories, and your joy with me in every chapter. And if I failed to mention a name, know that you are held in my heart and loved beyond measure.

To my beloved **Sister Circle Book Club** — Mary, Pam, Jo Katherine, Lenora, LaTricia, Carlotta, and Author Suzetta Perkins — thank you for twenty-six years of fellowship, laughter, and literary sisterhood. Your commitment to story, community, and one another has been a steadfast source of joy and inspiration.

To **Iris Martin** of Surreal Journeys Travel and **Sam Smith** of Sampton Safari Ltd — thank you for expanding my understanding of global connection and for your generosity of insight.

To the young people, mentors, and families who have trusted me with their stories — your courage is woven into every page. To the mentors who show up for youth every day: your impact is immeasurable.

To my community partners and colleagues in **Fayetteville, Raeford, and Buffalo** — thank you for building spaces of belonging, healing, and possibility. To the military families and veterans of **Fort Bragg**, your resilience and service shaped both this story and my own life.

To **Fayetteville State University**, the HBCU community, and the **Divine Nine** sisterhood — thank you for grounding me in legacy, excellence, and collective uplift.

To **Jeannine Cook** of Harriett's Bookstore — thank you for your fierce commitment to literary liberation and for affirming the heart of this work. And to the **Kensington Book Swap** in London — thank you for reminding me that stories travel farther when shared hand to hand.

To the Black-owned brands whose missions align with community uplift — including **Blk & Bold, Be Rooted, and Midunu** — thank you for inspiring small moments of joy and intention throughout this journey.

To Lakesha Parker — my best friend, my sister in spirit, the one who gives true meaning to "Fruitbelt for Life." Thank you for loving me with a loyalty that does not waver, for knowing my silences as well as my laughter, and for reminding me that home is not always a place — sometimes it is a person. Your presence in my life is a blessing I do not take lightly.

To **Swan Davis of Let's Make It Happen Together, LLC —** thank you for your vision for the Adopt-A-Neighborhood Program and for allowing Fayetteville-Raeford CARES and our Purple Beauty Mentoring Bus to be part of that vision. Your commitment to community uplift continues to open doors for youth and families in ways that will echo for generations.

To **Susan L. Taylor and the entire National CARES Mentoring Movement leadership team, along with the Affiliate Leaders across the nation —** thank you for the transformative work you do every day. Your dedication to healing, empowerment, and collective care has shaped this movement and strengthened communities far beyond what words can capture.

To the readers — thank you for holding these characters, their journeys, and their unfolding. May you feel seen, strengthened, and reminded that community is not a place we go; it is something we build together.

And finally, to every ancestor whose resilience made my voice possible — this book is an offering. A continuation. A prayer of gratitude.

Ubuntu, always.
— *Alberta Lampkins*

AUTHOR'S NOTE

Where We Hold Each Other was born from the belief that healing is not a solitary act. It is communal. It is ancestral. It is intergenerational. It is the quiet, courageous work of choosing one another again and again.

This story is rooted in the places that shaped me — the neighborhoods of Buffalo, the military community of Fort Bragg, the halls of Fayetteville State University, the sisterhood of the Divine Nine, and the youth and families of Fayetteville and Raeford who taught me what Ubuntu looks like in motion.

At its heart, this novel is also a sociological exploration — a reflection on how communities are shaped by systems, and how those same communities can rise to reshape the systems around them. The characters' journeys remind us that personal becoming is always intertwined with structural realities, and that collective care is a form of social change.

The Black-owned brands woven through this novel — including Blk & Bold, Midunu Chocolates, and Be Rooted — appear not as endorsements, but as cultural touchstones. They honor lineage, artistry, and the beauty of Black creativity, grounding the sensory world of the story in the same way community grounds our lives.

My hope is that as you close this book, you feel the truth that guided every chapter: we rise because someone held us, we heal because someone believed in us, and we become because community makes room for our growth.

Thank you for walking this journey with me.

— Alberta Lampkins

BOOK CLUB DISCUSSION QUESTIONS

1. Ubuntu in Action

How do Leha, Chemelu, and the wider community embody the principle *"I am because we are"* throughout the novel?

2. Becoming vs. Surviving

Which character's healing journey — Leha, Tyashia, Ron, or Melina — resonated with you most, and why?

3. Partnership & Emotional Safety

In what ways does Leha and Chemelu's relationship redefine partnership, vulnerability, and emotional safety?

4. Legacy & Lineage

What does "returning to the soil" mean for Chemelu, and how does the story honor African and African diasporic heritage?

5. Youth Rising

How do Tyashia, Malik, and Jalen each step into leadership, and what does their growth reveal about mentorship and community care?

6. Truth & Accountability

Which moment of honesty or confession — Ron's, Melina's, Delilah's, or Leha's — felt the most transformative, and why?

7. Fear, Identity & Expansion

How does Leha navigate the fear of becoming someone new, and what does "shedding" look like for her?

8. Local Roots, Global Reach

What does the Nairobi opportunity symbolize for Leha, Chemelu, and the Fayetteville community?

9. Symbols That Speak

Which motif — leaves, soil, breath, sensory elements like coffee and chocolate, or the yellow ladybug — stayed with you the most, and why?

10. Personal Reflection

Which character did you see yourself in, and how did the story shift or affirm your understanding of community and Ubuntu?

A NOTE FROM THE AUTHOR TO BOOK CLUBS

Thank you for choosing this book, for holding these characters with care, and for stepping into a story rooted in community, lineage, and becoming. My hope is that your conversations echo the spirit of Ubuntu — that you leave your gathering feeling more connected, more grounded, and more aware of the ways we hold one another through joy, grief, and transformation.

May your discussions be rich, your reflections deep, and your hearts open to the possibility that we rise together.

Ubuntu, always.
— Alberta Lampkins

ABOUT THE AUTHOR

Alberta Lampkins is a sociologist, novelist, and community advocate whose work lives at the intersection of healing, lineage, and collective care. She is the founder and publisher of A.L. Savvy Publications, an independent press dedicated to uplifting stories rooted in transformation, belonging, and the power of community.

A proud graduate of Fayetteville State University, Alberta has spent more than two decades supporting youth, families, and mentors across North Carolina through trauma-informed, culturally grounded programming. Her writing is shaped by the neighborhoods of Buffalo, the military community of Fort Bragg, and the vibrant youth and families of Fayetteville and Raeford — communities that taught her what resilience, connection, and Ubuntu look like in motion.

She is the author of several works, including the novella *Teach Me How to Fly*, the self-help book *Extracting the Good: The Importance of Self Love*, the community-centered anthology *Messages to Our Children*, and *Speak Young Brown People, Speak, We Are Listening*, a national collection amplifying youth voices on social injustice through essays, poetry, and visual art.

Where We Hold Each Other is her debut novel, blending sociological insight with storytelling to explore how communities rise, how families heal, and how love — in all its forms — becomes a structure strong enough to hold us.

Alberta lives in North Carolina with her husband, Al, and is the mother of two children, Ahmad and Alexis, and the grandmother of Elijah, Ahli, Chloe, and Carter. She continues to write, teach, and build spaces where people can unfold into their fullest selves.

www.ingramcontent.com/pod-product-compliance
Ingram Content Group UK Ltd.
Pitfield, Milton Keynes, MK11 3LW, UK
UKHW041631190726
13854UKWH00006B/2433